PURRFECT SECRET
THE MYSTERIES OF MAX 8

NIC SAINT

PUSS IN PRINT PUBLICATIONS

PURRFECT SECRET

The Mysteries of Max 8

Copyright © 2019 by Nic Saint

All rights reserved. No part of this book may be reproduced in any form by any electronic or mechanical means including photocopying, recording, or information storage and retrieval without permission in writing from the author.

This is a work of fiction. Names, characters, places, brands, media, and incidents are either the product of the author's imagination or are used fictitiously. The author acknowledges the trademarked status and trademark owners of various products referenced in this work of fiction, which have been used without permission. The publication/use of these trademarks is not authorized, associated with, or sponsored by the trademark owners.

Edited by Chereese Graves

www.nicsaint.com

Give feedback on the book at: info@nicsaint.com

facebook.com/nicsaintauthor
@nicsaintauthor

First Edition

Printed in the U.S.A

PROLOGUE

Dick Dickerson slipped his feet into his red velvet slippers and groped around on the nightstand for his glasses. Fumbling a little to put them onto his face, he glanced before him confusedly. Why was he sitting up in bed in what felt like the middle of the night?

Picking up his phone, he saw it was only a little after three. Too early to get up. And then he realized what had awakened him: loud music blasting from the speakers downstairs.

He drew a hand through his grizzled mane, got up with a groan and put on the white boxing robe that Sylvester Stallone had worn on the set of *Rocky IV*, Dick's favorite movie.

He moved out of his ornate bedroom, along his equally ornate hallway, down the no less ornate marble staircase, to arrive in his ostentatiously ornate entrance hall, where he only had to follow the music still blasting away to locate its source: his private study.

He couldn't remember having left the music on. Then again, lately he'd had so much on his mind he probably could have. As usual he took a Sonata before laying down his head, then some Provigil in the morning, along with a line of coke and his usual Prozac tablet. The Sonata knocked him out pretty good, so he might not have noticed leaving the music on.

Then again, if he heard correctly this was *What Goes Around... Comes Around*, the Justin Timberlake song. Not exactly Dick's taste. He liked Michael Bublé. He liked Michael Bublé a lot. In fact Michael Bublé was all he listened to lately.

With a sigh, Dick shuffled into his office, and that's when he saw it: the door to his giant walk-in safe was wide open. Dammit! Anyone could have just walked in!

"Dick, Dick, Dick," he muttered to himself. "You're losing it, pal."

Even though Doctor Mueller had told him to take it easy on the pills, and the coke, he couldn't help himself. He needed a little pick-me-up from time to time, and he was a firm believer in the old saying 'What doesn't kill you makes you stronger.' And since the coke hadn't killed him yet, or the pill-popping or even the vodka, it stood to reason it was making him stronger, right?

He shuffled to the safe door and peered inside. Odd. He'd even left the light on.

Shaking his head, he shuffled into the steel contraption. The moment he had, though, he saw that there was something seriously wrong with this picture: the countless stacks of files he kept in there, neatly organized in alphabetical order… they were all gone!

His jaw dropped as he stared at the empty shelves. Only a single file folder remained. He picked it up, his hands trembling, and opened it. Inside, there was a single picture. A picture he immediately recognized, and which sent his blood pressure rocketing skywards.

He gulped as he held onto the wall to steady himself.

This wasn't happening!

Just then, the giant steel door slammed shut with a thumping clang!

"Noooo!" he cried, pounding the door. But to no avail, of course.

And that's when things started to get even weirder. And a lot scarier!

A strange odor suddenly permeated the small space. Dick wrinkled his nose as he took a sniff. It smelled like… poop.

Had he just pooped himself? No way. He wasn't that far gone. He was only sixty-two, for crying out loud. And he didn't have problems in that area. Yet.

And then he saw it: some species of sludge was pouring into the safe through a vent in the ceiling. He sniffed again. Yup. Definitely poop. Horrible, liquid, greenish poop!

And then panic really set in. The song, the picture, the poop.

Oh, God. This wasn't happening. This couldn't be happening to him!

"Hey!" he screamed. "Let me out! I'll give you the files! Just let me out of here!"

But of course no response came. This wasn't a scare tactic. They had the files. They'd taken them along with all of the other secrets he'd assiduously collected over the years.

They weren't here to scare him off or send him a message.

They were here to kill him. Drown him in poop.

If he hadn't been so scared he might have laughed at the irony.

The poop was up to his knees now, streaming in at a steady clip.

The stench was unbearable and he was retching, wading in the toxic stuff.

And as he screamed in horror at the fate that was

awaiting him, a voice came from the other side of the door—muffled, of course.

"Little message for you, Dickerson. What goes around, comes around!"

"I'm sorry!" he bellowed. "Don't do this to me. Have a heart!"

"Yeah, right. Like you had a heart, huh? Screw you, Dickerson!"

The poop was reaching his waist now, ruining his nice Rocky boxing robe. And then he got an idea. He quickly took it off and waded over to the hole where the sludge was pouring in, then shoved the wadded-up robe into the hole, trying to stem the deadly flow.

In the process he got poop all over him. The yucky stuff got into his eyes—into his nose—into his mouth! But he would prevail. No one got the better of Dick Dickerson!

He shoved the thing home and held it in place in spite of his retching.

There. He'd done it! He was like that little Dutch kid who plugged his finger in the dike and saved his entire frickin' village!

Unfortunately Rocky's robe was no match for this particular hole. The pressure was too great, and soon the stuff was seeping in again. Pretty soon the safe was filling up so fast not even an army of little Dutch boys with little Dutch fingers could have stemmed the flow.

And the worst part? Dick knew exactly what he'd done to deserve this.

CHAPTER 1

I opened a lazy eye when some sort of light tapping drove away the slumber I'd enjoyed for the past couple of hours. I know what they say about cats: that they're never really asleep. That they take 'catnaps' and wake up in the blink of an eye, ready to fight or take flight when danger lurks. Poppycock. I'm a cat and I like to sleep. In fact I can sleep so deeply not even the sound of a cannon can wake me up. Not that I've ever heard an actual cannon being fired in my vicinity. Do people even still use cannons? Somehow I doubt it.

But whatever. The thing that woke me up wasn't a sensation so much as a nuisance. An annoyance. A burden, a plague, a pest or even a pain in the neck, if you catch my drift.

For I found myself staring into the impudent eyes of the latest intruder to invade my household: Milo, the cat that belongs to Odelia's across-the-street neighbor Mrs. Lane.

He was grinning at me now, the white menace. Grinning like a regular fiend.

I closed my eyes again, hoping he hadn't noticed he'd

managed to wake me up. But to no avail. He simply tapped me on the head again with that infuriating cheek he possesses.

"Wakey, wakey," he said. "Rise and shine, old man."

"I'm not old," I growled at him, and now he was grinning even wider—a regular Cheshire grin if ever I'd seen one.

"Oh, you are old," he said. "Ancient. In fact before I met you I didn't even realize cats could get that old. You even have hair growing out of your ears, did you know that?"

"You have hairs growing out of your ears."

"Yeah, but they're tiny and they're soft. Like fuzz. Yours are long and hard. Like the hair on the back of a pig."

I would have snarled at him, lifting my upper lip like a dog and actually snarled, but I'm a cat, and cats don't snarl. Instead I produced a soft hissing sound, hoping to indicate my displeasure. It only made him grin even wider, the annoying little runt!

"So how old are you, Max? If I'd have to make a guess I'd say you're pretty ancient. So you were probably around before humans drove around in cars, right? Did you see the horse and buggy? Were you alive during the Civil War? Were you here when the English were bopping around Long Island, creating trouble for Washington and the Colonists?"

I didn't even dignify this last jab with a response. Instead, I hopped off the couch with as much dignity as I could muster under the circumstances, and strode off, my tail high —and a little fluffed-up because of the residual annoyance— and was just about to take the stairs to the second floor to wake up my human when that human came stumbling down those same stairs, looking like death warmed over and almost tripped over me and fell.

"Max," she muttered. "Sorry, dude. Hey, there, Milo. Settling in all right?"

"Settling in just fine, Mrs. Poole," said Milo, now scratching his unhairy ears.

"Just call me Odelia, will you?" said Odelia. "I'm too young to be Mrs. Poole."

Milo cocked an eyebrow, indicating he thought Odelia was pretty ancient, too, and very deserving of the moniker he'd just awarded her, but then strode off in the direction of the kitchen, where Odelia had put out an extra bowl for our latest guest, and dug in.

I kept a keen eye on him, as Milo had been known to dig into my bowl, too, and even drink from my milk.

"What are you doing up so early?" I asked my human.

She gave me an 'Are you kidding me?' look and gestured with her head to the backyard, where Grandma Muffin was digging into the soil, dressed like a regular gardener.

"Oh, right," I said delicately.

Ever since Gran moved in with Odelia things have been a little rocky. Grandma has a way of doing things, and Odelia has a completely different way of doing things, and the twain are hard to reconcile. Like the fact that Gran loves her soap operas and her reality shows while Odelia prefers a good movie from time to time. And then there's the fact that Gran doesn't approve of Odelia's boyfriend hanging around all the time, and even sleeping over. She feels that Chase should just go ahead and propose and make an honest woman out of her granddaughter so she can get all this 'fooling around' over and done with.

I doubt whether Odelia approves. She probably feels she's too young to get married just so she can have her boyfriend stay the night from time to time. And since I'm a modern cat—in spite of what Milo might think—I heartily approve.

My name is Max, by the way, but I guess you already figured that out from the way Milo keeps addressing me. I'm a blorange cat—a very tasteful combination of orange and pink—while Milo is one of those horrible white cats with the bristly, stiff hair. He's also very young and was obviously raised by a woman who doesn't know the first thing about cats. She probably never taught him manners which has turned him into an obnoxious monster.

But enough about Milo. I'm sure he'll only be around for a few days—until Mrs. Aloisia Lane returns from her trip to Florida and is ready to assume command once again.

Just then, Dooley wandered in through the sliding glass door, followed by Harriet and Brutus. Those three are my best friends in all the world—yes, cats have best friends—don't you believe everything you read on the Internet about us being loners and curmudgeons and all that nonsense. We like our fellow felines just fine thank you very much.

"Hey, Maxie, baby," rasped Brutus by way of greeting, holding up a paw.

I high-fived him, then low-fived him, then hooked my nail behind his, gave a little tug while we both blew raspberries, then we paw-bumped and shared a hearty guffaw.

Once upon a time Brutus and I were mortal enemies but those days are long gone. Nowadays we get along like gangbusters, whatever a gangbuster might be. Brutus is a strikingly butch black cat, by the way, and Harriet, a gorgeous white Persian, is his girlfriend.

"Hey, Max," said Dooley, looking like he wasn't fully awake yet. Dooley is a Ragamuffin, which in his case means he's on the small side and has a thick gray coat. He's also very fluffy, which makes him very popular with his human, Grandma Muffin, and a little less popular with Marge, who has to vacuum the carpets and couches at least twice a week.

Milo returned from the kitchen, and immediately my eyes were drawn to the drop of liquid on his chin. It was milk, and I knew for a fact that Milo's milk bowl had been empty. I pointed an accusing paw at him. "You stole my milk!"

"I did not, sir," said Milo, quickly wiping away the incriminating evidence.

"I saw you! You had a drop of milk on your beard! Didn't he have a drop of milk on his beard, Dooley? Tell me you saw that!" I turned to my friends for corroboration but they appeared less than excited to wade into the argument.

"For your information, cats don't have a beard, Max," said Milo calmly. "Except for you, of course, but that's because you're ancient. Like Methuselah. He had a beard. At least I think he had. What do you think, Dooley? Did Methuselah have a beard? You're the expert."

Dooley stared at the young whippersnapper. "Huh?" he said finally.

"Odelia tells me you're a very smart cat. Smartest one she knows, in fact. A real know-it-all. So I'm asking you: did or didn't Methuselah have a beard just like Max?"

"I don't have a beard!" I cried. "You're just trying to confuse the issue!"

"And what is the issue, Max?" asked Milo kindly, like one addressing a feeble-minded old fogey.

"The issue is that I just caught you stealing my milk!"

Milo tsk-tsked mildly, probably the first time I'd ever seen a cat do that. "*Mi casa es su casa*, Max. Which means my milk is your milk and vice versa. Now what can I offer you guys?" he continued, this time addressing Brutus, Harriet and Dooley. "I've got milk, kibble, some excellent Fancy Feast Seafood and of course the always-tasty Cat Snax."

"Those are mine!" I cried. "Those are my Cat Snax and my Fancy Feast Seafood!"

"Oh, don't be a miser, Max," said Harriet as she strode right past me.

"Yeah, sharing is caring, pal," said Brutus as he did the same.

"Thanks, Max," said Dooley cheerily. "I love those Cat Snax of yours."

And then they were all digging into *my* bowls, snacking on *my* favorite food!

Sharing is caring my furry butt!

I sank back on my haunches, haughtily draped my tail around my buttocks, and gave them all the stare. And the first one I directed my fearsome stare at was Milo, who was overseeing the feast as if he was the one who'd personally arranged all of it, the impudent jerk!

I have to admit, though, that no matter how hard I stared, it didn't affect the others one bit or deter them from gobbling up all of my food. And when they'd finally polished off my last bowl, they all had drops of milk stuck to their beards, crumbs of Cat Snax decorating their whiskers, and Fancy Feast Seafood stuck to their lips.

Ugh. What a way to start the day.

CHAPTER 2

Odelia was staring out into the backyard, where her grandmother was digging holes into the ground, presumably to plant some of the bulbs she'd acquired. When Gran first moved in she'd mentioned how the backyard looked like a wasteland and that someone ought to do something about it. So now, since she didn't have a lot to do, she'd just decided to dig in and do it herself.

Problem was, Odelia liked her backyard just fine. She liked grass. She liked how low-maintenance it was. And she liked the few rhododendron bushes she'd planted near the back, because all she needed to do was prune them from time to time, deadhead them, and sit back and enjoy the riot of color come springtime.

And now Grandma was determined to turn her backyard into some sort of garden of Versailles! There was even talk of installing a water fountain, a rock garden, and a fish pond!

Odelia didn't know the first thing about fishes, or the dozens of plants Grandma had gotten at the garden center and was now transferring to the soil. They'd probably all need a lot of work to maintain, as would the fountain and the fish pond and its dozens of fishes.

She shook her head, still dressed in her Hello Kitty PJs, sipping from the coffee Grandma had made—extra-strong, just the way the old lady liked it—not so much the way Odelia liked it. And it was then that she noticed her cats seemed to be arguing about something.

"What's up, guys?" she asked, popping a slice of bread into the toaster.

She frowned when Max suddenly jumped up onto the kitchen counter, something he never did.

"Max?" she said when he gave her a look of annoyance. "What's wrong?"

"They're eating my food," he whispered.

She leaned in. "What was that? I didn't catch that."

"They're eating my food!" he hissed, gesturing with his head to the four cats who sat licking and grooming themselves.

And true enough, the bowls were all empty.

"Oh, right," said Odelia, and automatically reached into the cupboard where she kept the cat food and started filling up those bowls again.

"No, don't do that!" Max hissed, and she moved closer.

"Aren't you hungry, Max?" He rarely refused his food, and then only when he was sick. "Are you coming down with something?"

"Yes, I am! It's called Milo and it's worse than swine flu or flesh-eating bacteria!"

She smiled. "Max, I told you it's only for a little while. Now please be nice to our guest. Sharing is caring, after all." When Max produced a strange sound at this, like steam escaping from a pipe, she gave him a closer look. "Are you sure you're not coming down with a bug? If you want I could call Vena. She does house calls, too."

"No!" he yelled, horrified. "No, it's fine." Then, resigned, he added, "I'll handle it."

And he hopped from the counter, a defeated air about him.

Cats. Sometimes they had a hard time making new friends. Then she got a bright idea. She moved to the TV nook and turned on the TV, then fiddled around with the remote for a moment, flipping through the Netflix menus until she hit on the one she wanted.

This should do the trick.

"You guys!" she yelled. "Come in here for a moment, will you?"

Five cats came trotting up, Max the last one to join the small troupe.

On TV, an episode of *Kit Katt & Koh* was playing, the new Netflix show that was such a big hit. It told the story of Kit Katt, a regular young woman from a small town who worked as a reporter for the local newspaper and could talk to her cat Koh, who fed her bits of news he picked up from his feline friends. Almost as if the show's creators had taken a long, hard look at Odelia's own life!

"Ooh, it's Kit Katt!" Harriet cried happily as she hopped onto the leather couch.

The others quickly followed suit, and Odelia watched on as her cat family settled in for the duration of the eppy. They all loved Kit Katt and especially the funny and feisty Koh.

Just then, her phone belted out the latest Dua Lipa hit and she hurried to the kitchen, where she'd left it on the counter. Her toast had popped and she took it out and placed it on a plate while she pressed the phone to her ear.

"Yeah, Chase."

"Hey, babe. You're up early."

"Grandma," she said, only needing one word to make her meaning clear.

"I feel your pain," said Chase. "If it's any consolation, I've got a case for you—and a hot tip straight from the front lines."

"A murder? In Hampton Cove? No way."

"Way. Does the name Dick Dickerson mean anything to you?"

"He's the editor of the *National Star*, right? The supermarket tabloid?"

"He's also dead. Killed in a pretty creative—and gruesome —way, I'm afraid."

"You want me to join you?"

"Please. Your uncle is out of town for a couple of days, so I could use a hand."

Odelia's uncle, a widower, had recently met a woman. She worked for Dos Siglas, the famous beer company, and traveled the country handling the company's PR and overseeing the shooting of their equally famous 'Most Fascinating Man in the World' commercials.

"I know. He told me. He and Tracy are going hiking in the Appalachian Mountains. Tracy's company owns a cabin out there, where they often put up executives and guests."

"For some reason I never pictured your uncle as the hiker type," said Chase, and Odelia could hear the smile in his voice.

"He's not," said Odelia, also smiling. Uncle Alec was easily three times as big as she was, and had probably never worked out a day in his life. In fact he'd smoked like a chimney until only recently, and his cholesterol levels always made his brother-in-law, Odelia's dad, who was a doctor, give him that unhappy look doctors like to give their worst patients.

"He must like that woman a lot, to give up a lifelong habit of being a couch potato."

"Yeah, he's smitten," said Odelia, who was happy that her uncle, whose wife had died years ago, was finally 'playing the field' again, as they said. Even if there was only one woman on that field as far as Alec was concerned. "She's nice," she added. "I like her."

"I like her, too," said Chase. "So are you game, Poole?"

"Count me in, Kingsley," she said.

"Pick you up in five. Oh, and you better bring a clothespin," he said before hanging up.

CHAPTER 3

Watching Kit Katt and Koh and their adventures was all fine and dandy, but doing it under duress was not. For one thing, Milo clearly wasn't familiar with the etiquette involved in watching a TV show as a family. He kept getting up and moving about, then returning and sitting in a different place each time. And what was more, he kept accidentally stepping on the remote and pausing the show or even switching the channel. And the worst thing? He wasn't even doing it on purpose I didn't think. It was almost as if he couldn't help himself.

"Sorry, dude," he muttered when he suddenly planted his butt on my tail, then, when I extracted myself, started drumming his paw against my back for some reason!

His behavior was frankly driving me up the wall. So when he'd stepped on my toes for the third time, I snapped, "Will you just sit still for a second?"

He merely grinned up at me, then said, "Chill, dude. It's only a stupid show."

I gasped in shock, and so did Harriet, who was a big fan

of Kit Katt and her handsome sidekick Koh. "Only a stupid show!" I echoed. "This is Kit Katt we're talking about, Milo!"

He shrugged, now lying on his back and balancing his paws in the air. "Whatever."

"It's only the best cat show ever!"

"Yeah, it's not like there are a ton of great cat shows," said Brutus. "Dog shows? Too many to count. But cat shows? Nah. Almost as if Hollywood doesn't care about us cats."

"Yes, you've got your Lassie, you've got your Boomer and you've got your Benji, but no cats. What's that all about?" Dooley added, clearly also a *Kit Katt & Koh* aficionado.

"Simple," said Milo, now sticking his butt into the air and wiggling his tail. "Cats can't act. Dogs, on the other hand, can."

There were collective gasps of shock now, all of us staring at Milo like he'd just committed sacrilege, which he had. "Take that back," I said.

"Take what back?"

"That cats can't act."

"But it's true! Dogs can be taught to perform all kinds of tricks, which makes them the perfect actors. Only cats aren't so easy to instruct. Hence the lack of cat shows."

I was shaking my head. This was crazy talk. "You're wrong," I said vehemently.

"Actually he kinda has a point there, Max," said Brutus. "Cats are difficult actors, and we all know how Hollywood feels about difficult actors. They get sidelined."

I couldn't believe this. Cats are a superior species. Everybody knows that. Compared to cats dogs are nothing. We have the better reflexes, the bigger brainpower, the greater charm, the works! "What about *Tom and Jerry*?" I said. "That's a lot more popular than Lassie ever was."

Milo gave me a strange look. "*Tom and Jerry* is a cartoon, Max."

"So?"

"So there are no actual cats involved," he said slowly.

"Oh," I said, never having given this minor little detail a great deal of thought. "Well, I like *Tom and Jerry*," I said stubbornly. "Even though Tom is something of a loser."

Well, he is. What cat worth its salt keeps getting bested by a silly little critter?

The doorbell rang and immediately Milo jumped from the couch, where he'd been counting his belly hairs, and streaked off in the direction of the door.

"Poor Milo," said Harriet. "He probably thinks it's his human, here to pick him up."

"He doesn't," I scoffed. "He probably thinks it's the pizza guy with fresh food."

Harriet gave me a slightly critical look. "Why are you being so mean to Milo, Max? He means well. And it's not his fault he's here, having to miss his home and his human."

"Oh, please," I said. "He's like the guest you don't want. Like Owen Wilson in *You, Me and Dupree*. He looks like an angel but deep down he's just a spoiled little brat."

"Maxie, Maxie," said Brutus now, shaking his head. "How would you feel if Odelia handed you over to some stranger, and you suddenly found yourself having to share another cat's food, being at the mercy of a human you never met? Huh? Put yourself in his paws for a moment. Have a heart." He patted my chest. "I know it's in there somewhere."

That was rich, coming from Brutus. It wasn't that long ago that he'd been that cat, coming in here with his swagger and his bullying ways. Just like Milo.

"I don't like him," I said decidedly. "And there's nothing you can say that will make me change my mind." The others were all staring past me, and my heart sank. "He's right behind me, isn't he?" They all nodded, and I slowly turned. I was right. Milo was behind me, giving me a sheepish look.

"Some big dude is at the door. I think he's a cop?"

"Chase Kingsley," said Brutus knowingly. "He's my human."

"Way to go, buddy," said Milo. "He looks nice."

"Yeah, I don't see him all that much," said Brutus. "I practically live at Odelia's mom's these days. They shipped me around for a while but I've decided to settle here."

"I'll bet you can relate, huh, Milo?" I said, trying to lighten the mood. "Being shipped around from human to human. Ha ha."

But Milo wasn't laughing. Instead, he was picking at the couch cover with his nails, his eyelids flickering nervously. "Uh-huh," he said finally. "That's right, Max. You got my number, buddy." And then he promptly turned on his paw and padded off.

"Max!" Harriet said, and directed a reproachful look at me. "You're so mean!"

"Yeah, you're behaving like a first-rate bully, Maxie," said Brutus.

Coming from a former bully of bullies that was the last thing I needed to hear!

Still, I felt a bit bad about the whole situation. No idea why, though, as I knew I was right and Milo was wrong. I mean, he was the intruder and I was the intruded, right?

CHAPTER 4

The episode of Kit Katt ended and Brutus and Harriet drifted off into the backyard, probably to stare at Grandma while she dug more holes. Cats love to watch humans dig holes. No idea why. Probably so they can pick up a few ideas on skill and technique.

"Hey, buddy," I said to Dooley. "You're awfully quiet. Something wrong?"

He shrugged. "Have you ever felt superfluous, Max?"

I was surprised Dooley would even know a big word like that. "What do you mean?"

"I mean that Harriet has Brutus and Brutus has Harriet. You have Odelia and Odelia has you. Even Milo has his human—even though she's not here right now. But who do I have?"

"You have Grandma," I said. "And she has you."

He stared off in the direction of the garden, where Brutus was now giving Grandma a few tips on how to dig a hole by using her hands instead of that silly-looking shovel. "Grandma doesn't care a hoot about me, Max. In fact I don't think she ever did."

"I'm sure that's not true. Grandma loves you—she loves all of us."

"No, she doesn't. You know what she said to me the other day? That I shouldn't sleep on her feet. She said she's too old to have cats sleep on her feet. She also pushed me away when I tried to dig my nose into her armpit this morning. Said I was being silly and she was too old for that nonsense." He shook his head. "I'm telling you, she's getting ready to take me to the pound, Max. I can feel it in my bones."

"Now don't you talk like that, Dooley," I told him. "That's crazy talk. Maybe Grandma is acting a little weird lately but that's just because she's in a fight with Tex and Marge."

"She's in a fight with Tex and Marge and she's decided she doesn't want me anymore," he said sadly.

Grandma had worked for her son-in-law Tex for years and years at Tex's doctor's office. But since Tex and Odelia's mom Marge had protested Grandma's attempt to move away and go and live with the rich family of her ex-boyfriend Burt Goldsmith, Gran had moved out of their house and into Odelia's, and now things were very tense all around.

"I'm sure everything will go back to normal soon enough," I said. "Besides, Odelia is pretty much your human, too, right? She loves you just as much as she loves me."

"In my experience humans can only love one pet, Max," said Dooley somberly. "And since she already has you, there's no room in her heart for anyone else." He sighed deeply. "No, looks like I'm humanless." Then he cast a forlorn look at me. "At least I still have you, Max. You're my best friend, and you'll never leave me, right?"

"Of course I'll never leave you," I said, rubbing my friend's noggin with my furry knuckles. "Best friends forever, right?"

"Right," he said, a glimmer of hope lighting up his features. "So you won't mind if I permanently move in with you?"

I know I should have said yes wholeheartedly, so I don't know where that slight hesitation came from. Maybe from the fact that I was on edge with this whole Milo business. Or maybe because Dooley kinda took me by surprise. Fact is, I flinched. And Dooley saw that. And his expression hardened, and without another word he stalked off.

"Dooley!" I yelled. "Come back here! Of course you can move in with me, buddy!"

But he was already gone.

I felt eyes burning into my back so I turned. Milo was staring at me. Then he smiled. "Looks like you need a new friend, Max. Why don't you let me be that friend from now on?"

"I have no idea what you're talking about," I said, pensive now.

He strode up to me and placed a paw on my shoulder. "You look sad, Max. And no wonder. Your best friend just walked out on you. But not to worry. I'll be your new bro."

I gulped. A strange sensation was gnawing at me. A sense of foreboding. Then I stomped down on the sentiment. Harriet and Brutus were right. Milo was my guest. I needed to be nicer to him. Hospitable. Kind and understanding. So I relented.

"Of course," I told him. "From now on my milk is your milk and my Cat Snax are your Cat Snax, Milo. And you're welcome to stay under my roof for as long as you like."

His lips slowly curled up into a smile. "I knew you'd warm to me, Max. I just knew it. You're an old fogey, and old fogeys sometimes need time to adjust. But from now on we're besties. Besties for life." And he held up his paw, so I placed mine against it. And when he went low, I went low, too. But when we paw-bumped, I had a sinking feeling something was terribly wrong with this picture.

And I didn't even know the half of it yet.

CHAPTER 5

True to his word, Chase showed up right on the dot. Odelia grabbed her purse, took one final glance at her grandmother puttering away in the backyard and stepped out.

Chase pressed a quick kiss to her lips, then took a firmer hold of her, dipped her down and laid a real smoocher on her.

When he returned her to perpendicularity, she was swooning a little. Great way to start the day!

"And hello to you, too," she said, following him to his pickup, parked at the curb.

"You've got your grandmother to thank for that," he said with a grin.

"She give you pointers on technique?"

"As if. No, ever since she decided to stay with you I've been forced to become this pining, lonesome, sad figure, watching from afar."

"Somehow I'm having a hard time imagining you as a pining, lonesome figure."

"Well, it's true," he said, getting behind the wheel as she

slid in right next to him. "I'm sitting there all by my lonesome, in your uncle's big, old house, thinking of you."

"If it's any consolation I'm thinking of you, too." Especially since her grandmother was a poor substitute for having Chase's warm body next to her in bed at night.

"Maybe we have to educate your grandmother in the ways of the world."

"Gran is beyond education. Nothing I say or do has any effect on that woman."

Grandma liked Chase, no doubt about it, but recently she'd developed this old-fashioned idea that the male of the species should propose to the female of the species before they actually moved in together and slept in the same bed. No idea where this idea came from, exactly. Then again, Gran did watch a lot of those daytime soap operas and maybe some former mob boss's identical twin and reformed serial killer turned art therapist's illegal adoptive brother who was also a Navy SEAL had at some point conceived a son with an OB/GYN and Gran felt that if only they'd gotten married they could have saved themselves a lot of trouble.

Yes, Odelia enjoyed her occasional dose of the soap opera machine herself, too.

"She's redoing the garden now," she said, slumping down in her seat and putting her pink-and-yellow polka-dot Chuck Taylors up on the dash. "Says she's going to turn it into the kind of garden Louis Quatorze would have been proud of, water-spewing cherubs and all."

Chase laughed. "She's doing that just to spite your dad, isn't she?"

"Oh, yes, she is."

Grandma had always been in charge of Tex and Marge's garden, until she decided to skedaddle and move next door. But in spite of the fact that she'd hoped Tex would be pining for her and begging her to come back, instead Odelia's father had flourished and had never been happier. Getting his meddling mother-in-law out of the house had been a lifelong dream ever since the old lady had moved in when her husband Jack had taken his philandering ways to the seventh heaven or maybe in his case the seventh circle of hell.

Now, by turning Odelia's garden into the cream of the horticultural crop, Gran probably hoped to inspire a raging jealousy in Tex, as the latter was oddly proud of his own backyard and this had been the one thing he and Grandma had in common: a green thumb.

"Maybe I should ask Dad to take the first step and reconcile," said Odelia now.

"Fat chance. You'd have better luck asking your mother."

"Mom says to let things cool off. That Gran will come to her senses soon enough." She shook her head. "I'm not so sure. Gran seems to like this new arrangement, and so does Dad."

"Looks like your dad and grandma have reached a stalemate."

Chase was navigating his pickup through morning traffic and had reached the town limit. "So why did you want me to bring a clothespin, exactly?" Odelia asked.

"You'll see. It's not pretty."

"Don't tell me he got blown up. I just had breakfast."

"He wasn't blown up. In fact, as far as we can see, he drowned. Or I should probably say he suffocated."

"He drowned in his pool?"

"He drowned in a pool," said Chase mysteriously.

"A pool… of his own blood?"

"Duck poop."

"Duck poop?"

"Duck poop."

"Huh. And you're telling me this wasn't an accident?"

Chase looked grim. "Absolutely not. Dick Dickerson was murdered."

*I*t only took them about fifteen minutes to reach their destination. Dick Dickerson lived in one of those huge McMansions right outside of Hampton Cove, built almost on the coast, with access to a private strip of beach, a heliport, a heated pool on the patio, jacuzzi, too many rooms and bathrooms to count, and a fleet of servants at his every beck and call.

When Chase had directed his pickup down the asphalt driveway and parked in front of the house, Odelia wondered why it was that all the celebrities who came to Hampton Cove had a habit of getting murdered at one point or another. Within the past few months she'd visited the homes of singers, reality stars, actors... This small Hamptons town of theirs was quickly becoming the murder capital of the state if this worrying trend kept up.

She admired the ivy-covered brick exterior of the tabloid magnate's house, and the stone steps leading up to heavy oak doors.

"Security?" she asked as she followed Chase inside.

There was a hubbub of police activity, and Odelia nodded greetings to several Hampton Cove PD officers she personally knew. Having a police chief for an uncle awarded her a lot of advantages as a reporter for the Hampton Cove Gazette: often she was the first one on the scene, and the first one to glean interesting bits of information. And sometimes, like now, she was even invited to join in on the investigation. The only thing she didn't have was one of those windbreakers with the word WRITER printed across the front and back.

"Oh, he had security," said Chase, "only whoever did this was smart enough to know their way around the system."

They walked through an ornate entrance hall, every bit of wall space covered in laminated covers of the *National Star*. Clearly Dick Dickerson had been proud of his work.

They took a right turn past a huge statue of Dickerson dressed like Napoleon, complete with prancing black stallion, and walked into what looked like the tabloid king's private study. And that's when she saw it: a trail of greenish sludge on the floor, leading to the biggest safe she'd ever seen. It looked like one of those ginormous bank safes.

And then she caught a whiff of the smell and she winced.

"It gets worse," Chase said when he saw her expression.

And it did. As they approached the safe, she saw that the floor was covered with two inches of the same green-and-white sludge, and the stench was beyond horrible. Inadvertently she brought a hand up to her face to cover her mouth.

Lying face up in all of that muck, was Dick Dickerson.

CHAPTER 6

Odelia was glad she hadn't brought her cats. They didn't need to see—or smell—this. Two people from the Suffolk County coroner's office were examining the body. They were wearing face masks. Not a bad idea. She probably should have brought that clothespin.

"Poor guy," she said as they walked back out of the safe. "Not a pleasant way to go."

"No, it sure wasn't," said Chase.

"What was he doing in that safe?"

"We think he must have been lured there—did you notice he was dressed in his pajamas?"

Actually she hadn't. She'd been too busy trying to fight the nausea the smell created. "So how did they do that?"

"We have no idea. But he didn't lock himself up in that safe. And there are no signs of a struggle. So he must have walked in there voluntarily, then had the safe door close up on him."

"How did the duck poop get into the safe?"

"They thought about this," said Chase, as he led her out of the office and back into the hallway. "In fact this must have taken careful preparation. This wasn't some half-assed job they put together at the last minute."

"They? You think there was more than one assailant?"

"Oh, yes. This was not a one-man job."

He walked her around the house, along a wood chip mulch path that snaked along the side. She saw several patches of nice-looking petunias, geraniums, million bells and impatiens. And of course some of the popular deer-resistant annuals like angelonia, snapdragons and helichrysum. Like everywhere on the South Fork, deer liked to roam wild and free in Hampton Cove, devouring whatever they could dig their hungry teeth into.

They'd reached the back of Dickerson's huge house, and Odelia frowned when her eyes met a scene she wouldn't normally associate with the fastidious billionaire: a huge tanker had been backed up to the house, a five-inch hose connecting it to a wall vent. Next to the tanker, a tractor had been parked.

"This is how they got the duck poop into the safe," explained Chase, pointing to the hose. "That's where the vault vent used to be. Dickerson had a safety built into the vent to prevent liquids from being introduced or birds nesting in there but they simply ripped the whole thing out and fed the hose straight into the vault's HVAC system."

Odelia stared at the huge tanker, which looked just like any fuel tanker, only this one had obviously been used to transport something different from oil or gasoline. "Where did they get the tanker? And the duck poop?"

"Geary Potbelly. He's the only duck farmer left on Long Island. We already arranged for an interview. He says one of his tractors and one of his tankers was stolen last night, a tanker full of liquid duck poop ready to be taken to the poop processing plant." Chase gestured to the tanker. "This here tanker and that there duck poop."

Odelia pursed her lips. "This was an organized setup, Chase. Not some kid coming in from the street bearing a grudge against Dickerson. Whoever did this planned this out in advance." She studied the hole in the wall up close. "They must have had blueprints."

"Possibly," Chase admitted. "And you're right about this being a professional crew."

"So you're looking at organized crime?"

He nodded. "Like you said, they needed a lot of know-how to pull this off. Then again, there are crews who do this work for hire. Anyone could have contracted them."

"Anyone who wanted Dick Dickerson dead. Any candidates?"

"Oh, plenty," he said. "In fact we're working on a list right now. Turns out Mr. Dickerson was not exactly the people's favorite. Exactly the opposite, in fact."

"People he insulted with his articles?"

"Amongst others. If you want you can join me on some of the interviews. With Alec out of town I could use the extra pair of eyes and ears. Not to mention your keen mind."

"Oh, so now it's my mind you're suddenly interested in, huh?"

"Not just your mind," he admitted with a wide grin as he pulled her close.

There was some more kissing until a cough interrupted them. When Odelia looked up, she found a man dressed in coveralls staring at them. He was fiddling with his cap.

"So can I take her back then?" he asked.

"Yes, you can, Bert," said Chase.

"Is that…"

"Bert is in charge of the duck poop tanker," said Chase. "He works for Potbelly."

"What a way to make a living."

Bert mounted the tractor, adjusted his cap, spat on the

ground, then proceeded to maneuver the tractor in front of the manure tanker. He jumped back down, and hooked the tanker up to the tractor, then hopped back into the powerful rig, and then he was pulling that mastodon from Dickerson's lawn, giving Odelia and Chase a nod as he did.

"Murdered by duck poop," said Odelia as they watched the tractor drive off.

"There's a certain irony to it, though, right?" said Chase.

"You mean a peddler of poop being killed by poop?"

"Uh-huh."

"Yeah, I guess you're right. It is ironic. But it's still murder, Chase. And we still have to catch whoever did this."

"Oh, I couldn't agree more. But you have to admit there's a sort of poetic justice to the whole thing, if you consider the lives Dickerson destroyed by printing his brand of filth."

Chase was right. Even though she was a reporter herself, the kind of stuff the *National Star* engaged in could hardly be called journalism. Half of what they wrote was invented, and the other half grossly exaggerated. And all of it intended to provoke, intimidate, ridicule and cater to the lowest common denominator or possibly even lower.

No, she didn't think Dick Dickerson would be missed. But he was still a human being, and he'd been murdered, so whoever was responsible needed to be brought to justice.

And she was just about to follow Chase back to his pickup when her phone rang. When she took it out she saw it was an unknown number. Not unusual for a reporter.

"Odelia Poole," she said, picking up.

"Oh, hi, Miss Poole. Is this the Odelia Poole who works for the *Hampton Cove Gazette*?"

The voice was male and sounded oddly familiar. "Yes, this is she. Who is this?"

"My name is Otto Paunch, and I'm a great friend of President Wilcox. As you may have heard he's currently residing at his Hampton Cove residence, Lago-a-Oceano. And as his great, great friend and confidante, I can reveal to you exclusively that Van—that's President Van Wilcox—was surprised not to see his name appear on the list of Hampton Cove's wealthiest residents."

"Well, that's because President Wilcox doesn't officially reside in Hampton Cove," Odelia told the caller. "Officially he lives in Washington. At the White House."

"Yes, but his heart has always been in Hampton Cove. He loves it out here, you know—loves it. And if it weren't for this president thing, I'm sure he would have topped that list."

"There are some pretty rich people on our annual rich list, Mr. Paunch. Some of them probably a lot richer than your friend."

"Poppycock. Van is the richest man in the Hamptons. The richest man in the state, even. I'm looking at his bank statement right now and I can see he's got twenty billion dollars to his name. Twenty billion dollars, Miss Poole! Who can beat that? If that doesn't take him straight to the top of your list you're not the reporter I took you for."

"If you're sure about this, Mr. Paunch, I could always print a new version of the list."

"Do that, Miss Poole. Because I am sure about this. As Van's best friend, you can trust me on that. In fact you can trust me on anything I have to say about him. Van and I are so close you wouldn't believe. We're like brothers. Twins. Now don't let me keep you. I'm sure you want to get started on that new rich list straightaway, Van's name at the very top."

"Goodbye, Mr. Paunch."

"Goodbye, Miss Poole."

And as she put her phone away, she was still wondering who Otto Paunch's voice reminded her of.

CHAPTER 7

Vesta got up and looked at her handiwork with a nod of appreciation. Odelia's garden was a mess, but with a little bit of work, a dash of love, and a lot of manure, she could turn it into a work of art. She couldn't wait to see the look on Tex's face when he glanced over the hedge into his daughter's garden one fine morning and saw stretched before his stupefied gaze the most beautiful garden in all of Hampton Cove.

That would teach him to kick his own mother-in-law to the curb!

Not that he'd actually kicked her to the curb, but those were tiny details she didn't like to concern herself with. And that's when she saw the lone figure of Dooley sneaking through the hedge in the direction of Tex and Marge's backyard.

"Hello there," she said with a reproachful glint in her eye. "Now where do you think you're going, young cat?"

Dooley looked up, two paws on Tex's property and two paws on what Vesta now considered her own. "Um… home?" he said, an expression of confusion on his furry face.

"You come back here right this instance, Dooley," snapped Vesta. "Your home is with me, and since I live on this side of the hedge now there's no reason for you to go over there anymore." She accentuated the word 'there' with a wave of the hand and a look of distaste.

"But... my bowl is over there," said Dooley. "And my litter box. And my couch."

"Not anymore it's not. I'll buy you a new litter box. And a new bowl." Well, she would tell Odelia to buy them, at any rate. On the small pension she received she couldn't afford to spend money like water on such trivial stuff like litter boxes and cat bowls. Not since Tex had cut up her credit cards and thwarted her plans to become a millionaire heiress.

Dooley retracted his paws and sat on his haunches for a moment. "But... I don't want to be here, Gran. Nobody here loves me." He said it in such a sad tone that even Vesta, whose soul was calloused after having watched *General Hospital*, *The Young and the Restless*, *The Bold and the Beautiful* and *Days of Our Lives* all of her life, not to mention listening to countless sob stories from Tex's patients as they booked appointments, felt her heart constrict.

"What do you mean, nobody loves you around here? I love you. Isn't that enough for you?"

Dooley's eyes widened. "You love me, Gran?"

"Of course I do. I'm your human, aren't I? And you're my cat, aren't you?"

"I guess I am," said Dooley. "I just figured... you don't like me curling up at your feet anymore. And this morning when I tried to snuggle you pushed me away." He didn't say it in a reproachful tone. More like a tone that indicated he wasn't all that surprised that anyone would push him away.

"Oh, Dooley, Dooley," said Vesta, picking up the gray fluffy cat and cradling him in her arms. "You have to understand that I've been under a great deal of stress lately. What with being kicked out of my own home and my own family turning against me. It's enough to drive any woman to distraction. And if I haven't been very nice to you it's because sometimes humans get so wrapped up in their own problems that they kinda forget about their responsibilities. Like my responsibility to turn this crappy yard into a new Versailles. Or to make sure my granddaughter doesn't get involved with some impostor or evil twin. Or take good care of the only baby I've got left," she added, giving Dooley a squeeze.

"Who is that baby?" asked Dooley.

"You, of course! You're my baby, Dooley. In fact you're all I've got left."

"You're all I've got left, too, Gran," said Dooley softly.

"Why, you've got Max, haven't you? I'd forget about Harriet and Brutus if I were you—they live over there," she said, gesturing to the hedge. "Over on the dark side. But Max is your friend, isn't he?"

"No, he's not," said Dooley sadly. "I asked him if I could stay with him and he turned me down flat. Milo is right. Max doesn't care one hoot about me. He probably never did."

"Who's Milo?" asked Gran.

"He's the new guy. Bristly white hair? Pink nose?"

"Oh, right," said Gran vaguely. Odelia was always taking in strays. Hard to keep up. "Did you just say this Milo told you Max doesn't care about you?"

"Uh-huh. Well, he didn't say it straight out. He kinda suggested it when he said a real friend would have invited me to stay in his home a long time ago."

Gran was frowning at Dooley. "Sounds like a suspicious character to me, Dooley. Like Dr. John Branson, the identical twin of Dr. Richard Quartermaine, who turned out to be a basket case and ended up attacking his brother's wife with that bomb that time. He got sent to an asylum but managed to escape by switching places with his twin." She nodded pensively. "To be completely honest with you, I'm not sure he's not to be distrusted."

Dooley blinked, visibly enthralled with this bit of sage advice. "Okay," he said finally.

Feeling she'd dispensed enough wisdom for one morning, she poured Dooley from her arms, then suddenly had a bright idea. "You know what I'm going to do, Dooley?"

"What?" asked Dooley.

"I'm taking a leaf from your book."

"My book? What book?"

But Vesta wasn't listening. "I'm going over there to confront the guy. I think the time for dillydallying has come to an end and now it's time to act. Like Nurse Rebecca Webb when she told Jason she'd finally had enough of his affair with her devious half-sister and told him to choose. Of course that was before he was killed in that plane crash, but no matter."

And with a hint of steel glinting behind her glasses, she stalked into the house. Time to tell that no-good son-in-law of hers what was what and find out where his priorities lay.

CHAPTER 8

I saw Dooley take a nap on the bench on the deck and was just about to go over there and try and patch things up between us when Milo gave me a tap on the head.

I hate it when cats pat me on the head. Still, remembering Harriet and Brutus's words, I managed a polite smile. "Hey, Milo. What have you been up to?"

"Oh, just scouting the place," said Milo. "Looking around, you know."

"Great."

"So, Max. Is it true that you're the only one who's allowed to sleep at Odelia's feet? And that you won't let anyone else even get near her when she's asleep?"

I stared at Milo. "What are you talking about? Who said that?"

"Dooley. He told me you're very possessive when it comes to your human." He shrugged. "Can't blame you, though. She is a great human. If I had a human like that I'd make sure no other cat came anywhere near her either."

I stared at Dooley, who was licking his fur, now basking

in the sun. "Dooley said that? He actually told you I'm…" I swallowed away a lump of annoyance. "Possessive?"

"Obsessive is the word he used, actually. But hey, like I said, with a human like Odelia what cat wouldn't go a little nuts, right? She's only like the perfect human ever."

"Nuts," I said between gritted teeth. "Obsessive."

"Yeah. So why don't I sleep on the couch? I don't want to get on your bad side again, Max. I know now why you didn't take to me when I first arrived. Because I was too nice to Odelia and you felt threatened." He held up his paws. "I can dig that, brother. Respect. And I can assure you it won't happen again. She's your human. Paws off. I get it."

"I'm not like that!" I cried, aghast. "I'm not possessive or obsessive or… nuts!"

"Right-o, brother," said Milo, taking a step back. "Whatever you say."

"I'm just not! Whatever Dooley told you was a bunch of lies!"

Milo laughed. "Like that thing he told me about you being madly in love with Harriet? And how you and Brutus used to come to blows over her?"

"I'm not—" I paused, trying to keep calm. "I'm not in love with Harriet! Dooley is! He's the one who's always been nuts about her. And obscenely jealous of Brutus."

"Look, Dooley's just looking out for you, Max. Like any friend would. He knows you're sensitive about this whole Harriet thing and who can blame you? Being in love like that for years and years and years without having the guts to tell her? That takes a lot of self-control, brother. And I get it. If you love them, set them free, right? More power to you."

"I'm. Not. In. Love. With. Harriet," I said, parsing out the words between puffs of smoke now pouring from my nose. "I never was. Never will. She's just a friend, all right?"

"Sure," said Milo, but it was obvious he didn't believe me.

"Look, I know it's tough, buddy. Especially with the kind of cat Brutus is. And the things he's been saying about you."

I gawked at the cat. This was getting better and better. "What's Brutus been saying about me?"

"Oh, just that you're the dumbest cat he's ever met," said Milo, suddenly having developed a powerful interest in his nails.

"Dumbest cat he's ever met!"

"Look, I know you consider Brutus a friend," said Milo. "And the last thing I want is to cause trouble. But with the stuff he says about you, I'd reconsider that friendship, bro."

"What else has he been saying about me?" I demanded hotly.

"Only that you're so ugly no cat in Hampton Cove wants to be your girl. And so dumb you've never realized this before. And so deadly dull and boring nobody wants to be your friend. And that the only reason he and Harriet hang out with you is because your humans are related." He shrugged. "It's that old saying all over again, isn't it? You can choose your friends but you can't choose your family? It's a blessing and a curse. And in Harriet's case it's definitely a curse, as she's forced to spend time with you—time she could spend with her real friends downtown."

I had developed a tremor in my paw now, and a twitch in my whisker. "Thank you very much, Milo," I said hoarsely, in as calm and collected a way as I could muster. "Thank you for telling me the truth about my so-called friends."

Milo did the palms-up thing. "Hey. What are friends for, right?"

Friends were there so they could backstab other friends, I thought as I walked away. And as I directed a nasty glance at Dooley, now licking his butt as if he didn't have a care in the world, I vowed that from then on they were dead to me. Dooley, Harriet, and Brutus. They were dead to me and if I never saw or heard from them again that was fine by me!

"Where are you going?" asked Dooley as I slipped right past him.

"Out!" I snapped.

"Want me to tag along?" he asked.

I directed as cold a look at him as I could muster. Then I turned my back on him and stalked off. You're dead to me, that look said, and judging from Dooley's expression of surprise, he caught it right in the ribs.

CHAPTER 9

Chase rode his pickup to the farm where Geary Potbelly did his business. The rutted road led them to a farmhouse, long clapboard structures located right behind it, and huge silos where presumably Geary stored the food for the ducks or—and Odelia didn't even want to contemplate this—the poop the animals produced.

"So… I don't see no ducks," she said as Chase parked the rig next to the farmhouse.

"They moved them all indoors a decade ago," said Chase. "They used to roam free, but then environmental laws tightened and allowing the duck poop to drain into the ground and pollute the groundwater with nitrates became strictly prohibited. So now the ducks are all in those long white buildings over there, where they can poop through the mesh wire so it can be flushed into big holding tanks and then procured for processing."

"What do they use it for?"

"It ends up on huge compost heaps, where it's mixed with mulch and yard waste which binds the nitrogen in the manure and prevents it from leaking into the ground and leaching into the groundwater. Then it's sold to garden centers and Home Depot and such."

"How come you know so much about duck poop, Chase?"

He laughed. "Before you start thinking this is my latest hobby, let me assure you it's not. No, I talked to Geary on the phone to figure out how his poop ended up killing Dickerson and he explained to me a little about the process they have out here."

As they walked up to the house, the same guy in coveralls they met out at the Dickerson place, held up his hand in greeting. He was shoveling straw onto a wheelbarrow.

"Bert! Have you seen Geary around?" Chase yelled at him.

"Come on in!" Bert yelled back. "He's inside." He was pointing to the stable.

"I guess we're going to meet some of those famous Long Island ducks up close and personal," Chase quipped.

They strode into a large space, surprisingly light and airy, and immediately Odelia saw thousands upon thousands of ducks lounging around, buckets of feed attached to wooden poles, light fixtures dangling from the ceiling, and the ducks not in cages as she'd feared, but free to roam the large space, straw under their feet and happily quacking away.

"Wow. I don't think I've ever seen so many ducks in one place," she said.

"Me neither," Chase chimed in.

A man dressed in blue coveralls was crouched down over what looked like feeding troughs, and they walked up to him, the ducks scuttling away as they did.

"Mr. Potbelly!" Chase said as they joined the duck farmer.

Contrary to the name, he was a tall, reedy man with a tan, weather-beaten face and a ball cap with the name 'Potbelly Farm' lodged firmly on his head.

"Hey there, Detective," said Geary. "Nice to put a name to the face."

"Likewise," said Chase. "This is Odelia Poole. Odelia is a reporter for the *Hampton Cove Gazette*, but she also frequently helps us out in our investigations."

"Your daddy is Tex Poole, right?" asked Geary, nodding. "He's my doctor."

"I think my dad is pretty much everybody's doctor," said Odelia.

"He's a good one, though. Got me some of those patches for my chest pains." He slapped his chest. "Been feeling like a new man ever since. Real miracle cure, Miss Poole."

"Odelia. And I'm glad my dad could help you out, Mr. Potbelly."

"Geary," he said with a grin that displayed two rows of nicotine-stained teeth. "So what can I do you for?"

"You can help us understand how a tanker full of your duck poop ended up all the way out at Dick Dickerson's place."

He scratched his scalp. "Well, sir, like I told you over the phone, one of our tankers got stolen last night, along with one of our tractors. So that might explain things."

"Any idea who could have taken them?"

"Nope. Must have happened sometime after midnight, though, cause my youngest one just got back from checking on the ducklings in the hatchery and he says the tanker was still there when he did."

"He's sure about that?"

"Absolutely. That thing's an eyesore, and he would have noticed if it was gone."

"So walk us through this, Geary. Someone got onto your property and took off with a tractor and a tanker. How is that possible?"

"We sleep all the way out there," said Geary, pointing to the west. "The entire family lives on the perimeter, in houses we built ourselves. Five generations of Potbellies have lived there and still do, so we don't hear what goes on up here at night."

"Don't you have guard dogs? A fence? Security?"

"We have a fence, but they took out an entire section. Professional job, too. When my son told me I thought they'd come for the ducks. We were surprised they'd taken the tanker. Couldn't imagine what they wanted with nine thousand gallons of duck poop."

"Now we know," said Chase grimly.

"We have a couple dogs, too, but I guess those sneak thieves must have managed to get past them." He grunted. "At least they didn't hurt them. Those dogs are like family."

"So no cameras, huh?" asked Odelia.

"Potbelly Farm isn't the Chase Manhattan or Tiffany's, Odelia. We've had a few break-ins over the years but nothing major. The fence is more to keep the deer out and the ducks in than anything else. The rest is up to the dogs, and usually they're enough of a deterrent. But the visitors we had last night were something else. Real pros, if you ask me."

CHAPTER 10

Grandma was huffing a little by the time she reached the doctor's office. It was only a short walk from the house but still. She was seventy-five, not twenty-five, and even when she was twenty-five working out wasn't the hype it had become later on. Oh, she'd bought those tapes Jane Fonda had put out in the eighties. She'd even bought herself some of those funky leg warmers Jane was so nuts about, and those colorful leotards. But the workouts looked too strenuous even then, and she'd never gotten into them the way Victoria Principal or Linda Evans did. Or even that hot John Travolta in *Perfect*. Now there was a fine man.

She crossed the street on a huff. She'd prepared her little speech and Tex was gonna get it now. How she'd been waiting and waiting for him to apologize and how it was starting to look like she'd be waiting until she was dead and buried before he finally came round.

She opened the door and walked into the waiting room that had been her domain until a few weeks ago. When she walked up to the desk her jaw dropped when she caught sight of the woman seated behind it. Seated in her chair, behind her desk, in her exact spot!

None other than Scarlett Canyon herself was staring back at her, giving her that impudent look she was famous for. Not a day younger than Vesta herself, Scarlett nevertheless looked younger, thanks to the numerous procedures she'd undergone. Her boob lift-slash-enhancement especially had cemented her reputation with the senior center's male membership, but her face, too, had been extensively worked on, her eyes now resembling a cat's eyes and her lips plumped up way beyond what was esthetically pleasing.

Then again, with boobs like that, what hot-blooded male cared about the face?

"Scarlett," Vesta said curtly. "Patients are supposed to wait in the waiting room."

"I'm not here as a patient, Vesta," said Scarlett, tapping a single long nail on the keyboard spacebar. "I work here now."

Vesta's jaw dropped a few inches. "Work here? What do you mean, work here?!"

"I heard you abandoned poor Tex and how he was desperate for a new receptionist, so I volunteered." She smiled widely, or at least as widely as her collagen-filled lips would allow. "And I have to tell you, I love it, Vesta. I don't understand why you quit."

"Don't you mind why I quit. That's my chair, Scarlett, and that's my desk, and that's my computer. So you better walk out of here now, or I'll have you thrown out so fast not even those implants of yours will be able to break your fall when you hit the pavement."

A cough sounded behind her, and she whipped her head around. Half a dozen people were seated in the waiting area, following the altercation with rapt attention. She didn't mind. Scarlett was going to get what was coming to her and she didn't care who heard it.

"Are you threatening me with violence, Vesta?" asked Scarlett, bringing a shocked hand to her chest.

"If you don't clear out of here I'm kicking your enhanced booty so hard those butt implants will end up dangling behind your ears. And that's not a threat—that's a promise!"

Scarlett rose and jutted out her butt. "For your information, this booty is all-natural, just like my boobies," she said, a noticeable purr in her voice. "Unlike your bony butt and your flat chest, Vesta dear." She even had the gall to flash her eyebrows at her!

"That's it," Vesta snapped. "I'm coming for you, Scarlett."

And she would have mounted that desk, sciatica or no sciatica, and given Scarlett a piece of her mind, when Tex's door opened and the doctor himself came walking in.

"What's going on here?" he demanded.

With his shock of white hair and his kind face Tex Poole reminded some people of Dick Van Dyke when he was solving murders as Dr. Mark Sloan on *Diagnosis: Murder*. Now, though, he looked more like a masked avenger, without the mask, as he stepped up to his mother-in-law, and took her arm in a firm grip, then took Scarlett's arm in an equally firm grip, and dragged the two women apart.

"What the cuss do you think you're doing, Vesta?" he said. "Barging in here and threatening my receptionist with bodily harm?"

"She took my place!" Vesta croaked. "And on top of that she insulted me!"

"All I said was that you are very slim, Vesta," said Scarlett coyly. "I was paying you a compliment. I really was, Dr. Tex."

Tex was looking grim. "I don't get it, Vesta. First you quit on me and now you attack the woman who was so kind to step up and offer her help when she saw I was struggling?"

"Oh, she was offering to help, all right," said Vesta.

"Though I'm not sure my daughter would appreciate the kind of help Scarlett has to offer!"

Tex had the decency to blush. "Now, Vesta, you know that's nonsense talk."

"Filthy gossip, that's what it is," said Scarlett. "And mean-spirited, too."

"I'll give you mean-spirited," Vesta growled, and tried to poke her nemesis in the fake nose. She never got close, for Tex was still acting like a buffer between the two women.

"Now, now, Vesta," he was saying in that horribly soothing doctor's voice of his. "Calm down."

"Oh, all right," said Vesta, shaking off Tex's hand. "I'm going already. But I'm warning you," she spat in Scarlett's direction. "This is not the end."

"Oh, I wouldn't expect it to be, Vesta, dear," said Scarlett sweetly.

And as Vesta stalked huffily to the door, Scarlett even blew her a kiss. In return, Vesta blew her nemesis a raspberry, made a very rude gesture with one of the fingers of her right hand, and slammed the door shut behind her.

No, this was not the end. In fact this had only just begun.

CHAPTER 11

Dooley sat on the wooden garden bench, feeling miserable. He didn't understand why Max had suddenly decided to give him the cold shoulder. In spite of Gran's assurances that Dooley was loved, he was starting to think that Milo was right after all, and that Max didn't give a hoot about him. Or anyone else, for that matter.

And just when he was thinking of maybe sneaking after Max and asking his old friend what was going on, Milo jumped up onto the bench and made himself comfortable.

"Hey, buddy," said Milo. "You don't look so good. Are you sure you're not sick?"

Dooley blinked a few times. "Sick? Do you think I'm sick?"

Milo held up his paws. "Hey, I'm not a doctor, buddy, but you look kinda pale. Max just told me the same thing, so I figured I'd do the square thing by you and check it out."

"Max told you I looked sick?"

"Sure. Then again, he said you were born sickly. Been weak and prone to disease ever since Grandma brought you home from the pound."

Dooley's heart was beating fast now, a sickening sense of doom extending its icy tentacles into his soul. "The pound? Grandma brought me home from the pound? But she always said she got me from a very dear friend of hers. From a litter of eight little Dooleys."

"A little white lie, Dooley. Humans are big on little white lies. They think it's for the best, but they often end up doing a lot of damage. Anyhoo, I think maybe it's time for you to head on down to the vet, don't you think? You're coming down with something. And it wouldn't surprise me if isn't some parasite wreaking havoc inside your digestion system."

"A parasite!"

"Yup. Worms, probably."

"Worms! Inside me?!"

"Sure. You've got your tapeworm, your hookworm, your whipworm, your roundworm... Have you lost weight recently?"

"I-I think so," said Dooley, touching his shrinking belly. "Haven't been hungry."

"That's the worms for you," said Milo with a knowing nod. "Make you lose your appetite. You're probably full of them, crawling all over your insides. What about vomiting? Diarrhea? Coughing? Feeling bloated?"

Dooley felt sick, and suddenly retched. "How-how big are these worms, Milo?"

"Oh, the smallest ones are at least five inches long. The big ones?" He gave Dooley a worried look that spoke volumes.

Dooley could imagine dozens of worms moving around inside his gut, and when he glanced down at his belly, he could almost see them, wriggling underneath the skin! "G-get them out of there!" he cried. "Milo! Help me—you need to help me get rid out of them!"

"I want to help you," said Milo earnestly. "But Max told me not to."

"Max told you what?!"

"Yeah, he said you're such a crybaby it's better just to leave you to your own devices. He said he's tried to help you out before, but you end up making life a living hell for him, so nowadays he simply prefers not to tell you anything at all, and hope you won't notice that you're sick and…" He grimaced. "Maybe I should just follow Max's advice."

"Tell me!"

"I don't know, Dooley. Max said I shouldn't bother. Then again, I'm of the opinion that a true friend always tells his friends the truth—even when it's just… terrible, horrible."

Dooley stared at this newfound friend of his. "Tell me the truth, Milo. Just… tell me." Milo placed a paw on Dooley's shoulder and looked him in the eyes. One of those earnest, heartfelt looks. The kind of look a real friend gave his best friend and compatriot. And Dooley remembered the cold look Max had given him and he knew. Max was not his friend. No matter what Gran said. Max was simply a liar. "Just… tell me?" he whispered.

"You're dying, Dooley. This is the end of the line for you, pal. I give you two more days—three, tops—and then it's bye-bye, baby for Dooley."

"Oh, no!" he cried. "But-but is there nothing I can do? Milo—please!"

Milo looked doubtful, like a doctor after giving his patient the final verdict. Then he softened. "You need to get rid of those worms, buddy. Either you live, or those worms do. Only one of you can live. Just like Harry Potter and his old chum Voldemort, remember?"

"How-how do I get rid of these Voldemort worms?"

"There's only one way." He squeezed Dooley's shoulder. "Cat Snax."

"Max's favorite snack."

"That's right. Cat Snax contain a secret ingredient that worms hate. The more Cat Snax you eat, the greater your chance of survival."

"But Max hates it when we snack on his Cat Snax."

"Come on, Dooley. This is do or die, buddy. If you don't get rid of those worms you'll be dead inside the day."

"The day! You just said two or three days!"

"I didn't want to upset you."

"Cat Snax," said Dooley thoughtfully.

"Cat Snax. And you need to scoot."

"Scoot?"

"Wipe your tush across the floor."

"Why?"

Milo sighed. "Isn't it obvious? When those Cat Snax kick in, those worms are flushed out of your system. But they hang on for dear life, digging their little pincers into your butt. So you need to boogie-woogie those suckers. Crush them and turn them into poop smears."

"Poop smears," repeated Dooley, thinking that this sounded like music to his ears.

"Yeah, so don't you go poopy doopy in the litter box now, you hear? Those blood-sucking parasites love litter. They snack on that litter. And then they jump right back onto your fur, burrow their way through your skin, and you're right back where you started."

"You mean I have to… poop on the floor?"

"The floor, the rug, the bed, heck, you can poop on the kitchen table for all I care. As long as you scoot."

"Scoot."

"Scoot like your life depends on it, Dooley." He nodded seriously. "Cause it does."

CHAPTER 12

I'd been wandering along aimlessly, and finally reached downtown and I still had no idea where I was going. The idea that Dooley had been saying those horrible things about me, and so had Brutus and Harriet, had cut me to the quick. How could they even think that stuff? Me, in love with Harriet. Or possessive of Odelia. Or the dumbest and ugliest cat in Hampton Cove. So ugly, in fact, that no female cat had ever shown an interest in me.

A sneaking suspicion now entered my mind. The suspicion that Brutus and Harriet were right. That I really was that dumb and that ugly. I mean, why else was I still single while everyone else was involved with someone? The thought had never occurred to me before.

And as I finally reached my destination, Wilbur Vickery's General Store on Main Street, I looked around for Kingman, Wilbur's plump piebald. To my elation he was right where he always was: holding forth to three female cats who hung on his every word.

"Hey, Kingman," I said by way of greeting.

Then, to my surprise, the three females gave me a furtive glance then stalked off without even so much as a hello.

"And hello to you, too," I said as I stared after them.

"Hey, Max," said Kingman. "Are you feeling all right? You look a little… out of sorts."

"Did those girls say something about me?" I asked, still staring at the three females sashaying off, their heads close together and clearly sharing a tasty morsel of gossip.

"Nope. Why would they?"

"Just wondering," I said, frowning to myself.

"Did you hear about that murder case?" Kingman asked, changing the subject.

"What murder case? What are you talking about?"

"The *National Star* dude that got smothered in duck poop?"

"Duck sauce?" I asked, figuring I'd misheard.

"Duck poop, not sauce. Yeah, your human is all over that one. Went up to Dickerson's house this morning to investigate, along with her beefcake boyfriend. I figured you'd have tagged along—you and that ragtag gang of feline detective friends of yours."

"They're no friends of mine," I muttered darkly, wondering why Odelia would be investigating a murder case without inviting me along. This was definitely a first. And then the horrible truth came home to me: hadn't Milo said I was too possessive about Odelia? Too obsessive? Not allowing anyone else to even come near her? Odelia must have felt it. She must have felt the noose tighten around her neck and decided to take her distance. Investigate this murder case all by herself. Without possessive Max to cramp her style.

Gah. Now I'd done it. I'd gone and made my human mad.

Which could only mean one thing: she was getting ready to chuck me out.

My eyes widened. Could it be... Could it be that she was grooming Milo as my replacement? Maybe he didn't even belong to this Aloisia Lane woman. Maybe she'd gotten him from a friend, and she was going to keep him and train him and then she was going to kick me out! Maybe even hand me over to Aloisia Lane when she returned from Florida!

"Max!" Kingman was yelling, and only now did I notice he must have been trying to catch my attention for a while now. "What's wrong, Max? You don't look like yourself, buddy."

I gave him a sad look. "I haven't been myself for a long time, Kingman. Only it's taken me until now to realize it." And with these words, I slunk off. I didn't know where I was going. Home? But where was home? Not with Odelia, that was for sure. And not with Marge or Vesta either.

Home is where the heart is, the old saying goes. But my heart didn't belong to anyone, Milo had made that clear to me. And suddenly a surge of gratitude swept through me. Milo was the only friend I had in this world. The only cat who'd told me the truth.

The only cat who hadn't lied to my face all these years.

I passed a newsstand, and read the headlines about the *'Don of Dung Dunged to Death,'* but they didn't hold any interest to me. Someone else would have to catch the Don of Dung's danged killer. Someone smart and cool and popular. Someone who wasn't me.

My days as a feline sleuth were over.

˜

*H*arriet watched as Dooley stalked into the house, assumed the squatting position, and produced a nice little turd, right there on Odelia's new off-white IKEA rug, then proceeded to wipe his tush on the same rug, sashaying along while intently looking over his shoulder at his progression, as if admiring his handiwork—or rather his buttwork.

She blinked, wondering what had gotten into the cat. Then she suddenly noticed that she was no longer alone. Milo had materialized right next to her and was shaking his head.

"Sad, isn't it?"

"What is?" she asked.

"Dooley. I didn't want to tell you this before but he's finally lost it."

"He is acting a little weird," she admitted. "Why is he pooping on the rug?"

"Nobody told you? Oh, the little guy is head over heels in love with you, Harriet, and this is his way of showing you."

"What?!" she cried, horrified.

"Sure. He must have seen it on some *Discovery Channel* documentary, how some tribesmen in the Amazon rainforest smear their poop on trees as a token of their affection. Anthropologists say tribeswomen study that poop as an indicator of the health and vigor of the male, which greatly helps them in choosing the right partner so they can procreate. It's all true," he said, holding up two claws when Harriet gave him a look of horror. "So now poor, deluded little Dooley there thinks he can win your heart by spreading his stool around, in the hope you'll figure his stool shows he's a better potential mate than Brutus."

"Oh, my God, but that's just ridiculous!" Harriet cried, aghast. "Has he lost his mind?"

"Dooley's mind was never a very powerful instrument to begin with," said Milo, who seemed to know what he was talking about. "Which is why he's fallen prey to this state of delusion. But not to worry," he added, suddenly chipper. "I'm sure it's just a phase. After all, Max passed through this awkward stage and he came out more or less unscathed, right?"

"Max? Did he have this... stool phase?"

"Oh, yes. Max has been head over heels in love with you for years, Harriet. Only now the pendulum has swung the other way, I'm afraid."

"What do you mean?"

"Max hates you. It often happens with one who's loved as deeply and as passionately as Max has. When that love isn't reciprocated it turns into a violent, deep-seated hatred."

"Max hates me?"

"Max loathes you with every fiber of his being. Just watch him when he thinks you're not looking. You'll see the rage in his eyes. The pure, unadulterated murderous loathing."

"I don't believe this. Why has no one ever told me this before?" she demanded.

"Because they didn't want you to worry, Harriet," said Milo, his voice dripping with compassion. "And then there's the other thing. The violence."

"Violence?"

"Oh, yes. Max has these violent tendencies. When provoked he gets quite dangerous. Cats felt that as long as you didn't know how he felt about you, you couldn't provoke one of his outbursts." He touched her shoulder lightly. "I disagree. I feel that you have a right to know. And now that you do, and you're properly warned, you can prepare yourself."

"You mean... stay away from him?"

"Stay away, and in case you do need to come into contact with the madcat, don't look into his eyes, don't talk to him, don't do anything that might trigger an attack."

"Oh, dear. Well, I'm glad someone had the courage to tell me. Thank you, Milo."

"Don't mention it, Harriet."

They both stared at Dooley, who was now studying the brown smears on the carpet, sniffing them intently.

"Mad," said Harriet.

"And sad," Milo added with a sigh.

CHAPTER 13

"So what do you think, Chase?" asked Chief Alec, speaking from Chase's phone.

"No, what do *you* think, Chief?" asked Chase.

He could see Tracy Sting behind the Chief and an amazing view of the mountains the couple were currently hiking through. They were lucky they had reception.

"Yeah, we asked you first, Uncle Alec," said Odelia. She waved at Tracy, who smiled and waved back. A striking redhead with trim, athletic physique, she was a can-do woman who looked even more can-do with her sunglasses, hiking jacket and hiking boots.

Even Alec looked ready to tackle those mountains—and enjoy a nice crackling fire once they got back to their lodge or cabin. The rotund chief looked like he'd lost some weight, and his bushy brows suddenly looked a lot less bushy, as if he'd—gasp!—trimmed them. Everything to impress his date. In fact Alec looked years younger—a marked effect.

"Look, I don't have all the details, all right?" the Chief was saying. "Just what you told me. As far as I know Dickerson had a ton of files in that safe of his. In fact he was famous for having dirt on pretty much everyone who was someone and he kept it in that safe."

"The safe was empty," said Odelia.

"Not completely empty," said Chase. "There was one file and one picture."

"Yeah, a picture of a rose," said Odelia. "Ring any bells?"

"None," said Chief Alec. "But maybe you can start by looking at the usual suspects."

"Which are?" said Chase.

Alec frowned. "Um… Dickerson was rumored to be a close friend of the President but they'd recently fallen out over something. No idea what. You'd have to ask him."

"The President as in *the* President?" asked Odelia.

"Yup. So if I were you I'd start there. And then there's the professional aspect."

"Like a mob hit," said Odelia.

"Dickerson got in bad with Yasir Bellinowski."

"The Russian mobster?" said Chase.

"Alleged," said Alec. "At least that's what I heard. So I would pay him a visit. Maybe there was something in that vault Bellinowski wanted so bad he was prepared to kill for it."

"It does have mafia written all over it," Odelia agreed. "With the duck poop and all."

"You need to follow up about that theft at the Potbelly farm. Whoever stole that tractor and that tanker is your guy. Catch him, and catch the person who ordered the hit."

"Good luck!" Tracy said, moving into view again and giving them a wave.

"Thanks," said Odelia. "We'll need it."

"Oh, no, you won't. You guys are the best damn sleuths I've ever had," said Chief Alec with a grin. "And the fact that I only have to pay one of you makes it even better."

"Ha ha," said Chase. "Very funny."

"Take good care of my uncle for me, Tracy," said Odelia. "He's the only one I've got."

"Oh, I'll take very good care of him," Tracy assured her. "In fact I already am."

"She is," said the Chief with a happy grin, his face rotund and his cheeks flushed.

"I don't think I want to know," said Odelia with a laugh.

And on the image of the Chief and Tracy kissing, the connection cut out.

"They look happy," said Chase.

"They look more than happy," said Odelia. "They look like they're in love."

Chase had placed an arm around her waist. "You mean they look like us?"

"Something like that."

He kissed her deeply, and she almost dropped her phone, which he took as a good sign. Looked like he still had it. But then he wrenched his mind back to the investigation. They were holed up in the police station, where they'd decided to consult with the Chief and get his input. Now, though, they needed to follow up on his instructions and go and talk to the President. Gulp.

"Do you think the President will even talk to us?" asked Odelia, whose mind had landed on the same topic.

"I hope so. He was a close friend of Dickerson's."

"Until they fell out over something."

"We need to find out what that something was."

"Yes, we do."

They were seated side by side at the Chief's desk, so close together they were cheek to jowl. And since he was in the vicinity, Chase closed his lips on hers and for the next five minutes or so Dick Dickerson, the President and any possible mob connections between the tabloid mogul and this Yasir Bellinowski were the farthest thing from his mind.

But then a knock at the door surprised them and when the door swung open and Dolores appeared, they both looked up with flushed cheeks and a guilty grin on their faces.

"All right," said the policewoman with an eyeroll. "Guess I can come back later."

And then she walked out and bought them another ten minutes or so, which was all they needed.

CHAPTER 14

"I've never met the President," said Odelia as Chase steered the car through town.

"Me neither," he intimated.

"I mean, any president. Not this one or any of his predecessors."

He smiled and gave her a sideways glance. "You look excited."

"Damn right I'm excited. We're about to meet the frickin' President!"

"You look hot when you're excited."

She blushed. It wasn't the idea of seeing the President that made her feel all hot and bothered, but what she and Chase had done on top of Uncle Alec's desk. Good thing he'd never know. Unless Dolores told him. Which she probably would. And everyone else in that precinct. Shoot.

"So what did he say?" she asked.

"You mean what did his Secret Service detail say?"

"Uh-huh."

"They don't like the idea."

"He's not a suspect. Did you tell them he's not a suspect?"

"They don't like the idea of the President being interviewed by cops, period—suspect or no suspect. They don't like the story the media might spin this into."

"He's a friend of Dickerson's. He was in town when the guy was murdered. We have to talk to him."

"They know that. That doesn't mean they have to like it."

"Besides, it's not as if the President can just go and steal a tanker full of duck poop from a duck farm, back it up to his friend's house and kill him. The Secret Service would have noticed if he was traipsing around duck farms in the middle of the night."

"I think we established that whoever is behind this hired a couple of pros."

"Even so. The President probably can't even order a Big Mac or chicken nuggets without everybody knowing about it and blabbing about it."

"Yeah, I don't think we're seriously considering the possibility that President Wilcox killed his buddy the media mogul," said Chase. "But we have to start somewhere."

And so they did. "I like this mobster for the murder. And the picture of the rose left at the crime scene? Probably has some kind of mobster meaning. Like the dead horse in *The Godfather*. I mean, maybe the mob moved on from horses to pictures of horses. Or roses."

"Sure," said Chase with a grin.

"Did they find any fingerprints on that picture?"

"None. Nothing on that vault door, either, or anywhere else, for that matter. Like I said, these guys are pros. They wouldn't make a rookie mistake like that."

"Seems elaborate," said Odelia, still thinking this through. "They could have just shot him. Why go to all the trouble of the duck poop thing? That just seems like… overkill."

"Why aren't your cats along for the ride?" suddenly Chase asked.

"Mh?"

"Your cats. They usually tag along on these things. Like a good-luck charm?"

Yeah, why hadn't she brought Max and the others along? For some reason the thought hadn't occurred to her. Probably because Max seemed upset about Milo and the others eating his food. She'd just figured he wanted to be left alone. People thought cats were simply animals, with animal reflexes and driven by animal instincts. But they were smart creatures—a lot smarter than most humans gave them credit for. And they were also very sensitive, and when they were going through the kind of adaptation Max was going through with Milo, maybe it was better just to leave them alone to deal with it in peace.

"I'll bring them along next time," she said.

"Maybe it's for the best," said Chase. "I don't think the Secret Service would like it if we arrived with a bunch of cats in tow. They'd probably think they were Russian spies."

They finally arrived at Lago-a-Oceano, President Van Wilcox's expansive mansion. It was an impressive, sprawling structure, with several buildings apart from the main house, servants' quarters, an old hunter's lodge, and spreading grounds. It had a private beach where Van Wilcox was rumored to enjoy going for a swim, as did the First Lady Rima Wilcox, who hailed from Georgia and liked the privacy the mansion afforded her and her husband.

They announced their arrival to the burly Secret Service man at the gate, who eyed them stoically through glasses that obscured his eyes, spoke something into his wrist, then stepped aside as the heavy wrought-iron gate slowly swung open.

More burly men with sunglasses and dressed like Men in Black dotted the landscape, like garden gnomes on a front lawn, and Odelia swallowed away a lump of uneasiness.

"I hope they don't shoot us," she said as all eyes turned to them as they proceeded along the winding drive. "Do they also remind you of Agent Smith from *The Matrix?*"

"Don't think about it," Chase advised her. "Just keep your eye on the prize. We need to find out what the President figures happened to his friend."

"Or former friend."

"Exactly. All the rest is unimportant at this stage."

She gulped some more when the number of Agent Smiths seemed to increase the closer they got to the mansion. "I think they're multiplying. Just like in *The Matrix.*"

"Keep your cool, Odelia. This will all be fine."

"That's what you think. You're the cop. I'm the reporter. Everyone knows the President eats reporters for breakfast."

"He does not."

"He hates us. He hates us all."

"I'm sure he doesn't."

"If he orders his Secret Service to take me out back for a neck shot tell my parents I love them, all right?"

"You'll be just fine."

She wasn't too sure about that. She'd seen the way the President handled reporters. Chances were she wasn't going to make it out of there alive.

Chase seemed to sense her apprehension, for he said, "If worse comes to worst, just tell them you're with *Fox News*. The President loves *Fox News*. He'll think you're the best thing since sliced bread and he'll probably try to make you ambassador to Finland or put you in charge of Homeland Security."

She didn't respond. Just then, her phone sang out Dua Lipa's *One Kiss*. She saw it was that Otto Paunch guy again. Great timing.

"Hi, Mr. Paunch."

"Hey, Miss Poole. Have you changed that rich list yet? I'm

looking at the *Hampton Cove Gazette* website and President Wilcox's name is still absent from the list."

"I… have been a little busy, Mr. Paunch. But I'm on it."

"That's great. Oh, and while you're at it, could you also change the President's Wikipedia page? I see it says here that he was on the cover of *Time Magazine* twenty-one times. That's incorrect. He's been on the cover fifty times, more than any other president ever and certainly more than Richard Nixon, who was on the cover only forty-three times."

"Um…"

"Can I count on you for that, Miss Poole?"

"Well, I don't actually—"

"Thanks. You're amazing. Talk to you soon!"

"I don't actually work for Wikipedia," she said, but Mr. Paunch had already disconnected. She stared at her phone. So weird.

"Who was that?" asked Chase.

"Otto Paunch. He's one of President Wilcox's best friends and he keeps calling me to change stuff online."

"Like what?"

"Like the rich list we published, or now he was asking about his Wikipedia page."

"I guess Presidents do that kind of thing all the time. They're very sensitive when it comes to public perception."

"But… I don't work for Wikipedia."

"No one does. They've got editors who write those pages."

But then she forgot all about Otto Paunch and his strange requests. They'd arrived at the forecourt of Lago-a-Oceano and Odelia was duly impressed. It looked like something out of a fairytale, the porticoed entrance supported by columns, lending it a classical look. The mansion itself was huge, with dozens of windows looking out across the forecourt, the impressive building sporting a distinctly Spanish architectural style.

"It looks… amazing," she gasped, then, "I'm underdressed, Chase. Grossly underdressed."

"We're here in an official capacity, Poole. Not as guests."

And then a small army of Agent Smiths descended upon them and that was the end.

CHAPTER 15

⌘

Scarlett Canyon was filing her nails when the phone rang. Again. She sighed deeply, put down her nail file and picked up the phone. "Dr. Poole's office. How can I help you?"

"Hi," said a croaky voice. "My name is Ida LaBelle and I think I have a boil on my butt. Can you tell me what I have to do to get rid of it?"

"I'll schedule an appointment with Dr. Poole."

"No!" cried the voice. "I mean—I can't. I'm a busy woman with a lot on my plate. But you sound like a clever person. And you work for a doctor so obviously you must know a lot about medicine. So please just tell me—*advise* me—what should I do?"

Scarlett studied her nails. She'd just gotten new gel nails down at the nail salon but she wasn't convinced about the color. They were pink with little glittery ladybugs. She would have preferred the blue ones with the gold sparkly hearts. "I'm sorry, dear," she now intoned. "I don't know nothing about no butt boils."

"But… you work for a doctor, don't you?"

"Yah. So?"

"So you must be a licensed receptionist."

"Look, honey. If you want to make an appointment, make an appointment already. Otherwise stop wasting my frickin' time."

"You *are* aware that you're supposed to be a licensed receptionist to work for a medical professional, right? If not the inspectors might come in and arrest you for fraud."

"What inspectors? What are you talking about?"

"You can't just walk in from the street and start working for a doctor. You need to have the necessary paperwork. Didn't nobody ever tell you that, Scarlett?"

She stared at the phone for a moment. That voice… "How do you know my name?"

"Because… I read it in the yellow pages just now."

"I'm not in the yellow pages. Do people even still use the yellow pages?"

"Forget about the yellow pages and listen to me for a sec. I'm just trying to help you out here. If you don't got no license you're not even supposed to be in there, sitting at that desk and typing at that computer. Inspectors will come in and bust you if you don't quit."

"Vesta? Is that you?"

Silence. Then: "My name is Ida LaBelle. And I'm calling about my butt boil."

"Oh, fiddlesticks, 'Ida.' And your butt boil! I'm telling Tex you're harassing me!"

"You're denying me medical treatment! That's a federal crime! I could bust you for that, you booby bimbo!"

"Buzz off, Vesta," said Scarlett, and thunked down the phone.

Just then, Tex walked in from the office, a smile on his face. "And how is my favorite receptionist doing? Was that a patient?"

"Nah. Just your mother-in-law trying to mess with me."

The smile disappeared. "Vesta? What did she want?"

"I don't know. Something about a butt boil and a license." She waggled a nail. "She's going to make trouble for you, Dr. Tex, I'm telling you. That woman is like a dog with a bone. She'll keep coming back until you give her a kick in the bony rear end and be done with her."

"I can't kick my wife's mother in the rear end," said Tex, a little wistfully.

"Well, you should. I've known Vesta all my life. She's a terror. I know she's family and all, but sometimes you just have to draw a line in the sand, Dr. Tex. Take a stand."

Tex didn't look like he was prepared to take a stand. "If she calls again just tell her…" He hesitated, rooting around for a possible solution. "Just tell her not to call again," he concluded lamely, then turned on his heel and disappeared into his office.

Scarlett smiled. "I'll tell her just that and more," she said to herself, then resumed the study of her nails. She needed more sparkle, she thought. Sparkle was the new pink.

※

The Agent Smiths that had converged upon Chase's aged pickup now opened the door—both the passenger side and the driver's side—then proceeded to escort the cop and his assistant out of the car. They all had those black sunglasses, making it impossible for Odelia to see their eyes, and for some reason they kept pressing their fingers into their ears.

But instead of taking them into the house, they escorted them right around it.

"Where are you taking us?" asked Odelia. The men

assumed a dignified silence, though. She turned to Chase. "Where are they taking us?"

"To see the President. I hope."

He didn't seem worried, so Odelia tried to relax. If the hardened cop wasn't worried, she probably shouldn't be, either. But she couldn't help it—she was worried.

"I think they found out I'm a reporter, Chase," she said now. "They must have scanned my face or something and got a hit in their database and now the secret is out. It's just like I told you: they're taking us out back to give us neck shots and bury our mangled corpses in the woods!"

"And how would our corpses end up being mangled?" asked Chase, amused.

"They'll torture us first! Try to find out what we know!"

"Know about what?"

She flapped her arms. "I don't know!"

He placed a reassuring hand on her lower back. "See? You don't know. So there's no need for them to torture you."

"Okay, I'm taking back the mangled corpses thing. So they'll just shoot us and bury us. Where we'll never be found." She took out her phone. "I need to tell my parents."

"Tell them what?"

"Where we are! If they have a last known location maybe they can tell Uncle Alec to come and find us. Give us a proper Christian burial!"

"I think you're overreacting, honey. The President of the United States doesn't kill people in his backyard. At least not as far I know."

At this point, the Men in Black—or Agent Smiths—seemed to have entered the final straight, for they were talking into their wrists again, muttering incomprehensible jargon under their breaths. And then she saw it—or rather, she saw him: the POTUS.

They'd arrived at what looked like an animal enclosure. It

was a circular area, cordoned off by a three-foot-high fence, and offered the weirdest sight Odelia had ever encountered, and in her days as a reporter she'd encountered many weird sights.

This one took the cake, though: the President of the United States was… wrestling with a very large hog, both of them down and dirty in two inches of mud, and they were really going at it, the President holding the hog in a death grip, and the hog kicking its legs and desperately trying to escape.

Both man and beast were covered in mud from top to toe, but that didn't seem to bother either. And then Odelia saw that a second hog had entered the fray, and was now jumping on top of the President, presumably to open a second front and save its buddy.

"What's going on here?" Odelia asked as she watched the proceedings, wide-eyed.

"The President is wrestling a hog," said Chase, who seemed more amused than surprised. "Two hogs, in fact. Oh, look, there's number three. Raising the stakes."

About a dozen Secret Service agents guarded the hog enclosure's perimeter, their expressions inscrutable, and their stance vigilant and alert. If those hogs tried any funny business they'd be on them in a heartbeat, that stance seemed to indicate.

The leader of the free world, meanwhile, still had the upper hand, but with three hogs against one human, he was having to fight hard to maintain his advantage. The hog he was holding onto slipped out of his grip, perhaps due to the slippery conditions, and the President now rose to his feet and assumed a wrestler's pose, the hogs circling him warily. And then one of them moved in for the kill, squealing like… a pig, and went on the attack!

The President simply stepped aside and then landed a

crushing blow to the hog's back! Hog and man went down in a splash of mud, and now the other pigs joined in.

"I can't watch this," said Odelia, who'd never been a big fan of wrestling.

"My money is on the President," said Chase, who seemed to enjoy the show tremendously. But then suddenly it was all over.

From the house, a woman came hurrying over. Odelia recognized her as Rima, President Wilcox's wife of five years. She was a former model and looked absolutely stunning. Tall and willowy, with raven hair, a dark complexion and one of those hourglass figures you read so much about but rarely see in real life, she came teetering over on high heels, dressed in a skintight sparkly number that revealed some stunning décolletage.

"Van!" she was yelling, her voice plaintive. "Oh, Van!"

Van, who by now was holding the three hogs by the necks, looked up at the sound of his wife's voice. "I'm a little busy here, honey!" he yelled.

"Ooh, not with the piggies again, Van," she said as she surveyed the scene with a look of distaste. "How many times have I told you not to fight the piggies. You get dirty."

"And I love it!" her husband yelled, and got up, allowing the hogs a little break.

One of the Secret Service agents handed him a towel, and the President wiped the mud from his face.

"It's the President of France, Van," said his wife. "He wants to talk to you."

"Tell him I'll call him back," said the President.

"But he's called three times already. He wants your advice on a very important matter."

The President rolled his eyes. "What is it this time? The war in the Middle East? Russia? North Korea? A NATO emergency?"

"He wants to paint the Elysées Palace white. And he wants to know what paint he should use. He wants to make it look just like our White House."

"Ooh! I know that!" said the President, snapping his fingers. "He should use Whisper White exterior paint. Yup, that's it. It's manufactured by Duron. Tell him to look for Duron Exterior Alkyd Oil Gloss Whisper 248 paint. That should do the trick. Oh, and tell him this information is gonna cost him."

"I'll send him the bill," said the First Lady, then happily tripped away again.

"He who works for free is a dumbass," said the President with a wide grin, handing back the towel to the Secret Service agent. "Now how can I help you folks?"

CHAPTER 16

"We're investigating the murder of Dick Dickerson," said Chase.

The President, a large man with a square face and a blond mane, stepped out of the enclosure and straight into a large kiddie pool that had been set up right next to the hog enclosure. Steam rose from the pool surface. He submerged himself into the warm water and sighed happily. "Aaaah," he said, luxuriating. "This is the life. Who are you, by the way?"

"Oh, I'm sorry. My name is Chase Kingsley, and I'm a detective with the Hampton Cove Police Department. And this is Odelia Poole, our civilian consultant."

At least Chase hadn't mentioned that Odelia was a reporter, she thought with a silent sigh of relief. Her fear of being shot had lessened somewhat but was still at the back of her mind. "We understand Mr. Dickerson was a good friend of yours, Mr. President?"

"Just call me Van," said the President. "So you're Miss Poole, huh? I know about you. You work for the *Hampton Cove Gazette*."

Shoot!

"You wrote that article about the ten richest people in Hampton Cove."

"Guilty as charged," she said meekly, nervously glancing around at the Secret Service people and hoping they wouldn't go for their guns.

"I loved your article, Miss Poole, but I don't understand why you didn't give me top billing. I am the richest man in Hampton Cove, after all."

"Yes, that has been brought to my attention, Mr. Pre—Van."

He wagged a finger. "Don't tell me. Otto Paunch, huh?"

"He has been calling me," Odelia admitted.

"Good old Otto. He looks out for me."

"So what's up with the… hogs?" asked Chase.

The President laughed. "Have you ever been President of the United States, Detective Kingsley? Don't answer that. It's a rhetorical question. But if you had, you'd know that Washington is a tough town. Really tough. Those monkeys on the Hill fight dirty. So to be prepared I've been wrestling hogs. It's working, too. I think I got those politicians licked."

A Secret Service man had walked up. "Mr. President, sir," he said. "Will you be needing the hogs or can we return them to the pen?"

The President waved a hand. "You can put them back in the pen. Oh, and give them a nice treat, will you? They played a great game." He turned back to his guests. "I love those hogs. I even named them. Crazy Chuck, Nutty Nancy, Horrible Hillary and Bonky Obama."

"There's four of them?" asked Odelia.

"Yeah, Bonky Obama didn't want to come out today. Sulking as usual. Anyhoo!" He splashed his hands in the water and a plastic yellow duck popped up. He grabbed it and dunked it down again. "Dick Dickerson. Yes, he was a friend of mine. A dear, dear friend."

"Any idea who might have done this to him?" asked Chase.

"Well, Dickie had a lot of enemies," said the President, thoughtful. "In fact I think you should probably talk to Damon Galpin."

"The actor?"

"Yeah." The President's smile died away. "He likes to think he's me but he's not."

Damon Galpin had become famous for imitating the President on *Saturday Night Live*, and it was obvious the real President was not a fan.

"Why would Galpin have a grudge against Dick Dickerson?" asked Odelia.

"Well, Miss Poole, you'll have to ask him that. The only thing Dick ever told me was that Galpin hated his guts. He once even attacked him."

"Attacked him?"

"In an underground parking lot in New York. Became physical. He got in a couple punches before someone dragged him off Dick. Dick never pressed charges, even though I told him to. He was a softie, Dick was." The President's features softened at the memory of his dear friend. "Heart of gold. I'll miss him."

"There is a rumor that the two of you had fallen out. Is there any truth to that?"

The President gave Odelia a dirty look. "Now who put that idea into your head? Dick and I were like brothers. Never a bad word between us. I loved that guy. Loved him!"

"It's just… a rumor… Van," said Odelia uncertainly.

"That's Mr. President to you, Miss Poole," said the President coldly. He then hollered to his Secret Service people, "Can you get these bozos out of here? I don't have time for this nonsense. And someone get me President Macron on the phone!"

And with these words, their interview was terminated. The Secret Service people ushered Odelia and Chase out, first escorting them back to their car, and then watching as they drove off and left the premises.

At least nobody had shot her, Odelia thought, and thrown her body to be fed on by the hogs.

CHAPTER 17

Brutus watched as Harriet watched Max who was watching Dooley study a brownish smear on the wall. Next to him, Milo suddenly emerged, like a genie from a lamp, and tsk-tsked mildly.

"What's going on?" asked Brutus. He'd only been away for an hour but it felt more like a day. He'd popped around the corner to have a sniff at his favorite tree, only to discover three tomcats and two queens had tried to claim it as their own. To trump them all, he'd given the tree a rub and then, to finish things off, had sprayed it for good measure.

"It's a sad story, isn't it?" said Milo.

"What is?" asked Brutus.

"Harriet. She's gone full nympho."

He stared at Milo, goggle-eyed. "Full nympho? What are you talking about?"

"You do know what a nymphomaniac is, don't you, Brutus?" asked Milo kindly.

"Um… a female who likes… nookie?"

"A female who has an uncontrollable or excessive sexual desire."

He frowned at the cat. "And you're telling me Harriet is… that?"

Milo nodded mournfully. "Alas. She's always had a touch of nymphomania but lately she's gone full nympho, I'm afraid. She craves, Brutus—and it would appear you no longer have what it takes to satisfy those powerful cravings."

He looked back to Harriet, who was indeed looking at Max with the kind of fervor he hadn't noticed in her before. Almost like a mixture of repulsion and… rapt fascination.

"She can't possibly be in love with Max!" he said, thinking the idea laughable.

"She's not in love with Max. She craves him—like she craves any male. Look at her. See how she's yearning? How she's gobbling him up with her eyes? Devouring him?"

He did see, and he didn't like it. Time to put a stop to this nonsense. But then he noticed he'd stepped into a poop smear. Yuck! "What's up with this crap?!" he cried.

"I'm afraid Dooley's gone mad. It was bound to happen sooner or later. His is a mind that was going to become unhinged at some point in time. Soon he'll start covering himself in feces and it's only a matter of time before he becomes violent."

"Violent?"

"Out of control. He'll start attacking cats willy-nilly. Scratching, biting, trying to gouge out the eyes of any cat he considers a threat. When that happens there will be no alternative but to have him put down, I'm afraid."

Brutus shivered. No cat likes to contemplate having to be put down. In fact each time Odelia took them to the vet, Brutus couldn't help feeling this could very well be the last time. And when Vena took out those syringes she seemed to like so much, that liquid she filled them with could very well be some sort of little-known poison designed to euthanize.

"So Harriet wants to jump Max's bones and Dooley has

lost his marbles and is about to turn rabid. Anything else I should know about?" he asked, shaking his head.

"I'm afraid there is, Brutus. Have you seen the look on Max's face?"

He had. The otherwise tame feline looked pissed off. "He looks... angry."

"That's what I wanted to talk to you about," said Milo. "Max has just gotten the results back from that test."

"What test?"

"The test Odelia had Vena run on him."

"Oh." He didn't know nothing about no test but wasn't prepared to admit it. Sometimes stuff happened around here that nobody bothered to tell him about. Probably because he was the last acquisition—the last one to join Odelia's merry band of pets. With the exception of Milo, of course, but then he wasn't a fixture but a drifter passing through.

"I'm afraid the results of the test were conclusive."

"What did the results say?"

Milo took a deep breath. "Max is your brother, Brutus."

"What?!"

"I'm afraid so. The test doesn't lie. And not only that, Harriet is your aunt."

"You've got to be kidding me? How did this happen?"

Milo placed a paw on Brutus's shoulder. "And—are you ready for this?"

"Ready for what?" What could be worse than what this cat had already told him?

"Dooley... is your son."

From the shock, Brutus sank through his paws and dropped heavily onto the floor. For a moment, he merely stared mutely before him, then he finally managed to drag his head up and say, "Tell me all, Milo. Don't hold anything back."

And Milo did, and happily so. "See, the thing is that when

your and Max's mother was very young, she had an affair with Harriet's brother, which resulted in the litter that contained you and which was subsequently rejected by the cat your mother had been seeing before the affair. Your mother went on to have Max, who ended up growing up in a warm nest, while you, the illegitimate spawn of a doomed affair, were rejected and left to die."

"I was left to die?" asked Brutus, dazed. This was the first he ever heard of this.

"You grew up without a mother, without a father, unloved, unwanted, and forced to fend for yourself on the mean streets of New York, where a cat's life is worth nothing."

Odd. He couldn't remember these mean streets. He liked the story, though. It held a strange kind of fascination. Almost like the soap operas Granny liked to watch. "Go on."

"You became strong—because you had to be strong to survive. You became... Brutus."

"You mean I wasn't always Brutus?"

"Your mother christened you Whiskers."

Ugh. "What a dumb-ass name."

"Right? You're a self-made cat, Brutus. You even adopted a new name. To better indicate the kind of cat you'd become. Tough. Butch. A real cat's cat. Top of the heap."

He liked this story better and better. He was tough. And he was a cat's cat. The only thing he didn't like was the part about him being Dooley's dad. He watched as Dooley sniffed his own poop now and shook his head. No way was he that sad dude's dad. Milo must have sensed his discomfort, for he said, "If it's any consolation, Dooley's mother passed on a long time ago, Brutus." He quickly crossed himself. "May she rest in peace."

"Who was she?"

"Oh, just some bimbo you met on those mean streets of

New York. You wouldn't remember her. Just one of the many, many—*many*—notches on your collar."

It was true. He'd had a few conquests in his time—and Milo was right. He didn't remember any cat he ever met and knocked up on those mean streets—he didn't even remember those mean streets. Or New York. "So how did Dooley end up in Hampton Cove?"

"That's a very interesting story."

But the story would have to wait for another time, for at that exact moment Harriet suddenly made a pass at Max and that was something Brutus could not allow to happen!

CHAPTER 18

I'd been brooding for the longest time, and by the time I reached the good old homestead again, my mood had plummeted to the darkest depths of the feline mind. Which is why the scene as I encountered it upon my return didn't strike me as odd at first.

The fact that Dooley was chomping down pawfuls of Cat Snax was a little weird, especially since he and I had an understanding: he knew how much I loved Cat Snax, and how I considered them a special treat, only to be devoured at the end of the day, and only in small portions. The fact that he'd eaten all of them and must have induced Gran to open up another packet and had scarfed that down, too, irked me a little. No, make that a lot.

But since I wasn't on speaking terms with Dooley I found myself a little hamstrung. I made a mental note to tell Odelia later on, though. No more Cat Snax for Dooley.

And then there was the horrible habit he'd developed of pooping on the rug and then wiping his butt on that same rug. By the time I got home he must have been at it to a considerable extent, for the rug, which had once been off-white, was now off white completely. In fact it had turned completely brown. And smelly. And frankly disgusting. Not only that, but even as I watched Dooley was meticulously wiping his tush on Odelia's wall! Right underneath the intercom, in full view of everyone, and where it wouldn't be missed.

If I were Dooley, and faced with this sudden defecatory urge, at the very least I would pick a spot that was a little more discreet. Then again, it really wasn't my problem.

Still, it was odd. And you know what was even odder? The fact that Harriet had been staring at me ever since I'd arrived home. In fact she was looking at me the way one stares at a bug. The kind of bug one has never seen before. Bugs so ugly they fascinate and amuse.

I didn't want to acknowledge her, though, in light of what Milo had told me she thought of me. That I was too dumb and too ugly and too boring to spend time with. That's probably what this was. She thought I was so ugly she couldn't look away. Like a car crash.

And that was my life in a nutshell: an ex-friend who'd regressed to the scatological stage, and another ex-friend who reveled in my hideousness. And things would probably have stayed that way if Harriet hadn't suddenly approached, presumably to ascertain whether I was as ugly from up close as from afar, and Brutus hadn't come roaring onto the scene, claws extended, tail distended, back arched, and hissing like a rattlesnake!

"Take your paws off my lady!" he thundered.

"Brutus!" Harriet cried, as shocked as I was at this sudden outburst. "Stop it!"

The sound of his lady love's voice had an immediate effect on Brutus. His claws retracted, his tail returned to its normal size, and for a moment he seemed irresolute.

"Brutus, boogie bear," said Harriet, putting her paw on the

berserk cat's paw.

But the moment she touched him, he jerked back, as if stung.

"Don't touch me!" he yelled.

"What's the matter?" Harriet asked. "Are you in pain, care bear?"

Brutus opened his mouth to speak, then closed it again and stalked off.

"Brutus! Honey lamb!" Harriet called out, but Brutus was gone.

Harriet turned to me, then seemed to think better of it, and turned away.

What the huckleberry was going on? For a moment I locked eyes with Dooley, but he turned away, too, and moved off, his tail between his legs, disappearing into the backyard.

Milo then joined me, shaking his head commiseratingly. "I think Brutus has finally gone off the deep end, buddy. Did you see what happened just now?"

"Yeah, I was there, Milo," I said, still reeling from the turn of events.

"He was going to slug you, slugger. He was going to do you harm. Good thing he didn't, huh? Or you'd be dead meat."

"But why? Why would he suddenly turn on me like that?"

"Isn't it obvious? Brutus is your long-lost son, buddy."

"What?!"

"Sure. He's just had the results back from that test Vena ran. Turns out you fathered a son and Brutus is that son. He must have suspected this for a long, long time, which is why he came to Hampton Cove in the first place, hoping to meet the father who deserted him."

"But… that's impossible! I'm… neutered," I added, my voice dropping, for I wasn't proud of the fact.

"You think you're neutered but you're not, Maxie," said

Milo earnestly. "They lied to you, buddy. You're a fully functional tomcat."

"But... why would they lie about something like that?!"

"Because that's what they do! Humans, I mean. They lie and they cheat and they think it's one big hoot. We're dumb animals to them, Max. They're just having a bit of fun at our expense."

"I don't get it," I said, shaking my head. In fact my head was hurting. "So... Brutus is my son? So who is the mother?"

Milo gave me a cheeky grin. "Do you have to ask?"

"Yes, I do." I couldn't remember ever having been... intimate with any cat. Another big secret I wasn't willing to share with anyone. Except that one time behind that big cedar in the church parking lot. I was young and foolish and she was pretty and game and... Well, we sniffed each other's butts for the better part of an hour but nothing more came of it.

Milo was watching me intently, then nodded.

"I think you know, Max, don't you?"

I didn't know you could get pregnant from a kiss but there it was.

"So Brutus is my son?"

"Brutus is your son. Isn't this a blessed moment? You get to press your long-lost child to your bosom, Max!"

I didn't know about that. Seemed to me that Brutus was a little resentful towards dear old dad. Besides, he was a lot bigger and meaner than me, so maybe this teary reunion shouldn't proceed unsupervised. Oh, where was Oprah when I needed her? Or Jerry Springer?

Milo started to walk away, then turned back. "Oh, and before I forget. Harriet?"

"What about her?"

He shrugged. "Just thought you'd want to know. She's your sister."

CHAPTER 19

"That was quite possibly the weirdest interview I've ever been involved in," Odelia said once they'd put some distance between themselves and Lago-a-Oceano.

"He does have a point, though," said Chase.

"About what?"

"The hogs? I'll bet hog wrestling is as good a preparation to go into politics as any."

Odelia smiled. "He seems to love those hogs, too. And they genuinely like him."

"What's not to like? He's a lovable guy."

"Well, at least those rumors about eating journos for breakfast aren't true."

They were headed to their third interview of the day, the famous actor Damon Galpin, hoping to inch their way closer to solving this dreadful murder case.

"Who else do you have lined up?" asked Odelia.

"I've been trying to get a hold of this Yasir Bellinowksy guy."

"The mobster?"

"Alleged mobster. So far his lawyer has been stalling. But

I'll get him eventually. And then there's the break-in at Potbelly's."

"Anything new?"

"Uniforms are canvassing the area. Maybe a neighbor saw something."

She settled back. It was at times like these that she missed her cats. If only she'd taken Max, Dooley, Harriet and Brutus along, they could have gleaned something from the pets of the people they interviewed. Max would have loved to have a chat with President Wilcox's pigs. Or maybe they could have dropped them off at the duck farm and one of the ducks could have given them a description of the thieves. She sat up a little straighter.

Now that was a great idea! Why hadn't she thought of it sooner?

Chase looked over. "Everything all right?"

"Peachy," she said, commending herself on a brilliant idea. As soon as she got home she'd get right on it: drive Max and the gang over to the Potbelly farm and set them loose. They'd have a field day chatting up those ducks. One of them was bound to have seen something. Or one of the dogs. Max was great with dogs. In spite of cats' reputation as being afraid of canines he had no qualms about chewing the fat with any dog, big or small.

Just then, her phone sang out Dua Lipa's tune again, and she picked it out. When she saw that it was Otto Paunch, she groaned. "Yes," she said into the phone, not all that friendly this time.

"Oh, hi, Miss Poole. Just following up on that rich list business."

"I told you, I'm on a case right now. I don't have time to deal with—"

"About that. I think you should probably mention in your article that President Wilcox was Dick Dickerson's best friend. They were chums. Mates. Bosom buddies. Dick was Van's homeboy. His homie. His dawg. His—"

"Yes, yes. They were friends. I get it. So what about this rumor they had a fight?"

"Fake news!" suddenly yelled Mr. Paunch. "I swear if you print that garbage I'll—"

That voice. It sounded so familiar. But why? "Don't worry. I won't print any of it. I just want to find out who killed Dickerson. As a great friend of the President, who was a great friend of Dickerson, surely you must have some idea."

"I have. Two words. Brenda Berish."

"The former foreign secretary? Are you sure?"

"Absolutely. Dickerson had a lot of dirt on her. You know about the safe?"

"I do. It was emptied out."

"Whoever took it didn't want their secrets to come out. And that person is Secretary Berish. Just ask her. You'll see. She's the one who killed Dickerson. Oh, and don't tell her I was your source. She'll deny everything."

And with these words, Paunch disconnected. Odelia tucked her phone away.

"What did he say?" asked Chase.

"He says we should take a closer look at Brenda Berish."

"Secretary Berish?"

"Dickerson collected a lot of dirt on her. Paunch says she killed him over it."

They'd arrived at a residential neighborhood just outside Hampton Cove. A lot of the houses here were pretty sizable, with a few smaller ones to even things out. They passed the entrance to the Marina Golf Course and Chase slowed down. "He should be out here somewhere—ah, there he is."

A handsome man with perfectly sculpted blond hair, the even features of a Hollywood actor, dressed in white slacks and a green polo shirt and white golf shoes, stood waving at them from next to the golf course entrance.

"He looks younger than on television," said Odelia.

"They put a ton of makeup on him for when he plays the President."

Chase wedged his pickup between a Jaguar and a Porsche and they got out.

"Detective Chase!" Damon Galpin hollered, walking up, hand extended.

Chase shook it and then the actor turned to Odelia, took her hand and pressed a kiss on it, all the while fixing her with a pair of remarkable blue eyes.

"Miss Poole. Even lovelier in person than in your byline picture."

"You saw my byline picture?" she asked, oddly pleased.

"I read every single one of your articles. The *Hampton Cove Gazette* is a local treasure."

"I thought you actors only read *Variety* and *The Hollywood Reporter*."

He tipped his head back and roared with laughter. "That's a common misconception. Not all of us are dummies, Miss Poole—can I call you Odelia?"

"Please."

He pressed a hand to his chest. "Damon. And it is a pleasure to make your acquaintance. Now will you join me for a round of golf?"

"I'm sorry, Damon," said Chase. "We're just here to ask you a couple of quick questions."

"At the very least join me at the Legends Lounge. It's where I hang out most of the time anyway," he confessed. "Best part about golf is the socializing. Now come."

It was more of an order than an invitation, but so charmingly delivered it was impossible to spurn. So they followed the actor through the entrance and into a one-story building that was exquisitely appointed, all lacquered floors and polished wood paneling.

He led the way to the lounge he'd mentioned, and through the floor-to-ceiling windows they had an excellent view of the links, where folks were playing the noble sport.

"I have a terrible handicap, I don't mind admitting," said Damon as they took a seat in leather armchairs around a round glass-topped table. The actor held up his hand and a young pimpled waiter came scurrying over, a towel draped on his arm. "Vodka martini," said Damon, then turned a questioning gaze at Odelia and Chase.

"Just soda," said Odelia.

"Same here," said Chase.

"Still that same old gag about not drinking while on duty, eh?" said Damon with a twinkle in his eye. "I believe in starting early and keeping going unstintingly until the preprandial juices start flowing and digestion arrives at its peak."

"I would have thought vodka martinis were your meals of choice," said Odelia, who'd read the stories about the actor's famous binges.

"Oh, now, Odelia, you shouldn't believe everything you read in that paper of yours," he chided.

The waiter came over with their drinks and Damon quaffed deeply from his, then held onto it while he bowed his head. "Do your worst, Detectives. I'm ready for you now."

"Is it true that you and Dick Dickerson didn't see eye to eye?" asked Chase.

Damon nodded. "That is indeed true. Dickerson was filth, Detective. He was filth and he printed filth. And it didn't occur to him that the people whose lives he tried to destroy were human beings with feelings and friends and loved ones that could be hurt in his barrage of lies and horribly distorted 'articles.' I hated him and never made a secret of that."

"What did he say about you, exactly?" asked Odelia, who had some idea.

Damon gazed out across the spreading and rolling links. "Oh, this and that. You do know that he was a close friend of President Wilcox? And that he did all he could to secure him his election? In fact he went all out on that—slandering Wilcox's opponents and burying every single piece of gossip about Wilcox himself. And since I've been one of Wilcox's most vocal opponents from day one, Dickerson directed some of his vitriol at me, too."

"Do you think he kept some of those stories in his safe?"

"Right. Dickerson's famous safe. Where he kept Tinseltown's darkest secrets. Why?"

"His safe was emptied out by whoever killed him," said Chase.

"I guess that makes sense. Though I can assure you that whatever he had on me, he printed without delay."

"So he didn't try to blackmail you? To try and stop you from imitating the President?"

"He tried at first. But when I refused he responded with a barrage of garbage."

"That must have stung."

Damon smiled, and took another sip. "I wore Dick Dickerson's scorn like a badge of honor, Detective. In fact if he would have printed something nice about me it would have worried me more. Though there was one story that caused me to contact a defamation lawyer." When they both stared at him, he spoke a single word. "Hogs."

"Hogs?" asked Odelia, struck by the coincidence.

"Dickerson claimed I engaged in coitus with hogs." He grimaced. "And I have a fairly good idea who put him up to it, too."

So had Odelia. President Wilcox really did like to get down and dirty.

"Does a picture of a rose mean anything to you?" asked Chase.

"No, it doesn't. Why?"

"We found it in Dickerson's safe. We think the killer left it there on purpose."

"I see. To send a message." He mused for a moment. "No, I'm afraid I can't help you with that."

"Where were you last night between two and four, Mr. Galpin?"

"Home. Asleep."

"Alone?"

He grinned widely. "Come on, Detective. Do I look like a man who would kiss and tell?" Chase cocked an eyebrow at the actor and he relented. "Oh, all right. If you must know, I was in bed with Lauralee Gray. I'm sure she'll corroborate my 'alibi.'"

"The actress?" asked Odelia, impressed.

Damon nodded once. "I may be old but I haven't lost my touch, Odelia." He was wiggling his eyebrows at this, probably thinking it made him look more appealing. In reality it made him look like a lecherous uncle.

"One other thing," said Chase, who, if his frown was an indication, didn't seem to like the way Damon was looking at Odelia. "There's a rumor that President Wilcox and Dickerson fell out over something. Any idea what could have caused that rift?"

Damon's smile vanished. "I have a pretty good idea, yes. The thing is, Dickerson didn't own the *National Star*, Detective. He was merely its editor. The *Star* is owned by the Gantry family. And reportedly they didn't appreciate this love affair between their tabloid and Wilcox. There's a storm brewing for the President, and that fact hasn't escaped the

Gantrys. They wanted to distance themselves from Wilcox before they got dragged down along with him. So they pretty much ordered Dickerson to stand down, and possibly even dip into the treasure trove of dirt he'd collected on Wilcox over the years."

"Dickerson kept dirt on Wilcox?" asked Odelia.

"Dickerson kept dirt on everyone. He was like the J. Edgar Hoover of the tabloid world. Only he published some of the stuff he collected, used some of it to put pressure on people, and buried the rest to incur favors from his friends. He was a very dangerous man."

"Do you think his murder is related to his habit of blackmailing people?" asked Chase.

"I'm sure it is." He gave a slight smile. "Now all you need to ask yourselves is this: who amongst the people he blackmailed finally decided they had enough and struck back?"

CHAPTER 20

Tex Poole was generally a happy man. He'd married the woman of his dreams, had the most amazing daughter any doting father could ever have wished for, who'd recently become involved with a great guy and a fine cop, and he worked in a noble profession that fulfilled his every expectation and more. He even still had all of his hair and his own teeth.

The only thing that occasionally marred this blessed life he led was a little old lady who was a far cry from the sweet and loving mother-in-law he'd envisioned when he first met Marge Lip. He'd known from the moment Marge introduced him to her mother that this might not be the kind of easy-going relationship one often sees in Hallmark movies. Vesta Muffin adhered more to the cliché of the monster-in-law than the loving mom-in-law.

The first time he saw Vesta—when picking up Marge to go to the prom—she'd hit him over the head with a broomstick. Asked to explain herself by a horrified Marge, she said Tex had a face like a serial killer and she thought he was there to slaughter her daughter.

Things had gone downhill from that point. And Marge's dad, who at that point had already left his family to fend for itself, hadn't helped. He had an aversion to doctors that stemmed from a badly digested experience in the armed forces, when the barracks physician had given him a pill that had given him an itchy rash that had lasted weeks.

He'd never forgiven the medical profession—or any of its practitioners, whom he steadfastly referred to as voodoo priests.

Daddy Poole had died soon after Tex had started dating his daughter, though, which only left Marge's testy mother. And since Tex had taken an oath to save lives, he couldn't very well act on the impulse he sometimes felt to simply smother the woman in her sleep.

And it was with great reluctance that he had accepted his wife's suggestion to allow Vesta to move in with them—seeing as how she was increasingly having trouble taking care of herself. Forgetting to turn off the stove. Putting fresh laundry into the oven. Stuff like that.

So now, as a token of her gratitude, Vesta had set out to turn her son-in-law's life into a living hell every chance she had. Or at least that's the way it sometimes felt to Tex.

He'd just seen his last patient of the day when he walked out of his office and into the waiting room and was surprised to find it chock-full of people, all expectantly looking up at him.

He blinked and turned to Scarlett. "Scarlett?" he asked.

She smiled sweetly, then jiggled her boobage, as was her habit. "Dr. Tex?"

He approached the desk. "What are these people doing here?" he whispered.

Scarlet leaned in, in the process offering Tex a scintillating view of her cleavage. He fought against the sudden spell of vertigo. "I don't know what happened, Dr. Tex," she whispered back. "They started coming in twenty minutes ago. When I asked if they had an appointment they said yes. But I can't find them in your appointment book."

"So why didn't you tell them to make an appointment and come back? Are these even my patients? I've never seen any of them before."

"They said they arranged things with you, Dr. Tex," said Scarlett. "What was I supposed to do? I couldn't just kick them out. Some of them look really sick."

He glanced over his shoulder at the dozen or so patients. They did look sick. All of them. And unwashed. And when he looked closer, he saw they'd brought their raggedy bags with them. Almost as if they were…" He frowned, then turned back to Scarlett. "Did you get their names and addresses?"

"No, Dr. Tex," said Scarlett sheepishly.

"Insurance information?"

"I don't think they have any, Dr. Tex."

"Oh, for crying out loud," he muttered.

The door swung open and five more 'patients' stumbled in from the street. They all looked as grimy as their dozen colleagues. As soon as the door had closed, it opened again and five more walked in. This place was starting to look like Grand Central Terminal.

"Are you Dr. Tex?" asked one of the newcomers, a toothless older man.

"I am."

"Oh, great. I have a pain in my nose, doctor."

Tex studied the man's nose. It was one of those narrow, veiny noses. It also had a safety pin stuck through the fleshy part. "Maybe you should take out that pin," he suggested.

"What pin?" said the old-timer, feeling for his nose. "Oh, there's a pin in my nose!"

"Oh, for Pete's sakes." He addressed the small crowd. "How did you all get here? Who told you to come and see me?"

"Scarlett O'Hara," said the man with the pin in his nose.

"No, Scarlett Cannon," said an old lady with a glass eye. "She said you would treat us for free. Day or night. Any time."

Tex locked eyes with Scarlett, who was shaking her head. "I didn't say nothing, Dr. Tex! I swear! I don't even know these people!"

He had a sneaking suspicion he knew exactly who this 'Scarlett Cannon' was.

"What did the person who invited you look like?" he asked.

"A nice old lady," said one man. "Little white curls. Looks like Estelle Getty. I met her at the bus station. I like to hang out at the bus station. It's always nice and warm out there."

"I met her at the train station," said another man. "She even gave me your card."

"Lemme see that," grumbled Tex, and took the card from the man. It read, 'Scarlett Canyon, Unlicensed Receptionist, Dr. Tex Poole,' and even mentioned Tex's home address and phone number. "Vesta," he muttered under his breath, crumpling up the card.

"Hey, that's my card!" said the guy.

"You're going to treat us, aren't you, Doc?" asked a cross-eyed woman.

"Yeah, a promise is a promise," said another woman, who looked like a hobo.

In truth, they all looked like hobos. Probably because they were all hobos.

Scarlett was eyeing Tex with a knowing look. 'I told you,' that look said. And she had. And even if she hadn't, he should have known Vesta wouldn't leave well enough alone.

"All right," he said resignedly. "The first one come with me."

And he returned to his office, determined to murder Vesta the moment he saw her.

CHAPTER 21

I was in Odelia's bedroom when she finally arrived home that night. I had no idea where the others were nor did I care. After the bombshell Milo had dropped on me—the second one that day—I had a feeling I'd never really known these cats. They were like strangers to me. Except for Harriet, who apparently was my sister, even if she looked nothing like me, and Brutus, who was my son, and, again, looked nothing like me.

I had a hard time processing all these revelations, so for the rest of the afternoon I'd been hiding in Odelia's bedroom, behind the bed, my only companions the dust bunnies Odelia had missed when she'd last vacuumed there. Or maybe she didn't like vacuuming behind the bed, which was entirely possible, and those bunnies had been there forever.

Milo had come looking for me, but I'd managed to outsmart him by holding my breath. Tough, too, with those dust bunnies tickling my nose.

Finally, a familiar voice sounded. "Max? Where are you, baby?"

In spite of the sneaking suspicion I had that Odelia was

prepared to get rid of me and exchange me for Milo, a big smile lit up my face and a warm tingle spread inside my chest.

My human was home, and she would help me make sense of a senseless world.

"Odelia?"

It was Milo's voice.

"Yes, honey?"

"Can I have a quick word before the others arrive?"

"Sure. What's wrong?"

"A lot. You wouldn't believe what I've been through today."

"Oh, my God. What happened?"

"It's Max and the others, though mainly Max. He hates me."

"Hates you? What do you mean?"

"He's been torturing me all day! Denying me food and water, telling me I should probably jump under a truck and rid the world of the ugliest feline it has ever known. It's been awful. Awful!"

The bed shifted, and the box spring groaned. Odelia had taken a seat. "Jump up. Tell me all about it. This is not the Max I know, Milo. I don't know what could have happened."

I was too stunned to move an inch—or even to utter a single word. Instead, I just lay there, my ears pricked up, and listening to every horrible utterance from Milo.

"It all started when they held a meeting—Max, Dooley, Brutus and Harriet—and decided that from now on they won't be helping you out anymore."

"They won't? But why?"

"Frankly they hate it. They never wanted to tell you this but they hate this whole sleuthing thing."

"But I thought they loved it!"

"Trust me—they hate it. The only reason they went along

with the scheme is because they got extra kibble when they caught a killer or provided you with a clue."

"I didn't know," said Odelia, and she sounded distraught.

"So I asked them about it, but they said I should butt out. That I was an intruder and I'd be gone soon enough if not sooner and they didn't want me here—they never wanted me here and yadda yadda yadda. And that's when Max really went to town on me. First he told me I was too fat and that all I did was lounge about and steal his food and his milk and he wasn't having it anymore. So no more food for me. Then he said his human didn't want me here, either, but was too nice to say no to *my* stupid human which is why I should do everyone a favor and jump under a passing UPS truck and make the world a better place."

At this point, Milo took a breath and Odelia gasped in shock.

This was just too much. This cat was lying through his teeth!

"I'll talk to Max," said Odelia. "This kind of behavior is intolerable."

"I didn't want to tell you at first," said Milo. "I figured it would upset you to know what Max is really like." He sighed dramatically. "In fact I thought you wouldn't believe me."

"Oh, I believe you. And I'm going to deal with this right now. Where is Max?"

The box spring moved again. Odelia was getting up.

"No idea. I haven't seen him since he told Dooley to smear his poop all over the carpet and the walls."

"He did what?!"

"Yeah. Max can be really mean sometimes. He figured you'd punish Dooley and kick him out of the house."

"But Dooley is his best friend!"

"Not anymore. Dooley's been digging into Max's Cat Snax and Max went ballistic when he found out. Told me he hated that stupid cat. That Dooley was even dumber than me and that he was going to make sure you kicked him out once and for all."

"Oh, I don't believe this."

"I knew you wouldn't, Odelia."

"Oh, no. I do believe you, Milo. And I'm glad you're telling me all this."

"You should probably talk to Brutus and Harriet, too."

"What have they done?"

"They hate Max, and they hate each other, and Max hates all of them, too. In fact if I were you I'd separate them. Make sure they don't kill each other, I mean."

"I can't separate them. They all live under the same roof."

"Then I guess there's only one solution."

"You're not asking me to…"

"I know the pound has a bad rep but it's really not such a nasty place as they say. Aloisia got me from the pound, and a wonderful time I had there, too. Made lots and lots of great friends. Just look at it as a place where cats can find a new and happy home."

I shook my head disgustedly. I finally had Milo's number. My first impulse was to crawl from under the bed and tell Odelia the truth. But would she believe me? This cat was such a skilled liar she might not. So then I got a better idea. The only solution to the Milo problem. The solution I should have thought of sooner, if I hadn't believed his lies myself.

CHAPTER 22

I walked into the TV nook and found Odelia ensconced on the couch, Milo on her lap, Grandma next to her, and no sign of Brutus, Dooley or Harriet. Odelia & Co were watching the adventures of Kit Katt & Koh, though judging from the frown on Odelia's face she wasn't really following the story. And Grandma wasn't looking too attentive either, her thoughts clearly miles away. Only Milo was having a grand old time, enjoying Odelia's loving caress.

I now knew what his endgame was. To usurp my position in Odelia's home and heart.

So I casually strode up to them, ignoring the foul smell emanating from the wall where Dooley had done his business and which no one had bothered to clean up, and plunked myself down at Odelia's feet.

She gave me a dark frown. "Max," she said. "I've been looking for you."

"I know, I know," I said, bowing my head. "I have a confession to make. But first I want to apologize to you, Milo."

"To me?" asked Milo, clearly surprised.

"Yes. I know I haven't always treated you the way I should have. The fact of the matter is that I felt threatened when you first arrived. I guess..." I shrugged, and gave Odelia my best Puss in Boots face. "I guess I don't feel as secure in this relationship as I thought I did. I saw Milo as an intruder—someone who would take my place—and I lashed out. And for that I'm deeply, deeply sorry. In fact I feel so ashamed I only managed to work up the courage to face you now, Odelia."

"Oh, Max," said Odelia, softening. "It's so nice of you to apologize. What do you say, Milo?"

Milo wasn't saying anything. A suspicious expression had rearranged his face into a frown, and he was staring at me intently. Then, finally, he gave me a slight nod, almost like a Godfather nod. "Thank you, Max. It must have taken a great deal of courage to admit this."

I held out my paw. "Friends?"

Milo touched his paw against mine. "Friends," he agreed.

"Oh, you guys," said Odelia, wiping a tear from her eye. "I love you both so much. And I'm so proud of you. Especially you, Max. Like Milo said, it must have taken a lot of courage to own up to your mistakes like that. So now how do you feel?"

"Better," I said. "Like a weight has been lifted from my heart."

"See?" asked Odelia, scratching Milo behind his ears. "Max isn't so bad. And I'm sure you guys will be best friends from now on."

"Don't count on it," Grandma muttered.

"What?" asked Odelia, confused.

"Nothing," said Grandma. "I didn't say nothing."

. . .

I entered Marge and Tex's house through the kitchen and immediately went in search of my former friends. Milo was at Odelia's, who was giving him some of my favorite food, and I hoped he'd stay there. So far he'd limited his domain to Odelia's, but I had a feeling he might expand his reach as soon as he felt he'd conquered my human's place.

I traipsed through the kitchen, and was surprised to find Marge home alone, Tex nowhere in sight. She smiled down at me. "Dooley is in the family room, Max."

"Thanks," I told her. I walked through to the family room, where Dooley was watching on as Kit Katt instructed Koh to infiltrate a mobster's lair and talk to a pair of mice.

"Mice!" Koh growled. A black cat with distinct green eyes, Koh always growled for some reason. Possibly because it made him look more butch. "I hate mice."

"Please talk to them, Koh. You're the only one who can," implored Kit, an auburn-haired beauty played by the popular up-and-comer Virginia Salt. "Only you can save that little girl now. I know she's in there somewhere, and those mice might lead you to her."

"All right," Koh snarled. When he wasn't growling, he was snarling. "I'll see what I can do."

"Thank you, Koh," said Kit. "You're the best."

"No, you're the best."

"No, you're the best."

Figuring this lovefest might go on for a while, I walked up to the couch and hopped on next to Dooley. He didn't even look up.

"Hey, Dooley," I said.

"Don't bother, Max," he growled—probably got that from Koh. "I know what you really think about me so just go away."

"What did Milo tell you? That I hate you and that I think you're ugly and dumb and blah-blah-blah?"

His frown deepened and his whiskers twitched, indicative of a powerful emotion.

"He said you knew I was dying and you didn't even bother to tell me because you figured I just couldn't handle the truth. But you don't care about me and *that's* the truth."

"Wanna know what he said about you?"

He continued morosely. "What?"

"He said you tell everyone who will listen that I'm possessive and obsessive about Odelia and want to keep her for myself. You also tell them I'm deeply, madly in love with Harriet."

Dooley looked up for the first time. "What? I never said that."

"That's what Milo told me you said. He's been lying, Dooley. Setting us up against each other. And do you know what he told Odelia just now? That we hate sleuthing and that the only reason we go along with it is because of the special treats she gives us when we come up with a clue."

"Well, there is some truth to that," he admitted. "I like those super-special treats."

"But that's not the reason we do this! He also told her I tortured him today—made his life a living hell—even denied him food and water and told him to jump under a UPS truck. And then he said we all hate each other and Odelia should just do herself a favor and dump us all at the pound."

Now I really had Dooley's attention. "The pound!"

"Yup. That's been his plan all along. He wants us out of here so he can take over."

"But he has a human. This Aloisia person."

"Maybe she doesn't treat him as well as Odelia does? I don't know. Fact of the matter is that he's been setting us up with a bunch of nonsense."

"What nonsense?" asked a voice from my rear. When I turned I saw that Harriet and Brutus had snuck up on us and had jumped onto the couch, too.

"It's Milo," said Dooley. "He told Odelia how much we all hate each other and how she should drop us off at the pound."

"Milo also told me that you're my son, Brutus," I said. "Which, now that I've had some time to think about it, seems impossible. For one thing we're the same age, and when I had… relations… with… that cat… I wasn't a kitten and neither was she." I blushed. Luckily no one saw it, on account of my blorange fur. "Oh, and he also said Harriet is my sister. Which seems unlikely, as we look nothing alike."

"Milo said you used to be in love with me but now you hate me so much you want to kill me, Max," said Harriet softly.

"What?! That's crazy!"

"Yeah. He also said Dooley poops the walls because he's in love with me, too," she added with a sly smile.

"I only poop the walls to get rid of all of those worms!" Dooley cried.

"What worms? Who gave you that crazy idea?" asked Harriet.

"Milo," said Dooley, understanding finally dawning. "Oh, boy. I've been punked."

"Milo told me you're my brother, Max," Brutus grumbled. "And Dooley is my son and Harriet is my aunt. He also told me you're a raging nymphomaniac, Harriet."

"What's a nymphomaniac?" asked Dooley.

"Um, someone who likes nymphs," said Harriet, looking startled.

"Oh, I like nymphs," said Dooley.

"This cat's been having a big laugh at our expense," I said.

"Do you see me laughing?" asked Brutus.

"Is that why you were acting so cold and distant, buttercup?" asked Harriet, placing a paw on Brutus's face.

"Yup," he said. "I thought you were in love with Dooley and Max and—hell—every male cat out there."

"Oh, snookums. He was lying!"

"I know that now," he said, looking a little embarrassed.

"We need to get back at that cat," I said.

"We need to get that cat out of our lives," Brutus grunted.

"No more lies," said Harriet. "From now on we take everything he says with a grain of salt."

"More like a truckload of salt," Brutus agreed.

"Problem is, Odelia believes everything he tells her," I said. And then I told them my bright idea. They seemed to agree it was the goods, and soon we arranged the whole thing—just like in the old days. The days before Milo entered our lives and started spreading his poison.

CHAPTER 23

Odelia was surprised when her four cats walked in through the kitchen pet door. She'd just started dinner and looked up when the procession made the door flap.

"Hey, you guys," she said. "I figured I wouldn't see you again."

The foursome took up position right next to the kitchen counter and Odelia looked down. "We have held a meeting and have decided something," said Max.

"Uh-huh?" she said as she licked her fingers. She'd been chopping tomatoes. "What did you decide?"

"We want to formally invite Milo to join our small band of feline sleuths."

This was the absolute last thing she'd expected but it warmed her heart. "Hey, that's great." Then she was reminded of Milo's words. "It's just that... I know you don't really like this sleuthing business all that much. That you just go along with it for the treats. No, you don't have to deny it. Milo told me how you feel," she added when Dooley made to speak.

"We want to do this, Odelia," said Max emphatically. "And we want Milo to join us. I know we didn't always see eye to eye in the past but we feel we should put all that behind us and make a fresh start."

"I like it," she said decidedly. "In fact I love it." Then she hollered, "Milo! Come here a minute, will you?"

Milo came walking up, cool as a cucumber, until he saw the four cats seated side by side. He looked a little startled, and Odelia didn't wonder. They'd given him a really hard time.

"Hey there, Milo," said Max.

"Max and his friends have a proposal for you," said Odelia.

"Is that so?" said Milo with a touch of suspicion.

"We want you to join us on our sleuthing quests," said Harriet.

"Join the gang," Brutus added.

"Be part of the team," Harriet finished.

"And I think it's a great idea," said Odelia proudly. "So what do you say, bud?"

Milo narrowed his eyes at Max for a moment, then seemed to smile. Sweetly, he said, "Of course. Of course I want to be a part of your sleuthing gang."

"Band," Max corrected him. "We're a band, not a gang, Milo."

"Sure, sure," said Milo vaguely. "Part of the band. I love it. I love it."

"And I have your very first assignment all worked out for you," said Odelia, happy that her cats were getting along again. "I want you guys to go to the Potbelly duck farm and talk to the ducks—and maybe the dogs, too. There's been a murder and the murderer stole a tractor and a tanker filled with duck poop. We find the thieves, we find the murderers."

Milo was looking decidedly unhappy now. "Duck farm? Duck poop? Talk to dogs?"

"This is what we do, Milo," said Max. "You have a problem with that?"

"Nah, not me," said Milo, brightening. "If this is what it takes to be part of the gang—pardon me, the band—then count me in. Dogs. Ducks… Poop. Bring it on!"

It could have been Odelia's imagination but Milo seemed less than excited about the prospect of engaging in a little bit of detective work. Then again, this was probably because he was still feeling the sting of Max's words of that afternoon.

Oh, Max, she thought as she returned to her meal prep. Milo would need more than a simple apology to get over those harsh words Max had spoken. And frankly so did she. But this visit to the Potbelly farm was a good way to start making amends.

And she'd just finished peeling the potatoes when the sliding glass door was shoved all the way open and her father walked in.

"Vesta!" he roared, looking a little flushed. "I know what you did!"

"Always loved that movie," Gran croaked. "And the sequel. *I Know What You Did Last Summer 2*. Real classic."

"You sent those hobos into my office, didn't you?" Dad cried.

"It's offensive to call them hobos, Tex," said Grandma. "Didn't they teach you anything in that Political Correctness 101 course you took in that doctor school of yours?"

"Admit it," said Dad, his face now red like a lobster.

"What's going on?" asked Odelia, wiping her hands on the kitchen towel.

"She deliberately sent two dozen hobos into my office, and pretended Scarlett rustled them up. She's trying to poison my mind against Scarlett."

"Scarlett?" asked Odelia with a frown. "Scarlett Canyon?"

"Of course Scarlett Canyon!"

"I don't get it. Take it from the top, Dad."

Mom also walked in now, completing the family portrait. And with five cats following the altercation with rapt attention, it was almost like the nativity scene, if Max was a donkey, Dooley an ox, Brutus a camel and Milo Baby Jesus.

"What's with all the shouting?" Mom asked.

"She sent two dozen hobos into my office!" said Dad, still not making one lick of sense.

Mom must have thought so, too, for she said, "You're not making one lick of sense, Tex."

Dad took a steadying breath, planted his hands on his hips and started from the top, just like Odelia had suggested. "Two dozen hobos walked into my office."

"Is this a joke?" asked Gran. "Cause I'm laughing already."

"Two dozen hobos, Scarlett Canyon and I were in the office."

"This is a joke!" said Gran. "I love it!"

"You sent them," said Dad, doing the pointing-finger routine again. "I was in there for over two hours. One of them had a pin through his nose and one woman thought she had two growths on her chest but they were just two old raisins that had gotten stuck there."

Mom threw up her hands. It's one thing for a woman to know that her husband, being a doctor, will be forced to look at other women's chests from time to time but quite another to be given these kinds of graphic descriptions of the lurid act.

"They're called breasts, Tex, for crying out loud," Mom said now.

"Raisins," her husband insisted stubbornly. "When I touched them they came right off. Look, that's all beside the point. Your mother hates the fact that I hired a new receptionist, and she'll go to any lengths to sabotage my work."

"I don't know what you're talking about," said Gran. "If this Canyon woman is such a lousy receptionist why do you let her work there in the first place? Besides, you don't even pay her, so what's up with that?"

Mom turned on her husband. "Scarlett Canyon is volunteering for you?"

"Yes, she is," said Dad. "And she's doing a great job, too—until your mother started interfering."

"You do know that Scarlett Canyon had an affair with my dad, don't you?" said Mom.

Uh-oh, Odelia thought. Things were about to get ugly.

Dad opened and closed his mouth like a fish on dry land for a moment, then stammered, "I... she didn't... she didn't mention that on her—are you sure that was her?"

"Of course I know that was her. It's the whole reason Dad walked out on us in the first place. And you know about that. I told you."

More of the fish on dry land routine. Odelia was starting to feel sorry for her dad. She decided to put in her two cents. "Look, none of this would have happened if Gran hadn't deserted Dad when he needed her the most."

"Oh, don't give me that crap," said Gran. "None of this would have happened if Tex hadn't deserted me when *I* needed him the most!"

"You were pretending to be a man's mother!" Tex cried. "That's a felony!"

"Just a little fib," Gran insisted. "Besides, I did it for this family."

The argument would go on all night if not nipped in the bud, Odelia knew, so she held up her hands and yelled over the yellers, "I think this calls for a time-out!"

That got their attention. Mom gawked at her, Gran blinked, and Dad frowned.

"We're not toddlers, honey," said Mom. "You can't give us a time-out."

"I can if you behave like toddlers. So not a peep from you for the next five minutes."

She would have put them in the corner but that was probably too much. To her relief, the three other adults in the room respected her decision to call for a time-out under her own roof, and she went right back to preparing the spaghetti bolognese she was making. Five minutes wasn't much, but it was amazing how peaceful things suddenly became.

Dad was glaring at Gran, though, who was scowling at him, and Mom was alternately glowering at both her husband and her mother, so this time-out wouldn't solve the bigger issue, which was that these grownups had to learn to behave like adults. As it was, Odelia's cats were better-behaved than the humans who were supposed to take care of them.

Five minutes later, Dad stalked out angrily, Mom followed suit, and Gran settled in to watch *Jeopardy*.

Ugh. At least the shouting had stopped.

And then Dua Lipa began to sing and she frowned at her phone. Wiping her hands once more, she picked it up. "Mr. Paunch?"

"Hey, Odelia. Can I call you Odelia? I feel like we know each other. And I love this connection we have." When she didn't respond, he cleared his throat. "Anyway, just wanted to congratulate you on the updated rich list. Van is a very happy camper right now. How is that Wikipedia article coming along?"

"I told you—I don't work for Wikipedia, Mr. Paunch."

"Yeah, yeah, yeah. Now could you mention in tomorrow's

piece that President Wilcox is the tallest president that ever served this country? The absolute tallest?"

"Tomorrow's piece? How did you know I'm writing a piece for tomorrow's edition?"

"Oh, please, Odelia. Must we play this game? I'm one of the best-informed people in the country, okay? So why wouldn't I know what you and Dan Goory are up to?"

Odelia was surprised this Paunch person would know her editor. Then again, he seemed to know everyone else. "Okay, I'll try to squeeze it in. I'll have to fact-check it first, though."

"No need. I already took care of that for you. Consider it fact-checked. Tallest President in history. Oh, and he's also the President with the most hair."

"Most hair?"

"Most hair. I counted them myself. Also the softest hair."

"Softest hair?"

"That's right. Touched it myself. Soft as a baby's bottom."

And with this startling revelation, he disconnected.

Odelia stared at her phone. Otto Paunch was her own personal Deep Throat, only the information he imparted wasn't exactly groundbreaking or earth-shattering. Still, it was something. Like her own personal line to the President.

CHAPTER 24

The nocturnal blanket of darkness swept down on Hampton Cove, covering the picturesque Hamptons community in a cloak of peacefulness, most of its human inhabitants now fast asleep, while its cat population moved out of their houses in droves, led by that ancient hunting instinct and the desire to protect their domain from other felines.

And so it was that Odelia hopped into her car, watched her small cat menagerie gracefully jump into the backseat, and launched us on what she hoped would be a very fruitful night of snooping around on someone else's property. For where humans fear to tread, cats have absolutely no compunction to trespass with absolute impunity.

Our destination? Geary Potbelly's duck farm.

Our mission? Elicit the descriptions and possibly the names of the miscreants who had so dastardly stolen Mr. Potbelly's equipment to carry out their murderous scheme.

Five cats rode in the backseat in relative silence. Relative, I say, because wherever there is more than one cat present, banter inevitably enters the picture. Cats hate those uncomfortable silences even more than humans do and are quick to fill them with chatter.

"Is duck poop smelly?" asked Dooley now.

"All poop is smelly," I said.

"No, but I mean is it more smelly than cat poop—or even human poop?"

Harriet wasn't in a chatting mood. "Didn't you hear what Max said? All poop is smelly."

"I know. But what I want to find out is how smelly duck poop is in comparison with our own poop and human poop. On a scale of smelliness, where would you place duck poop?"

Brutus was grunting something. He was keeping a close eye on Milo, who he suspected of having secretly developed a crush on Harriet. Why else would he have gone to such lengths to try and break up this love affair he and the feisty white Persian enjoyed? "Who cares how smelly duck poop is?" the black cat said now. "It's a nonissue, Dooley."

Dooley seemed to beg to disagree. He was also begging for a smack on the snoot if he kept this up.

"I think duck poop probably rates a five on the Richter Poop Scale," said Milo, throwing his two cents in. "Human poop rates a six, and cat poop a solid seven."

"Richter scale?" I said with a frown. "I thought the Richter scale was for earthquakes?"

"Oh, Dr. Richter worked on a lot of scales," said Milo. "The earthquake thing was only one of them. For a long time he was actually more famous for his Poop Scale than for the Earthquake Scale. Of course he didn't call it the Poop Scale. Scientists dislike simple names. He called it the Defecation Magnitude Scale. Worked very hard on it. Involved a powerful olfactory machine of his own design called The Sniffer. Now mainly used in the perfume industry."

Dooley was interested. "So if cat poop is a seven on the Richter scale, what's an eight or a nine or even a ten?"

"Elephant poop, obviously, is an eight. Mice poop a nine. And it will surprise you to know that fly poop is a ten. But because fly poop is so tiny it is very hard for us to detect its odor. Richter set up this massive experiment where he collected fresh fly poop in large Mason jars then subjected its contents to The Sniffer. It registered as a ten."

"Wow," said Dooley, wide-eyed. "That's amazing, Milo. Fly poop. A ten!"

"Yes. It is said even The Sniffer was impressed. And out of commission for a while."

"Out of commission?"

"A smell that registers as a ten on the Richter scale is lethal for humans and very disruptive even to machines."

I have to say that I took this Richter story with a sniff of salt. Then again, stranger things have been examined by the leading scientists of our time so why not fly poop?

"We're almost there, you guys," said Odelia. "I'm going to drop you off at the fence, all right? From there it's not that far to the duck houses."

"We'll just follow our noses," Milo suggested mildly.

Odelia parked the car and opened the door. "Good luck," she said. "I'll wait here, okay? And watch out for those dogs."

"We'll be fine," I said. "We've handled dogs before."

"Yes," said Brutus. "I still have to meet the first dog who can best us."

Odelia smiled. "I'm so happy you invited Milo onto the team. This is what friendship is all about." And with these words of encouragement, she sent us off on our secret mission.

The fence was designed to keep deer out, and therefore presented no obstacle for five clever cats. For one thing, we're a lot smaller than deer, and for another, we can climb trees that are located right next to the Potbelly fence, with a nice overhanging branch that drops us right on the other side.

"I'm worried about the smell," said Dooley as we deftly landed on all fours.

"Oh, will you shut up about the smell," said Harriet irritably.

"If fly poop is deadly for humans, duck poop might be deadly for cats!" Dooley said.

"I'm sure we'll be fine," I said. "Now keep your eyes peeled, you guys. And remember: we're on a fact-finding mission. So first let's see if we can't talk to one of those guard dogs. If anyone knows what went down here last night, it will be them."

"Maybe we should spread out," said Brutus. "Isn't that what Bruce would do?"

Brutus was right. When on a dangerous mission, always ask yourself what Bruce would do. And right now Bruce would probably tell his team to spread out. And since I seemed to have assumed the role of team leader, I now said, "Brutus and Harriet, head up to the farm and talk to those ducks. Dooley and I will look for the dogs."

"What about me?" asked Milo. "What important task do you have in store for me, Max?"

He was giving me a slightly mocking look, as if on the verge of challenging my authority.

"You better go with Brutus and Harriet," I said, as there was no way I was going to have Milo cramp my style.

But Brutus and Harriet weren't all that eager either. Still, they relented, and I watched the trio stalk off in the direction of the stables—or the duck houses, as Odelia had called them.

And then it was just Dooley and me. Just like old times. And I suddenly felt almost cheerful. Dooley might not be the brightest bulb in God's big bulb shop, but he's my buddy, and

I was glad we'd ironed out those Milo-made differences. Or at least I thought we had.

"Max, if Brutus is my father, and you're Brutus's brother, is Harriet my mother?"

"Milo made all that up, Dooley," I said. "Brutus is not your father and I'm not his brother. My guess is that his human loves her daily dose of *Days of Our Lives* as much as Gran does and watching all of that stuff for years has somehow turned Milo into a mythomaniac as a consequence. Either that or a psychopath. The jury is still out."

"A mythomaniac, is that like a nymphomaniac, Max?"

"Not... exactly."

"Do you think Milo is evil?"

"Like I said, the jury is still out on that one. He does seem to enjoy wreaking havoc in other cats' lives."

We'd been traipsing around the duck farm without a single sighting of a dog, duck or other living creature and no hope of catching Odelia's thieving killers—or killing thieves—when suddenly I caught sight of two large ears sticking out of a hole in the ground. They were twitching anxiously, as if aware of our presence.

I hunkered down behind a tractor tire someone had conveniently discarded.

"Dooley!" I hissed. "Over here!"

"What is it?" he asked, excited. "Do you see something?"

Instead of replying, I pointed in the direction of the ears. And then he saw it, too. A face had surfaced, like a snail from its shell. It was a white, furry face with twitchy nose.

It was a rabbit. A big, white rabbit.

CHAPTER 25

"What is that, Max?" asked Dooley, both intrigued and terrified.

"That, my friend, is a rabbit," I said, and emerged from our hiding place.

"Watch out, Max!" Dooley cried. "It could be dangerous!"

"It's just a rabbit," I said. "Rabbits aren't dangerous."

"It could be a rabid rabbit!" he said.

The fluffy bunny didn't look rabid, though. So I approached it in the spirit of friendship. "Hey, there, buddy," I said by way of greeting. "My name is Max and I come in peace."

"What do you want, cat?" asked the rabbit in a gravelly voice. Almost as if it had been smoking a pack of cigarettes a day for its entire life. It could have been a pipe, too.

"My friend and I are trying to ascertain whether intruders burgled this farm last night," I said. "They would have stolen both a tractor and a tanker filled with duck poop?"

The rabbit stared at me—insolently, I would have

thought. Impossible, of course. Rabbits are fun and cuddly creatures. Lovable and full of joy and love and good cheer.

"I don't know what you're talking about, cat," said this rabbit, with distinct lack of good cheer. "What I do know is that you're trespassing, and if you and that other cat don't get out of my face in ten seconds I'm siccing the dogs on you."

"Hey! I said I've come in peace!"

"I don't care. We don't like strangers around these parts. So you better buzz off."

"I'm not a stranger. I live in Hampton Cove!"

"You're a stranger to me, stranger. Plus, you're a cat."

"So?"

"Didn't you get the memo? Nobody likes cats."

"Everybody likes cats! In fact people love cats!"

"Now, see, that's where you're wrong. People love rabbits. They hate cats."

This was one weird rabbit, I thought. Dooley, who'd also emerged from behind the tire, seemed to think so, too, for he said, "I never met a cat-hating rabbit before."

"And I'm not the only one. All rabbits hate cats—and so do humans."

"No, they don't. Our humans love cats," said Dooley.

"Huh," said the rabbit. "Your humans must be weirdos."

"No, they're not. They're perfectly normal humans," I said.

"If they like cats there must be something wrong with them."

"They're normal humans!" I cried. "And like all normal humans they love cats!"

"Look, I'm not having this conversation," said the rabbit. "You better clear out now before I call in the dogs."

"What has happened to you that you hate cats so much?" asked Dooley.

The rabbit frowned. "I don't understand the question. The whole world hates cats."

"No, it doesn't!" I said.

"You're obviously delusional, cat. Of course it does. All life on this planet agrees on only one thing: that cats are the most loathsome creatures ever brought into this world."

"Who are you talking to, Alfie?" asked a muffled voice.

"Stay where you are, Victorine," said the rabbit. "It's not safe out here."

A second rabbit rose up from the hole. Like its cat-hating friend, it was white and fluffy and looked harmless. When it caught sight of us, it even smiled. "Oh, hi, there, cats."

"Don't talk to them, Victorine!" said Alfie. "You know we don't talk to cats."

"Oh, don't be rude, Alfie." She gave us a look of apology. "Don't mind Alfie, cats. Ever since he was attacked by a pack of wild cats he hasn't been the same." She turned to Alfie. "These are two perfectly nice cats, Alfie. Gentlecats. They're not going to hurt you."

"Yeah, we're nice cats, Alfie," I echoed Victorine. "All we want from you is some information."

Dooley was eyeing the two rabbits with trepidation. "Did you say that a pack of wild cats attacked you?"

"Yeah, there were at least a dozen of them," said Victorine. "Vicious creatures. Not you, of course," she quickly added. "You're nice. Now what was it you wanted to know?"

I repeated my request, and I could see this set the rabbits thinking. Alfie probably about calling in the dogs, but Victorine was actually contemplating my question.

"I did see two men last night. They cut a hole in the fence. Before driving off."

"Don't help them, Victorine!" her cat-hating mate implored. "We don't help cats!"

"Oh, shush," she said kindly. "Um, one was short and one

was tall. And the tall one had a little mustache and the short one had a very big nose. Like one of them strawberry noses. He also had a purple spot on his upper lip. I thought maybe he got stung by a bee."

"Or attacked by a cat," Alfie growled.

Now we were getting somewhere. "That's great, Victorine," I said. "Did you ever see these men before?"

"Oh, no," she said. "And I haven't seen them since, either. Did you see them before, Alfie?"

But Alfie was now engaged in a silent protest.

"Oh, don't be like that, Alfie. Not all cats are bad. These are two perfectly nice cats."

"I don't like cats," Alfie insisted, his fluffy tail twitching defiantly. "Any cats."

Victorine shook her head. "I'm afraid he's become one of them whatchamacallits, um…" She thought for a moment, thumping her paw, then her face cleared. "A racist!"

I'd never met an anti-cat racist rabbit before, so this was definitely a first. "Well, if it's any consolation, there are some very nasty cats out there," I said.

"Darn tootin' there are," said Alfie.

Victorine pursed her lips. "Still. No sense in tarring all cats with the same brush, is there? I'm sure there are more nice cats than nasty ones. And the same goes for rabbits."

"Hey!" said Alfie. "Don't you go talking smack about your own kind!"

"Oh, Alfie, you have got to admit that your mother can be quite a handful. Like when I brought her that perfectly good carrot yesterday and she told me it had mildew. Mildew!"

"Okay, fine. My mother is a handful. But that doesn't mean all rabbits are like her."

"And what about your seven million sisters? They're always perfectly mean to me."

"All right. I'll give you that. My sisters are absolute pests."

"Or your fifteen million brothers."

"I get it! You've made your point!"

"And there was that time when your father called me a stuck-up little—"

"Fine! I get it! Rabbits can be horrible meanies, too."

"And don't get me started on your five million aunts."

"Hey, your family hasn't exactly rolled out the red carpet for me, either!"

"Don't you say a bad thing about my family, Alfie!"

Dooley and I kinda drifted off after that, feeling we didn't need to be there for this domestic scene of spousal discord. We had the information we'd come here to find, and that was good enough for me.

"I didn't know rabbits could be racist, Max," said Dooley as we walked away, the sounds of Victorine and Alfie arguing now growing distant.

"I guess all animals can be racist," I said.

"Do you think flies are racist? Against bees, for instance?"

"Probably so."

"And fleas against lice? Rats against mice? Cats against bats?"

"You bet. I don't even like bats. I think they're creepy."

We were both silent for a moment while we contemplated this. Then Dooley said, "It's a strange world out there, Max."

Truer words have never been spoken.

CHAPTER 26

*H*arriet wasn't as keen to venture into the duck's lair as she should have been. The truth of the matter was that this detective stuff was more Max's thing. Creeping into duck farms at night, talking to ducks and dogs, sniffing out secrets and mysterious clues. It wasn't really her bag. But since they'd already agreed to do this, she couldn't back out now. Besides, Brutus liked a bit of action, and she didn't want to let her hunky sweetums down.

The part of the farm where the ducks were kept were these long, white clapboard one-story buildings. She could hear the quacking even as they approached, and had a hard time adjusting to the smell and the muck that was spread all around the ducks' homes.

She tried to put her paws down where no mud or—worse —duck poo covered the ground, but it was hard going. As a prissy and fastidious Persian, she hated getting her flawless white fur soiled, and this trip to the duck farm was proving a real challenge.

Oh, how she wished she were home right now, blissfully resting her front paws on her human's lap. Marge was the finest human a cat could wish for. Odelia wasn't bad either, but she was too much of an amateur detective in Harriet's view. Marge, who worked at the local library, was a real homebody, which was perfect for Harriet, for she was just the same.

"Hey, you guys," said Brutus now. "I think this is it. Do you smell that?"

Harriet wrinkled her nose. "I've been smelling nothing else for the past half hour."

"Duck poop," said Milo, who was proving himself to be somewhat of a poop specialist.

"We better head on inside," said Brutus. "And talk to those birds."

"Is a duck a bird?" asked Milo. "I'm not so sure."

"Of course they're birds," said Harriet, who'd grown to detest Milo. She hadn't forgotten how he convinced her Dooley's poop-smearing antics were a seduction technique.

"There's a growing consensus in the scientific community that ducks are actually small humans with wings."

Oh, this was rich. "Humans! Are you crazy? Ducks aren't mammals!"

"Actually, they are. They're an ancient peoples, who lived on a small and sheltered island paradise, where they had developed a very sophisticated and technologically advanced society. They lived in peace and harmony for thousands of years, until a great cataclysm destroyed the island and forced them to evacuate. The creatures we now know as ducks are the descendants of that original society. Very sophisticated. Highly intelligent."

They were staring out across the stable, where thousands upon thousands of ducks were resting on a bed of straw. Softly quacking, they spread a distinct and musty odor.

"They don't look so sophisticated to me," Brutus grunted skeptically.

"They're so intelligent our own intellect is too weak to grasp the message they're trying to purvey," said Milo. "These gentle creatures are way ahead of us. Way ahead." He then directed a kindly glance at his compatriots. "Though you guys are the most intelligent felines I've ever encountered. Definitely a lot more intelligent than Max or Dooley."

"Well, that's not so hard," said Brutus with a grin.

Harriet gave her mate a critical look. Had he already forgotten who they were dealing with? Milo's modus operandi seemed to be to turn cats against each other.

"Especially you, Brutus," said Milo now, placing a paw on the black cat's shoulder. "You're probably the smartest one of the bunch. Handsome, intelligent, kind, with a big heart and a noble character. A real leader, in fact."

"I'm glad someone finally noticed," Brutus grunted.

"And I'm surprised Max doesn't appreciate you more."

"Well, Max is… Max, I guess," said Brutus. "He's been here longer than me."

"That's no excuse. You're clearly leadership material, Brutus. You should be the one in charge."

"Don't get me wrong," said Brutus. "Max is a great friend. But he probably shouldn't try to do everything himself. I've told him over and over again he should delegate more."

"Not delegate. Acknowledge your strength and relinquish the crown he's taken."

"Brutus," said Harriet crossly. "Can I have a word with you in private?"

"Later, petal. Milo is saying some very interesting things here."

"Brutus. Now!" she snapped, and stalked off to a corner of the stable.

Brutus followed reluctantly. "What's wrong?" he asked.

"He's doing it again!" she loud-whispered. "He's setting you up against Max!"

"No, he's not. He's just pointing out a few facts. Facts I happen to agree with."

"He's sucking up to you!"

"Hey, he's telling the truth."

"Oh, Brutus," she said, rolling her eyes.

Then she saw how Milo had stalked over to a small group of ducks and was now holding forth on something, the ducks all listening intently.

"What is he doing?" she asked.

"How should I know? Probably speaking in ancient duck."

"That duck story sounded a lot like the *Wonder Woman* story," said Harriet.

"I didn't like that movie. It had no cats in it."

They snuck closer and listened in.

"Thank you so much, dear ones," Milo was saying. "I owe you a debt of gratitude. Now remember what I told you about Farmer Potbelly."

"Yeah, he can't keep us locked up in here," said one of the ducks.

"He's a dictator and a tyrant and we're not going to take this anymore!" said another duck, who seemed like a very excitable one.

"Rise up!" said a squat duck. "Rise up, brethren and sistren! The revolution is here!"

"Spread the word!" an elderly duck croaked. "Spread the word far and wide."

And spread the word, they did. Before long, the stable was abuzz with revolutionary chatter.

"Looks like Potbelly is in big trouble," said Brutus.

"You see?" said Harriet. "This is what he does. He's a hate speaker."

Brutus stared at her. "I don't know what that is."

"He incites hatred! Stirs up all kinds of trouble just for the heck of it."

Brutus scratched himself behind the ear. He looked sheepish. "I guess you're right."

"Of course I'm right. Don't listen to him, Brutus. From now on we stick to Max's plan."

"Max's plan," scoffed Brutus, who seemed to have been infected by Milo's talk.

"Our plan," said Harriet, placing a kindly paw on Brutus's shoulder.

He nodded reluctantly. "Fine. We stick to the plan."

It was obvious Harriet would have to keep an eye on her mate. He seemed very susceptible to Milo's brand of nonsense. More so than any other cat in their coterie.

CHAPTER 27

⁂

"So? What have you found out?" asked Odelia the moment the cats were back. When she saw them coming she'd opened the door and they immediately hopped in.

"That the farm was robbed by two guys, one short with a strawberry nose and a purple spot on his lip, the other tall with a little mustache," said Max, who was the first to speak.

A pervasive smell of duck permeated the car and Odelia wrinkled her nose. "That's great! Did the ducks tell you that?"

"No, the wife of a cat-hating racist rabbit," said Dooley.

"And we discovered that Wonder Woman is a duck," said Harriet.

"And that Max is a great leader," said Brutus, his voice dripping with sarcasm.

Odelia decided not to go down that particular rabbit hole. "Uh-huh. Interesting."

Milo was uncharacteristically quiet, and in the silence Odelia thought she could hear furious quacking. And when she squinted in the darkness, she thought she could see lights flash on all around the Potbelly farm. "What's going on down there?" she asked.

"I think we better get out of here," said Harriet, shuffling uneasily.

"Why? What happened? Did they find out you were in there?"

"They might have," said Harriet.

There was a lot of commotion on the farm, Odelia now saw. People moving about and plenty of ducks, too. They seemed to be flocking together, moving as one flock of ducks away from their stable and in the direction of the houses the Potbellies had erected.

"Looks like the ducks are moving towards their owners' houses," said Odelia, surprised.

"Rise up," Milo muttered softly. "Oh, rise up, ye mighty race."

Odelia directed an odd look at Milo, then figured she'd better heed Harriet's advice and return home. Whatever was going on at that farm, it was probably better if she wasn't discovered lurking around.

During the ride home, the silence that had descended upon the car stretched on. She didn't mind. She had some thinking to do about the murder case, and she figured her cats were probably tired from all that traipsing around on the Potbelly farm.

Soon enough they were home and she let them out of the car again. They walked in a straight line, still cloaked in silence, then into the house and to their respective perches. All of them except for Max and Dooley, who were off to choir practice as usual.

And as she was about to close the door, the tall figure of a man walked up to her. When he stepped into the light cast by the streetlamp in front of her door, she saw it was Chase. He watched as Milo walked into the house, tail up, followed by Brutus and Harriet.

"Now there's something you don't see every day," said Chase as he casually leaned against the doorframe. "I always thought cats didn't need to be taken for a walk, only dogs."

"My cats are special," she blurted out.

"That, they are," he said with a slight grin.

"How long have you been out here?" she asked, noticing his parked pickup.

"Not that long. Half an hour, maybe. I tried calling but got your voicemail."

Shoot. She'd turned off her phone when she set out for the farm. "I must have forgotten to switch it on again."

He leaned in and took a sniff at her hair. "Smells familiar. In fact there's only one place I can think of that ships out this particular scent in bulk." He fixed her with a curious look. "Any particular reason you decided to go snooping around a duck farm at night?"

"I... just wanted to have another look at the farm—spend some time thinking."

"So you didn't go inside?"

"The cats might have. I just let them out of the car and let them wander about."

"You're such a terrible liar, Poole."

"I'm not lying! I sat there, in my car, thinking about the case, and I figured since I was driving anyway, I might as well bring the cats along. For company. And because they like it."

"And how would you know what your cats like and don't like? Do you speak cat?"

It was such a direct question she almost replied in the affirmative. But then her sense of self-preservation kicked in and she laughed lightly. "Speak cat? Very funny, Chase."

He gave her that cop look again, as if trying to figure out if she was telling the truth. She projected as innocent and careless a look as she could manage, which was a little hard as he was a very good cop, and he could look in a very piercing way when he wanted to. Finally, he relaxed. "So what do you think? Any bright ideas?"

"I think we should talk to some more people tomorrow."

"Very clever, Poole. Now why didn't I think of that?"

She narrowed her eyes at him. "And while I was out there I met a source who gave me a description of the two men who burgled that farm. One was short with a strawberry nose and a purple spot on his upper lip, the other tall with a small mustache. That ring a bell, Kingsley?"

The moment she'd said it, she regretted it.

"Source? What source?"

"You know I can't disclose my sources, Chase."

He gave her a withering look. "I disclose mine, so I don't see why you shouldn't disclose yours."

"I'm a reporter. My sources trust me to keep their identity confidential."

"And I shouldn't even be dragging you along on my interviews!"

They squared off for a moment, staring each other down.

"You look pretty sexy when you're angry, Poole."

"You look pretty hot yourself, Kingsley."

"Your grandmother home?"

"Watching a movie."

"Dammit."

"How about a quickie in your car?"

A wolfish grin spread across his features. "Now you're talking."

CHAPTER 28

To be absolutely honest, I was glad to be out of that car. Harriet and Brutus and Milo had really gone all out on the duck smell. In fact I was afraid I now smelled of duck dung myself. Dooley must have thought the same thing, for he said, "Do you think duck dung is as deadly as fly dung, Max?"

"Oh, don't listen to Milo. He's full of dung."

"Brutus was acting weird, though, wasn't he? Do you think the dung got to him?"

"Could be," I admitted, though it was far more likely Milo had gotten to him.

The silence in the car had been deafening, and I blamed it all on the intruder. Before Milo things had been fine, and now there was this constant tension. It was starting to affect me adversely. As in, my digestion wasn't as robust as it usually is. Could also be the fact that Dooley had eaten all my Cat Snax to get rid of his make-believe worms and Milo had eaten all of my Fancy Feast Seafood and now all that was left was my usual kibble and some milk.

Bummer.

"You know, Max? I'm glad we finally got to go out with Odelia again. I missed it."

"Me, too, buddy."

"And I'm glad we were able to help her. Do you think she'll catch those killers?"

"I'm sure she will. How many men with a strawberry nose are out there?"

"Not many, I'll bet."

"Nope."

Dooley gave me a sideways glance. "Max?"

"Mh?"

"I'm glad we're friends again."

"Me, too, Dooley."

"I don't like it when we fight."

"I love you, buddy."

"I love you, too."

And it was with a lighter heart that I pranced along the sidewalk, on our way to cat choir. The choir convenes every night, though not all members show up each time. Cat choir is not so much an expression of our artistic sensibilities as an excuse to hang out and shoot the breeze. Cats used to hang out on rooftops and such, but the park is a much better place. Plenty of trees to climb—us cats love climbing trees—and plenty of critters in the undergrowth—us cats love catching critters even more than climbing trees—so it's all good.

We arrived at the park and saw that it was already humming with activity. Not musical activity, even though some cats were already warming up those vocal cords by performing deep-breathing exercises and singing scales.

"Ooh, eee, aah," they were screeching.

A sporadic boot was already tumbling down from the windows of the houses overlooking the park, but it was clear the boot-throwers' hearts weren't in it, as these boots were old and worn-out. The real nice boots only came later, when choir practice really kicked in and stupefied humans picked up any footwear they could lay their hands on.

"Hey, you guys," said Shanille, who was cat choir's conductor. She's a gray cat with white stripes and belongs to Father Reilly. She sniffed the air. "What's that terrible smell?"

"Duck dung," said Dooley before I could intervene.

Shanille looked thoughtful. "I don't know if I shouldn't dismiss you. There's a hygiene rule in the cat choir rulebook about making sure you're properly bathed and washed before you arrive. Some of our members are very sensitive to pervasive odors, you know."

"We are washed and bathed," I said. "This is not our smell. It's Brutus and Harriet's. They're the ones who mingled with the ducks."

"We only mingled with the rabbits," Dooley explained helpfully. "One was racist and the other wasn't."

Shanille blinked as she took this all in. "I'll have to consult the other members. We are a democratic organization, after all. I'll put it to a vote."

And before I had a chance to file a motion to stay, she'd stalked off.

"Oh, darn ducks," I muttered.

"Now don't be a racist, Max," said Dooley. "Those ducks can't help how they smell."

"I'm not racist! I just don't want to be kicked out of cat choir because of a trifling thing like duck dung."

"It's not a trifling thing. Remember, duck dung registers a five on the Richter scale. That's not something to take lightly."

"How many times have I told you not to believe a word Milo says?"

"He wouldn't be lying about something like that. The Richter scale is real. I've heard about it on your *Discovery Channel*."

"Oh, Dooley," I muttered.

Moments later, Shanille returned. "Well, I've put it to a vote," she said. "And I've got some good news and some bad news."

Oh, crap. "What's the good news?"

"A majority of the members feel that a slight odor is acceptable."

"Yay," said Dooley.

"And what's the bad news?"

"A new member has joined cat choir and you know how new members are granted a veto during their very first cat choir practice?"

"So?"

"So this new member has vetoed your and Dooley's presence here tonight."

I had a sinking feeling I knew exactly who this new member was. "Don't tell me. Is his name Milo?"

Shanille looked surprised. "How did you know?"

"Milo? But how did he get here so fast?" said Dooley.

"He must have run like the wind to get here first," I said bitterly.

"Or maybe he apparated like Harry Potter!" Dooley said excitedly.

We'd sat through a Harry Potter marathon the other day and my head was still hurting. Dooley had enjoyed it, though. "Cats don't apparate, Dooley," I said.

"Professor McGonagall does. And she's at least half cat."

"Milo is not Professor McGonagall."

"Maybe he is. Maybe Milo is a wizard!"

"Milo is a pain in the butt," I said, turning away. At least soon he'd be ancient history.

"Hey, Max," Milo's voice sounded behind me. "Dooley. So weird to see you here."

"Nothing weird about it," I said, turning sharply. "We're out here every night. Isn't that right, Dooley?"

But Dooley was studying Milo intently. "Are you a wizard, Milo?"

Any other cat would have laughed off the silly notion, but not Milo. "How did you guess?" he said seriously.

"Oh, please," I said. "Don't fill Dooley's head with more nonsense, will you?"

Milo turned those placid eyes on me. "And what nonsense would that be, Max?"

"The worms! The scooting! The smearing poop on the walls!"

"Scooting is a very effective remedy for a life-threatening condition, Max."

"See?!" Dooley cried, the color draining from his nose. "I've got worms!"

And instantly he ran for the nearest tree and started rubbing his butt against it.

"I can see right through you, you know," I told Milo coldly.

He lifted one corner of his mouth. "Can you now?"

"And I'm going to expose you. The game is up, Milo."

He yawned. "If you say so. Now I'm very sorry, Max, but I have choir practice. And you, I guess, don't." And with a supercilious little grin, he stalked off, leaving me fuming.

CHAPTER 29

The next morning, Odelia was awakened by the smell of duck dung. She grimaced as she blinked against the sunlight streaming in through the curtains. The first thing she saw were five pairs of cat's eyes staring back at her. It appeared that overnight a regular clowder of cats had convened at the foot of her bed, and gradually, as dawn approached, they'd moved up in the direction of her pillow and now they were practically surrounding her.

Max had placed his paws on her chest, and was breathing heavily. Dooley was still at the foot of the bed, and seemed puzzled why he was the one left behind. Harriet had draped herself across the pillow Chase used when he slept over. Brutus was scowling at her from under her armpit. And Milo had somehow managed to squeeze himself between the headboard and the pillow and was like an oversized pair of earmuffs now, or a hat.

"Hey, you guys," she said as she yawned and tried to stretch. "Could you... move over a scooch? I need to get up."

But the cats weren't budging. If anything, she had the

impression they were eyeing each other as much as they were eyeing her. Like the showdown at the O.K. Corral.

"I've got a question for you, Odelia," said Brutus now.

"Shoot," she said, hoping they'd get this over with soon.

"Who's your favorite?"

Uh-oh. "My favorite what? Movie? I really like *Frozen*."

But he was not to be distracted. "Who's your favorite cat?"

"I don't have a favorite, Brutus. I love all you guys the same."

"That's scientifically impossible," said Milo. "The human mind likes to make sense of the world by turning it into a perfectly ordered set of lists. Favorite foods. Favorite socks. Best boyfriends. Best kisses. You get the drift. So you must have a favorite cat, Odelia."

"Well, I don't, Milo. Now can you move? I want to get up."

"Max is your favorite, isn't he?" Brutus insisted.

"Oh, Brutus," Harriet snapped. "Not again with this nonsense."

"It's not nonsense when it's true! Nobody blames you, Odelia," Brutus continued. "Max is, after all, your cat. Dooley is Grandma's, Harriet is Marge's, I'm Chase's, and Milo is this Aloisia person's. So it stands to reason you would like Max the mostest."

"That's not even a word," said Max.

"Yes, it is! And you be quiet, Max. I don't want you to influence Odelia."

They were all staring at her so intently it was slightly disconcerting. Something was going on here—she could feel it—but she couldn't exactly put her finger on it. She had to admit that there was some truth to what Brutus was saying. She did like Max the most. And this probably was because he was hers and had been with her the longest. But that didn't mean she didn't love the others. She loved all of her cats, though right now they were scaring her a little. "Look, the human mind may work like you say it does, Milo, but my mind doesn't."

"It has to," said Milo. "You're human, so you have a human mind."

"I don't care, all right?" she said, now dislodging the cats. "I like all of you guys. I don't have a favorite and that's that." A little white lie but she didn't think cats could read minds. Or could they? Brutus was trying his best to do just that. But finally he relented.

"I believe you," he announced seriously.

She laughed. "I'm glad you do. Now are you going to help me catch a killer today or are you going to poop all over the house like you did yesterday?"

"That was Dooley," said Brutus immediately.

"But only because I've got worms!" Dooley cried.

Yep. Something was going on with her cats, but right now she had a killer to catch—and a grandmother and a father to reconcile—and an article on President Wilcox to write.

When she got downstairs, Gran was digging holes in the backyard with such a fervor she reminded Odelia of a gang of moles. She walked to the door. "Gran? What's going on?"

Gran looked up with a resolute expression on her face. "I'm building a mausoleum."

"A what?"

"Your father has decided to send me to an early grave so I'm building a mausoleum. And I hope he'll spend the rest of his life staring at my tomb and remembering he was the one who put me there!"

And with these words, she dug her spade into the ground and returned to her grim endeavor.

Shaking her head, Odelia set foot for the kitchen. She needed coffee. Lots of it.

CHAPTER 30

Odelia and Chase were on the road again, only this time five cats rode in the back, much to Chase's amusement.

"You're the only one who treats her cats like dogs," he said.

"That's because they are almost like dogs," she retorted. She cast a quick glance in the rearview mirror and saw that the cold war still hadn't thawed. Usually her cats kept up a pleasant chatter but today there hung a silence like the tomb between them. She didn't know who was fighting with whom but it looked to her like they all had some kind of beef.

At least they'd come back last night with some valuable information. "So what have you got on those two men? One short, one tall—"

"Strawberry nose and mustache. I got it. So far nothing. It's not exactly a very detailed description. Can't you bring your source in and let them work with a sketch artist?"

She glanced back at Max, who shook his head. "Rabbits won't like it," he intimated.

No, the rabbits wouldn't like to come in and talk to the sketch artist. "Nope," she said therefore. "They won't come forward, I'm afraid."

"They? There's more than one?"

"One rabbit is called Alfie, the other Victorine," said Dooley helpfully.

"Odelia?" Chase prompted.

She shook her head resolutely. "I already said too much."

"But why? Have you explained to them they could be helping to solve a murder?"

"They know but they still won't come in. They—"

"Hate cats," said Dooley.

"Have an issue with the police," she said.

Chase was frowning. "I see. So they're implicated somehow. Did they sell information to the killers? Give up the location of Dickerson's safe? Are they members of his staff? No, I got it." He nodded grimly. "They're members of the Potbelly farm staff, aren't they?"

"Bingo," said Dooley. "He's good, Odelia."

"The rabbits aren't staff, though," said Max.

"But they work hard. Did you see that tunnel? Must have taken them ages."

"It's called a burrow," said Milo. "Rabbits are master architects. Like ants."

"Ants aren't rabbits," said Max.

"And how would you know, Max?" asked Brutus. "You're not a scientist."

"Max watches a lot of *Discovery Channel* documentaries," said Dooley.

"I watch a lot of WWE. That doesn't make me Hulk Hogan."

"Oh, shut up, Brutus," said Max.

"No, you shut up, Max!"

"Guys, guys," said Milo. "Enough with the violence. There are ladies present."

Odelia realized Chase was waiting for her to respond. "I'm sorry," she said. "I can't reveal my source. But you're right. They work at the Potbelly farm. They just happened to see the burglars. They never sold them any information, though. And they don't have any connection to them or Dickerson or the murder. They just—"

"Don't want to get involved," he said. "I get it."

"They don't want to risk their position on the farm", Odelia confirmed.

"They could always create another burrow," said Milo. "Rabbits are pack animals. They could simply up and leave and find some other place to live and hunt."

"Rabbits aren't pack animals," said Max heatedly. "And ducks aren't smarter than humans. You're so full of—"

"Max!" said Brutus, gesturing to Harriet. "Lady present!"

"—dung! I was going to say he's full of dung!"

"What's going on with your cats?" asked Chase, darting a quick look over his shoulder. "They're so feisty today. Meowing up a storm. Is it the weather, you think?"

"Yup. Weather is about to change," she confirmed.

Dua Lipa broke into song and she picked out her phone. "Yes, Mr. Paunch."

"Otto, please. Mr. Paunch is my dad. So have I got the scoop for you, Odelia."

"Yes?"

"Van Wilcox just got a call from the mayor of New York. They want to erect a statue in his honor. In the middle of Times Square if you please! And lemme tell you that it's going to be the biggest, grandest statue ever erected for any President anywhere in the world."

"The biggest? You mean bigger than the six hundred feet Sardar Vallabhbhai Patel statue in India?"

"Sure! Much bigger. This will be the greatest thing ever built. It's gonna be huge! And tall. Really tall. Incredibly tall. Like I said, the biggest statue in the world. In history!"

"That's quite an achievement, Mr. Paunch—Otto. The President must be excited." She glanced over to Chase, who was listening intently.

"Oh, he is. He's over the moon. He can't wait to pose for the thing."

"He's going to pose?"

"Sure! Only the best pose ever, in front of the best artist ever."

"Who's the artist?"

"I'd have to get back to you on that, but it's the best artist in the world. The greatest."

And promptly Paunch disconnected again and left Odelia pensively staring at her phone. "Have you ever had that feeling where you're sure you've heard a voice before but you just can't place it? I'm getting that all the time with this Paunch guy."

"What did he want?"

"Oh, New York is building a statue for President Wilcox in Times Square. He wanted me to have the scoop."

"Great," said Chase, shaking his head. "Another eyesore. Just what the city needs."

"Oh, you don't know that. If it's really the tallest statue ever built, it will attract a lot of tourists, and tourists bring in the big bucks, right?"

"Right," said Chase dubiously. "Well, here we are." He directed his car up to a tall gate, a guard approaching them from a guard booth. He showed the man his badge, got a nod, and the gate swung open.

Moments later they were driving up to the house, which looked almost as majestic as President Wilcox's Lago-a-Oceano, only smaller in size and painted a pale orange, resembling the setting sun, with the roof tiled in pink tiles and the gutters a bright blue.

"I like the color scheme," said Chase as he parked the car next to a stone fountain. They got out and Odelia opened the door so the cats could jump out, too.

"You weren't kidding," said Chase. "You're going to let them sniff around, huh?"

"They love to discover new… stuff," she said, and watched as the five cats pranced off. As usual, they'd formed pairs: Max and Dooley, Harriet and… Wait. Harriet was going off alone, and Brutus and Milo had paired up. Weird. Maybe they were making new friends?

CHAPTER 31

"Did you see that?" asked Dooley.

"What?" I asked.

"Brutus and Milo. They went off together!"

He was right. And Harriet was staring after her mate, an annoyed look on her face.

"The loser," she said as she joined us. "I told him not to listen to that guy but he insists Milo makes a lot of sense."

"I guess Brutus is more susceptible to Milo's manipulations than most," I said.

"Don't worry, Harriet," said Dooley. "He'll come around. I saw through Milo's lies, too, you know. Like the stuff he told me about the worms? Max convinced me those were all lies."

Even though Dooley had had a relapse, I'd finally managed to convince him he had no worms. Otherwise Vena would have found them during our last checkup.

"We have to get that cat out of our lives," said Harriet now. "When are we going to put your plan into action, Max?"

"As soon as we lay the groundwork," I said.

"You better do it soon, all right? I'm starting to lose it."

"Lose what?" asked Dooley.

"It!" I could tell from Dooley's expression that he wanted to ask what 'it' was but Harriet's outburst gave him pause.

"So what's the plan, Max?" asked Harriet.

"We chat with anyone who'll talk to us," I said. "Find out what they know."

"Fine," said Harriet, who didn't seem particularly motivated for this mission.

Nor could I blame her. Now that Brutus had fallen for Milo's deceit, there was no telling what that cat was up to next. Short of outfitting Brutus with an explosive belt and sending him on a suicide mission to take out all of Milo's enemies or incite a revolution amongst Hampton Cove's ant population, I figured we could expect anything from him.

We walked around the drive, which was covered with butter-yellow gravel and looked like the kind of sugar Odelia likes to put on her pancakes, and arrived at the back. No swimming pool here, or even a Jacuzzi. Secretary Berish did have a nice patch of lawn that stretched all the way to the ocean, where two deck chairs were set out and a nice parasol.

A chilly breeze wafted in from the ocean. It was too early in the year to go for a swim. Springtime in the Hamptons might be occasionally sunny, but it's not exactly warm. Still, it was probably nice to sit and gaze out across the vast expanse of the North Atlantic.

"I don't see any cats," said Dooley. "Or dogs. Or ducks. Or even rabbits."

"Me neither," I confessed. I did see Brutus and Milo, who'd hopped up on those deck chairs and were now lazing about, probably talking deep philosophy.

"I hate them," said Harriet, who'd noticed the same. "I hate them both."

And she stalked off in the direction of the house. Dooley

and I followed suit. There wasn't a lot for us to do out here. At least the patio door was open, a man smoking a cigarette and standing in the doorway holding it open for us. If he was surprised to see three cats slip into the house, he didn't show it. He had a cook's hat placed on top of his head, and wore one of those white smocks, so I figured he was probably part of the kitchen staff.

Once inside, we traipsed through the house, in search of pets, but found no sign of them. No cat bowls, or dog bowls, or any bowls for that matter. Could this place be petless?

"Looks like Odelia managed to find the one person who doesn't keep pets," I said.

"Bummer," Dooley agreed, as it also meant there was no food for us to steal.

We'd arrived in a large office, and saw that Harriet was staring intently at a stuffed animal mounted on the wall. It was a stuffed fox, and the sight of the thing gave me the willies. People who stuff animals should probably get stuffed themselves, as I can't think of a more cruel hobby.

"Yikes," I said. The three of us were staring up at the fox now, wondering what the poor creature had done to deserve such a terrible fate.

Just then, a voice rang out through the room. "What are you three doing here?"

We turned around as one cat, and saw that the voice belonged to an odd-looking reptilian creature in a glass terrarium, which had been placed on a table near the window.

"What are you?!" Dooley exclaimed, forgetting his sense of propriety. We were guests here, after all. Well, not guests so much as intruders.

"I, sir, am a bearded dragon," said the creature superciliously.

"You're very small for a dragon," said Dooley.

"I'm not a dragon. I'm a *bearded* dragon," said the lizard.

"And I'm a tiger," said Dooley, happily prancing up for a closer look.

As he did, the dragon's beard suddenly extended and the creature hissed.

Dooley shot about two feet into the air, then scooted off with the speed of light and disappeared underneath the desk.

"It's all right, Dooley," I said. "He's inside a cage. He can't hurt you."

But Dooley wasn't taking any chances. He was under that desk and he was staying put.

"We're here to conduct an official police investigation," I told the dragon, who by now had stopped hissing and whose beard had morphed back to its normal size. At least now I understood why he called himself a bearded dragon. He actually had an actual beard! "A man was murdered. His name was Dick Dickerson and he was the editor of a tabloid named the *National Star*. Apparently he printed a lot of bad things about your human—at least I assume Brenda Berish is your human—and what we're trying to discover is if she had something to do with Dickerson's death or if she knows of someone who did."

It was a long speech and I patiently waited for the bearded dragon to take it all in. I had no idea if this creature was intelligent or not but judging from the way he'd reacted to Dooley I assumed he was.

"This is a waste of time, Max," said Harriet finally. "Let's get out of here and see what kinds of lies Milo is filling Brutus's head with this time."

And she made for the door. "Dickerson did print some bad stuff about Brenda," said the lizard suddenly. "And she did hate him with quite a fervor. But she didn't kill that man."

"Oh, thanks, lizard," I said. "How can you be so sure?"

"Please don't call me 'lizard,' cat. I have a name and it is Humphrey."

"Sure, Humphrey. Whatever you say. So how do you know Brenda didn't do it?"

"She was in here talking about the murder last night. Her and her husband. They weren't broken-hearted over it, as you can imagine. But they didn't celebrate either. Brenda is a very kind woman, and she would never gloat over the death of another human being."

"What do you eat?" asked Dooley suddenly from his position under the desk.

"Pardon me?" said Humphrey.

"What kind of food do they give you?" asked Dooley. "Usually when Odelia sends us into these places there's food waiting there for us. But I don't see anything around here."

"Dooley—it's not polite to demand food from your host," said Harriet.

"Technically Brenda is not our host," I said. "We snuck in, remember?"

"If you must know, I'm quite partial to worms," said Humphrey.

"Worms?" asked Dooley, wriggling from under the desk. "What kind of worms?"

"Oh, waxworms, silkworms, butterworms, red worms, earthworms, mealworms, superworms…"

"I didn't even know there were so many different worms!" Dooley cried, looking horrified. He was clutching his tummy and I just knew he was thinking of Milo's words again.

"I like crickets, too," said Humphrey conversationally. "And the occasional leafy greens, of course. I'm not choosy. Oh, and pinky mice. I am a sucker for a juicy pinky mice."

Now he had Harriet's attention. "What's a pinky mouse?" she asked.

"Frozen baby mice. A real delicacy."

We were waiting for him to offer us some, but that was apparently asking too much. If we wanted mice—pink or otherwise—we'd have to catch them ourselves.

"So... about Dick Dickerson," I said, returning to the topic under discussion.

"Oh, right. How am I so certain Brenda didn't do it. Well, she was here, for one thing, working at her desk in this very room, under my watchful eye."

"You watch your human work?" asked Harriet.

"Why, yes. She seems to enjoy my company. Often she has remarked that I have a soothing effect on her, and why not? I am, after all, very easy on the eyes and pleasant to be around." For some reason he'd lifted his paw in greeting, so I lifted mine in response.

"So... who do you think might have done Dickerson in?" I asked.

He was lifting his other paw now, so I followed suit. Weird.

"Mr. Dickerson seemed to have a lot of enemies," said the reptile. "Brenda often fumed about some of the stuff he wrote about her. He did the same to others, as well. One of his frequent targets was a man who liked to portray the President to humorous effect on television. Brenda also expressed the opinion that the man might have killed himself."

"Suicide?" said Harriet. "That doesn't seem likely, considering the way he died."

"Yes, he drowned in his own feces, did he not?"

"Not his own feces," said Harriet. "Duck poop."

"Another species' feces. How extraordinary." The lizard frowned, or at least I thought he did. Tough to read facial expressions on a lizard. "I thought he died in his own excrement."

"Why would he kill himself?" I asked.

Dooley had approached the glass terrarium, probably looking to get in on the pinky mice action. The lizard eyed him with suspicion. "Brenda said Dickerson was under investigation. Apparently he'd aided the President in his election by engaging in some form of illegal activities and prosecutors were going through his business with a fine-tooth comb. He was looking at dismissal from his own company and possibly prison, hence the suicide theory. Though as you say, the duck poop thing seems to preclude such a possibility."

"Unless he staged the whole thing to make it look like murder," said Harriet, who was thinking hard. "All so he could cast the blame on one of his opponents."

"But who?" I asked. I turned to Humphrey. "Does the picture of a rose mean anything to you? It was left at the scene of the crime."

Humphrey regarded me sternly. "I don't like roses. They give me stomach cramps. I will eat fruits and vegetables, provided they're nicely chopped up, but no flowers thank you very much." He'd climbed a tree branch that had been placed inside the tank.

I had a feeling we'd gleaned as much information from Humphrey as we could, so I held up my paw in greeting and he did the same, though I had the impression he was merely trying to protect his stash of frozen baby mice from Dooley.

"Dooley, let's go," I said. "Thanks, Humphrey. You've been most helpful."

"Glad I could help, cat," he said.

"Max," I said, realizing my social faux-pas. "And this is Dooley and that's Harriet."

"Lovely," said Humphrey graciously. "Fare-thee-well —cats."

And we'd just stepped out of the room when we bumped

into an angry-looking female. Judging from the cap she was wearing, and her blue apron, she was part of the cleaning crew. "Cats!" she screamed the moment she saw us. "We've got cats!"

And then she was coming at us with a very large broom!

CHAPTER 32

⚜

Brenda Berish—Secretary Berish to her friends—was a motherly woman in her late sixties. She had a round face and a bouffant blond-gray hairdo. As in all the pictures I'd seen of her she dressed in a brightly colored pantsuit, this one a dazzling heliotrope.

The drawing room where she met us was light and airy, a floral motif extending from the upholstery to the wallpaper and even the carpet. Light slanted into the room, lending it a pleasant atmosphere, and the window had been cracked to allow some air in.

"Detective Kingsley—Miss Poole, how can I be of assistance?" asked Brenda, a kind smile playing about her lips.

"As I told your assistant over the phone, we're looking into the death of Dick Dickerson," Chase said, flipping open his notebook and taking a firmer grip on his pencil. "Mr. Dickerson was known to be a fan of your political opponent—not so much of you."

"Which led you to think I might have done him harm,"

said Brenda, nodding. "First of all, the night Mr. Dickerson was killed, I was in my study, working until late at night."

"Can anyone verify that, Secretary Berish?" asked Chase.

"Oh, please, Detective. You don't really think I drove a tractor up to Dick's house and poured nine thousand gallons of duck poop into his safe, do you? So what you're really asking is if I hired a crew of professionals to do that for me. I can assure you I didn't. There was no love lost between Dickerson and my family but I'm not the kind of person who settles her scores by going around murdering people." She'd placed her hands in her lap and sat poised and calm. "And to answer your question, my husband can verify that I was right here at the house. And if not him, my pet lizard can. Although I can't imagine he'll be willing to testify on my behalf." She threw her head back and laughed a tinkling laugh.

"What about your husband? Did he have reason to harm Mr. Dickerson?"

"Of course he did. Do you have any idea what that man did to us?" She took out her phone and held it out to them. A few choice covers of the *National Star* appeared. 'Brenda's Cancer Scare.' 'Brenda Admitted—Her Fatal Collapse.' 'Brenda's Abortion—Her Secret Love Child.' 'Brenda Going To Jail!' 'Brenda Confesses: I'm a Crack Addict!' 'Brenda Is A Lesbian!'

"That's quite the collection," said Odelia. She'd always known journalistic standards at the *National Star* were low, but she'd never fully realized how low they really were.

"Dickerson was the President's hatchet man," said Brenda, placing the phone on a gateleg table that held a portrait of her, her husband John and their daughter. "So he tried to destroy us. Naturally John wanted to hurt him. But he didn't. He would never stoop that low."

"Does the picture of a red rose mean anything to you?" asked Odelia.

Brenda shook her head. "No. Why?"

"It was found inside the safe—in fact it was the only thing found in that safe."

"Dickerson's files?"

"Gone. Every last one of them."

She mused on that. "Dickerson had many enemies. And he kept extensive files in his safe. Everybody knew that. He propagated the idea he was the new Hoover. That he could break anyone with the dirt he collected on them. But this rose business doesn't ring a bell."

"Do you know of anyone else who could have done this?" asked Chase.

Brenda laughed. "Do you have a couple of hours? Like I said, he made a lot of enemies over the years." When they both stared at her, she relented. "You want names? Well, I'll give you names. There was the President himself, of course. The DA was coming after Dickerson for election fraud and he was prepared to make a deal in exchange for giving up Wilcox. Then there was that Russian mobster he was rumored to be blackmailing."

"Yasir Bellinowski."

"That's the one. And there was the feud with his own daughter, who was suing him after he'd written her out of his will."

That was a new one, and Chase was furiously scribbling this all down.

"Um. Who else? Oh, Olaf Brettin, owner of the *Daily Inquirer* and Dickerson's biggest competitor."

"Why was he upset with Dickerson?" asked Odelia.

"You'd have to ask him. All I know is that they hated each other's guts. Probably because they were competing over the same shelf space and audience. Dickerson was winning, obviously. The *Daily Inquirer* only has half the circulation of the *National Star*."

Just then, a tall man with white hair walked in. It was Brenda's husband John Berish. He looked fit and healthy for a man who'd had a heart scare not that long ago.

Chase and Odelia got up to greet him but he gestured not to bother.

"What's wrong?" asked Brenda when she saw the look on her husband's face.

"Oh, nothing to worry about, darling," he said. "Just some trouble with cats."

"Cats?" asked Brenda.

"Vivicia caught them sneaking into your office. They were probably going for Humphrey." He held up a hand. "He's fine. Vivicia got there just in time."

"How in heaven's name did they get in?"

"The cook must have left the door open again when he went for a smoke."

Odelia's heart sank. She knew exactly who those cats were, and why they'd snuck into the house. "Um, those cats are probably with me," she said now.

The cool gaze of Brenda raked over her. "What do you mean?"

"They're my cats. They… like to go exploring from time to time."

"Yeah, they must have escaped from the car," Chase said, coming to her aid.

"Oh," said Brenda, and she didn't seem very amused. "Well, then. I guess you better come with me and gather them up before Vivicia turns them into meat for my pet lizard."

CHAPTER 33

For the first time in my life I'd been caught and locked up by a human. This cleaner was definitely a force of nature. In one fell swoop she'd grabbed us by the scruff of the neck and had thrown us into a dark cupboard, where we now resided.

"Um, I don't like this, Max," said Dooley. "It's dark in here and it smells."

"Oh, do shut up, Dooley," Harriet said irritably, as if Dooley was to blame for our predicament. "Instead of complaining, why don't you help us find a way out of here?"

"There is no way out of here," said Dooley. "I checked. It's some kind of cloakroom."

He was right. It was a cloakroom. A very small one, and all it contained were musty-smelling coats and sweaters and shoes. Not a nice place for a cat to be cooped up in.

"We have to keep our heads, you guys," I said. "The trick is to be ready when that door opens—and sooner or later it will open—and shoot out as fast as we can—away from that horrible woman with the broom."

"Maybe you can send a telepathic message to Brutus," said

Dooley, who didn't seem to give a lot of credence to my escape plan. "Tell him to come and save us."

"Brutus is only thinking about himself right now," said Harriet with a bitter undertone to her voice. "And how Milo is his new best friend. It wouldn't surprise me if those two are plotting to get us all chucked out of the Poole family's lives and shipped off to the pound."

"They'll have to take a number," said Dooley. "That woman with the broom looked like she was going to send us to the pound first."

"Or turn us into minced meat," I muttered.

"Max, you're scaring me," said Dooley. "Don't say things like that."

"Fine. I won't," I said.

"That was one scary-looking lizard, though," said Harriet. "I wouldn't be surprised if he told that cleaner to capture us and turn us into tasty morsels to snack on."

"Harriet!" Dooley cried. "Please!"

"Fine!" she retorted. "Maybe you can telepathically connect to Odelia and tell her to save us."

Dooley closed his eyes and muttered, "Odelia, please save us. Odelia, please save us. Odelia, please—"

"Oh, shut up already," said Harriet, who was one of those cats prone to fickleness.

But Dooley was not to be deterred. "Odelia, please—"

Suddenly the door opened and I shot out like a rocket—or even faster!

"Max!" suddenly a voice arrested my progress. Reluctantly, I applied the brakes and when I looked back I saw that it was Odelia and she was holding Dooley in her arms, Harriet having jumped up in Chase's arms, and accompanying them was the horrible woman who'd imprisoned us and a woman with a big glob of gray hair and a tall guy with white hair.

"It's all right, Max," said the woman with the big hair, crouching down until her knees cracked. "Odelia explained everything to me. Come here, little guy. You're just fine."

I stepped up to her, wondering why no one had ever told this woman that heliotrope was not a color that suited her skin tone. And as I approached, I sniffed a decidedly delicious aroma. It was Paloma Picasso, the scent Odelia sometimes applies when she goes out on a date with Chase. So I crossed those final few feet, and jumped into the woman's arms. She rose, her knees cracking some more, and groaned from the exertion.

She smelled nice, and with Odelia and Chase present I didn't think she'd dare stuff me into the mincer and turn me into lizard food.

"That cat looks good on you, darling," said the white-haired man jovially.

"No, I'm not taking a cat, John," said the woman, but from the way she was stroking my fur, and enjoying the sound of my purr, I could tell she was a goner.

Us cats have a secret weapon when dealing with humans: the softness of our fur and the burr of our purr. It soothes the nerves and warms the heart and makes humans fall head over heels in love with us and give us everything we need, until half of their kingdom.

Some people are impervious to our secret charm, though, and the cleaner who'd corralled us into the cloakroom was clearly one of them. She stood eyeing me with one of those skeptical expressions on her round face, her bushy brows wiggling with ill-concealed menace. And the thought occurred to me that she might be Dickerson's killer.

Serial killers often hate pets. And this woman definitely looked like a serial killer.

"Are you sure about that?" asked Brutus.

"Absolutely," said Milo.

The two cats were seated side by side on two deck chairs, looking out at the waves gently lapping at the shoreline. This was the life, Brutus thought. No bossy Max to contend with. No girlfriend trying to force her opinions on him. The only thing missing was his bowl of food and a television playing *Kit Katt & Koh*, his new favorite TV show.

"Cats are needlessly afraid of the pound," Milo repeated. "Trust me, I've been there, and the only reason that place gets such a bad rep is because the cats who've been there purposely perpetrate that rep. The pound, my friend, is paradise for pets. They treat you like royalty down there. In fact it isn't too much to say that every cat's dream is to live in the pound for life."

"So all those horror stories?"

"Bald-faced lies. I mean, who's told you that the pound is a wicked place?"

Brutus's own non-bald face hardened. "Max."

"And that's because Max knows. He knows how much better your life would be if you were sent to the pound."

"But why doesn't he go and live there?"

"Because Max is one of those cats who's got it made. He's his human's favorite, isn't he? Odelia gives him everything he needs. The best food, the best home, the best cuddles. And when you're not looking she gives him all that and more. But he doesn't tell you that, does he?"

"Max gets special treatment?"

"Of course he does. When you're not around the liverwurst comes out, and the gold-crusted chicken nuggets, and the hand-caught lobster and the Arenkha caviar and the crab!"

"Oh, my god!"

"Exactly! I'm not jealous, Brutus. I've lived at the pound, and I've sampled all these delicious foods myself. In fact I've eaten so much lobster that I can't stand the taste anymore. But you? You shouldn't be denied this nectar of the gods, my friend."

"Max!" Brutus said between gritted teeth.

"You get the crumbs from his table. And for what? So you can be at his every beck and call. Do as he pleases. Follow his orders and cater to his every whim. Do you really want that for yourself, Brutus? Or do you want to live like a king yourself for a change?"

"I want to live like a king," said Brutus decidedly.

"Of course you do. And you deserve to. But is Odelia going to give you the kind of life you deserve? No, she's not. For some strange reason she's determined to keep Max on as her favorite pet, while she treats the rest of you like mere serfs. Underlings. Max's minions."

"I don't want to be Max's minion any more, Milo."

"I commend the sentiment, Brutus. You have nothing to lose but your chains."

Brutus growled something to himself, then a thought occurred to him. "But what about Harriet? And what about Dooley?"

"They'll have to choose, too. If you convince them to join you, all the better."

"I might be able to convince Harriet. She loves me. Dooley? He's loyal to Max."

"His loss," said Milo. "Some of us are born to be slaves, Brutus. And some are born to be emperors—masters of our own fate." He placed a hand on Brutus's chest. "I think you know, deep inside, what you want to be, don't you?"

"An emperor," he growled, the fire of desire burning bright now.

"So convince Harriet that she can be an empress or stay on as Max's slave. The choice shouldn't be too hard."

He turned to Milo, suddenly overcome with emotion. It was very rare that he felt this strongly about another cat. "Milo," he said with a quiver in his voice.

"I know, Brutus," said Milo magnanimously. "I know."

"You are my savior. My hero. My messiah."

Milo sighed. "It's a tough job, but someone has to do it, Brutus."

"Is that why you left that pound—that paradise—to save the rest of us?"

"Yes, indeed. I could have stayed there forever—basking in the kind of life only the richest cats on earth ever get to experience. Instead I chose to take up the noble quest to free my fellow cat. To be a beacon of light and hope for the downtrodden and the oppressed. Cats like you, Brutus, and Harriet. Even Dooley," he added after a pause.

"Thank you," said Brutus, from the bottom of his heart. A tear stole across his furry cheek. He was deeply moved.

"Don't cry for me, Brutus," said Milo, touched.

"They are tears of joy, Milo. Tears of gratitude. Tears for you."

"Thank you, Brutus," said Milo with a gentle wave of the hand. "Now go forth and spread the word, my child."

CHAPTER 34

Once again, Odelia's cats were awfully quiet on the ride back into town. She didn't mind. She had a lot to think about after the interview with the former secretary. Obviously Dick Dickerson hadn't exactly been a choir boy. He'd made a lot of people very angry over the course of his career as a tabloid publisher. Chase was thinking, too, judging from the thought wrinkle creasing his brow, and so were the cats. A whole lot of thinking going on.

Max hadn't discovered anything of significance, so that was a disappointment.

As they rode into town, Max piped up, "Can you drop us off here, Odelia?"

She directed Chase to stop the car, and Max and Dooley hopped out. Harriet and Brutus and Milo preferred to ride along with her and Chase for some reason. So they dropped the three cats off at the house and Chase took her to the office before he cruised off in the direction of the police station to write up a report on the Brenda Berish interview.

And as she stepped into the *Gazette* office, ready to write up some of her notes, she saw that a visitor was in Dan's office. It was a man she'd never seen before, but then that wasn't so unusual. Dan knew pretty much everyone who was anyone and a lot of someones who were no ones, so he was bound to know people Odelia didn't.

She popped her head into his office. The aged editor was puffing from a nice cigar and sipping from what looked like a glass of port, his white beard waggling happily and his short frame relaxing on the wingback chair he'd installed in his office for when he needed a think.

His guest was a stocky man with a shiny round face and an equally shiny bald dome. He looked like a cartoon of a Wall Street banker, complete with stubby cigar and beady little eyes.

"Hey, there, Odelia," said Dan jovially. His cheeks were red and this was obviously not his first glass of port. "I want you to meet an old friend of mine. This is Olaf Brettin. Olaf runs the *Daily Inquirer*. Just about the nastiest tabloid on the East Coast."

"Not *the* nastiest," said the tabloid editor good-naturedly.

"No, the *National Star* got you licked in that department."

"The *National Star* got us licked in every department," said Brettin. "Not just nastiness but political clout, too. Not to mention circulation, of course." He didn't seem bothered by this fact too much, though, judging from his indulgent smile.

"That will probably all change now that Dickerson is dead," said Dan.

"I don't think so," said Brettin. "Except maybe for the political thing. The *Star's* owners never liked the direction Dickerson took the paper. They'll probably hire an editor who'll return to its core business: digging up dirt on celebrities and exposing scandals."

"Did you know Dickerson well, Mr. Brettin?" asked Odelia.

"We met occasionally. Dinner parties, galas, conferences,

industry events, that sort of thing. We didn't socialize, though. We weren't exactly chummy." His face sagged. "Dick Dickerson had a ruthless streak, Miss Poole. I know you'll probably say that we were like peas in a pod—publishing the same sort of tabloid muck—but I never set out to damage anyone's reputation or even use blackmail to further my own ends."

"And he did."

"And he did," Brettin confirmed.

"It probably got him killed, too," said Dan. "People will only take so much abuse."

"Did he ever try to damage your reputation?" asked Odelia.

Brettin pursed his lips. "Oh, he tried. There was a time our publications were neck and neck, and he used his full barrage of dirty trickery on me. But then he pulled ahead of the *Daily Inquirer* and he stopped bothering. Didn't think I was worth the trouble."

Dan's eyes were gleaming. "Odelia works with the police, Olaf. So you probably should be careful what you tell her."

"You work with the police?" asked Brettin, surprised.

"Occasionally," she said. "My uncle is Chief of Police."

"And her boyfriend is a detective," Dan added, a mischievous glint in his eyes. "So if you confess now, you wouldn't merely give me the biggest scoop in my career, Odelia would probably bring out the handcuffs and arrest you on the spot—isn't that right, Odelia?"

"I'm not a cop, Dan," she said. "I'm not allowed to arrest anyone, I'm afraid."

"I didn't kill Dickerson, if that's what you think, Miss Poole," said Brettin. "There was no love lost between us but what we had was a professional enmity, not a personal one. Besides, it's not as if losing an editor is going to cost the *National Star* its readership. A new editor will come in and take over. The Gantrys won't kill the goose that lays the golden eggs."

"Have they asked you to be the new editor by any chance?" asked Odelia.

"Oh, she's smart," Dan said cheekily. "Watch what you say now, Brettin."

"You trained her well," said Brettin indulgently. "No, Miss Poole. They haven't asked me. And even if they did, I would turn them down. I like my position at the *Daily Inquirer*. That tabloid is my life and I wouldn't trade running it for anything in the world."

Odelia started to leave. She had her own articles to write. And she was sure Chase or one of her uncle's officers would interview Brettin soon enough anyway, asking him about his alibi and stuff like that. But then she thought of something. "Does the picture of a rose mean anything to you, Mr. Brettin?"

"A rose?"

"There was a picture of a rose left in Dickerson's safe. Left there as a message, I presume."

He shook his head slowly. "I'm sorry. That doesn't ring a bell, Miss Poole."

She gave him a smile. "Thanks. Pleasure to meet you, Mr. Brettin."

"The pleasure is all mine," the tabloid editor said graciously.

CHAPTER 35

"Brutus was awfully quiet, Max," said Dooley.

I'd noticed the same thing, and it worried me. "Milo must have been filling his head with nonsense again," I said.

"What kind of nonsense?"

"Nonsense about me, probably. And maybe Harriet."

"What about me? What nonsense would Milo say about me?"

I had a feeling Milo's arrows weren't exactly aimed at Dooley, but I decided not to mention this. "I don't know, buddy. But it won't be good."

We were walking along Main Street, hoping to meet someone who knew something about this Dickerson business. We arrived at the barber shop, but no cats were in sight. The door was slightly ajar, though, so we snuck in anyway. You'd be amazed how much you can learn at the barber's. People waiting for their turn tend to gossip about the people having their hair cut, and the people having their hair cut tend to gossip about the people waiting for their turn. It's one big gossip machine, and from time to time some of that gossip is interesting enough to make it into print—in Odelia's numerous articles for the *Gazette*.

Today was a slow day, though. Only three people were waiting, with two seated in chairs and being worked on by the barber—a handsome man in his fifties named Fido Siniawski—and his assistant. In spite of his age, Fido still sported a full head of shiny black hair, and a wrinkle-free face. People said he'd had work done both on his face and his hair—implants, if the rumors were to be believed—but he looked pretty natural to me.

All cats like Fido. The barber is the proud owner of a Maine Coon named Buster, and any human who loves cats is a human after our own heart.

"Did you hear about Dick Dickerson?" asked one of the two women in the chair. Fido was dabbing at her hair with a brush, presumably applying some sort of dye or gel.

"Oh, such a horrible way to go," said Fido, his voice dripping with relish. "Duck poop. Really. Can you imagine?"

"Horrible," the woman agreed.

I recognized her as Aissa Spring, who runs No Spring Chicks, the vegan restaurant.

"Have they caught the killer yet?" asked Fido.

"No idea. That Odelia Poole has been trucking around with that cop Chase Kingsley again. They seem to be onto something. Marisa saw them drive by the store this morning in Detective Kingsley's pickup."

"That Detective Kingsley," said Fido unctuously. "Now that's one drop-dead gorgeous man."

"I wouldn't know," said Aissa, who is a lesbian. "I don't play for that team, Fido."

"But I do, Aissa!" said Fido, much to Aissa's hilarity. "And he's simply scrumptious!"

"What is scrumptious, Max?" asked Dooley.

"Um…"

"It means he's one handsome devil," said Buster, who'd snuck up on us and was studying us intently. "What are you two doing in here? Soaking up more of that gossip, are you? Whispering it into your Odelia's ear so she can fill her newspaper with a lot of nonsense." He shook his head. "You're all the same, you tabloid cats."

"Um, we're not tabloid cats, Buster," I said. "Whatever gave you that idea?"

"I'll bet you're here to collect gossip on me, too, aren't you? Write about me in that lousy little paper of yours? Well, let me tell you something, Maxi Pad. Maybe you should stop gossiping about others and start putting your own house in order first."

I had absolutely no idea what had gotten into Buster. "I don't understand," I said therefore.

"Sure you do. He told me all about you," said Buster.

"Who did?"

"Some white cat came in here yesterday. Telling me all the stuff you told him about me." He was balling his paws into fists now, and I had a feeling whatever Milo had told Buster wasn't good.

"What did I supposedly tell him about you?" I asked resignedly.

Buster frowned. "That I should be in the Guinness Book of Records as the Ugliest Cat Alive. That I'm so ugly mirrors crack when I look in them. That I'm so ugly I make onions cry. That I'm so ugly I give Freddy Krueger nightmares. I don't get that last one, though. I'm pretty sure I don't know any cat named Freddy Krueger. So why is he having nightmares about me?"

"Oh, Buster," I said. "Don't listen to Milo."

"It's not him that said all those nasty things about me—it's you!"

"No, it's not," I said. "Milo is a liar—he likes to spread

175

these nasty rumors and pit cats against other cats. It's what he does. He seems to draw some kind of perverse pleasure from creating trouble for others."

"He told me I have worms," said Dooley mournfully.

"You mean you don't think I'm stupid?" asked Buster, surprised.

"Of course not! I would never think that, Buster." And even if I did, I wouldn't be stupid enough to tell anyone, I thought. "It's all lies."

"I can't believe he would say something like that."

"He told me I should scoot my tush across the floor—squish the worms."

Buster blinked. "I'm sorry, Max. I didn't know."

"He barged into cat choir last night, too," I said, remembering the veto Milo had exercised against me and Dooley. "Made a lot of trouble for us there as well."

"Did you know that worms don't like Cat Snax?" Dooley asked. "It's true. They hate it. So if you ever have worms, Buster," he said earnestly, "eat a lot of Cat Snax. And scoot." I gave him a critical look and he had the decency to look embarrassed. "I'm sorry. I forgot. Scooting is not really a thing. And neither is eating Cat Snax to get rid of worms." He kicked at a small pile of hair that Fido had swept into the corner. "Damn that cat is convincing!"

"He is," said Buster. "I believed every word he said. He'd make a great politician."

"Or a great lawyer," I added.

"Or a Cat Snax salesperson," Dooley said.

A harrowing thought suddenly occurred to me. "Do you think Milo's been talking to other cats, too?" I asked Buster.

"Sure. Up and down the block. He's real chatty." Then his expression darkened. "Did you know that Kingman tells everyone who wants to listen that my mother was a bald cat? My mother wasn't bald. She had beautiful fur, just like me.

Big, beautiful fur. Orange, too. Lovely color. Now who would say such a horrible thing?" I gave Buster a keen look. He stared at me for a moment, then understanding dawned. "Kingman never said anything about my mother, did he?"

"No, he did not."

"Milo invented that story to make me upset with Kingman."

"Yes, he did."

"Fooled again! Oh, man!"

I patted him on the back. "Don't be too hard on yourself, Buster. He fooled us, too."

And as we walked out of the barber shop, I had the sinking feeling that Hampton Cove's entire cat population would soon be on the verge of war. And all because of one cat.

Ugh.

CHAPTER 36

Down at the precinct, Chase had just walked in when Dolores, who ruled over the station reception with an iron fist, yelled out, "Kingsley!"

He joined her at the front desk. "Dolores?"

Dolores was a big-boned woman with blond, curly hair, a no-nonsense expression tattooed on her face, and a fondness for mascara that made her look slightly scary. "You got a visitor, Kingsley."

"Who is it? Santa?"

She grinned. "Santa only visits boys who've been good."

"I've been good."

"That's not what I hear. Word on the street is that you've allowed yourself to be muscled out of the Chief's niece's house by his own damn mother!"

"Hey, what do you want me to do, Dolores? Kick out Odelia's granny so I can move in?"

"You could make an honest woman out of Odelia by putting a ring on her finger."

"And all this from the word on the street, huh?"

"The street is wise, Kingsley."

"The street's a wise-ass," he said as he walked away. "Who's my visitor?"

"Yasir Bellinowski. Said you'd told him to come in."

And so he had. Only he'd never expected Mr. Bellinowski to actually comply.

He walked through the station office, where several of his colleagues were hard at work answering phone calls, typing out reports on their computers, and generally doing their darndest to keep the peace in the rustic little town of Hampton Cove.

Yasir Bellinowski was waiting in one of the interview rooms. He was dressed in a Brooks Brothers suit that probably cost more than Chase's paycheck for that month, and was glancing annoyedly at a gold watch that might have cost more than Chase's paycheck for the whole year. The man's hair was slicked back, and Chase wondered if no one had bothered to tell him that people didn't wear their hair like that anymore.

He waltzed in and took a seat across from the guy. "Mr. Bellinowski. I wasn't expecting you."

The other man smirked. "Don't tell me. You're pleasantly surprised."

"I wouldn't go as far as that." He opened a file folder on the table in front of him. "You probably know why I asked you to come in."

"Sure. Dickerson, right? Scumbag that got whacked the other day. So ask away, Detective. Do your worst." He checked his watch again, auspiciously this time. "Though I should probably warn you I'm a busy man and I've got a busy schedule today."

Bellinowski was rumored to be in charge of a network of illegal gambling outfits throughout the area, and was probably the biggest loan-shark in Hampton Cove. Chief Alec had been trying to put him out of business for years, but so far he'd dodged that bullet.

"So rumor has it that Dick Dickerson kept some files on you in his safe," said Chase, deciding to cut to the chase. "And that you weren't too happy about that."

"So he might have kept tabs on me," said Bellinowski with a shrug. "What can I say? The guy loved his celebrities."

"And you consider yourself a celebrity, is that it?"

"Something like that," the mobster said with a grin.

"I sure would like to know what was in those files, Yasir."

"I couldn't tell you. Probably a bunch of made-up stuff."

"There's also a rumor—"

"Don't believe everything people tell you, Detective."

"—that you once loaned some money to Van Wilcox. And when he wasn't able to pay you back at the rates you like to charge he turned to Dickerson who decided to lean on you with some of the information he collected over the years. So you wiped Wilcox's slate clean, even if that meant taking a huge loss yourself, and you've never forgiven Dickerson."

"Rumors, rumors," murmured Bellinowski, looking bored now. "What else have you got?"

"Does this man work for you?" asked Chase, placing a picture of a short guy with a strawberry nose and a purple spot on his upper lip on the table in front of Bellinowski.

He glanced at it. "Possibly. You'd have to ask my personnel manager."

Bellinowski ran a few clubs in town, one of which, the Club Couture, was currently in vogue with the weekend crowd. He also organized the popular Beach Beats Festival in the summer, which attracted thousands of dance fans.

"What about this guy?" asked Chase, placing down another picture, this one of a tall man with a wispy little mustache.

"Did you really drag me in here to ask me about my staff, Detective? Cause quite frankly I've got better things to do."

"What about this picture?"

Bellinowski glanced at the picture, then frowned. "A rose?"

"You are the current owner of the Happy Petals flower store on Grant Street?"

"You know I am." For the first time he was looking a little flustered. "Why?"

"I think you know why, Yasir," said Chase, leaning in. "I don't know what Dickerson had on you but it must have been enough to make you go after him. So you hired two of your goons to steal a tanker full of duck poop from the Potbelly farm, empty out Dickerson's safe to make whatever he had on you disappear forever, and then you made him go away forever as well. But not before you made it perfectly clear to him that you were the one that did this, by putting this picture in his safe. So he could have a good think before he died."

Bellinowski arched an eyebrow. "This is all you got?" He picked up the picture and flicked it from the table. "A picture of a flower? Come on, dude. You can do better than that." He got up and smoothed out his suit jacket. "Next time you call me in make sure you've got a real challenge for me, Detective. This?" He gestured at the file. "Not even the *National Star* would print this garbage. No, don't get up. I'll let myself out."

CHAPTER 37

Scarlett Canyon was playing a game of Solitaire. It was the only game installed on the computer in Dr. Tex's office, and what Vesta must have been playing all these years while she pretended to be hard at work.

Frankly Scarlett was bored. The waiting room was empty. The phone hadn't rung in ages, and Dr. Tex was ensconced in his office. When she took this job she figured she'd have some fun at Vesta's expense. But dealing with patients all day long and listening to their sob stories and the details of their illnesses was so tedious she sometimes wanted to scream.

And then there was the fact that she'd been so dumb to volunteer for the job, so she didn't even get paid to sit here and do the worst and most boring job in the whole world. She'd raised the topic of giving her a contract to Dr. Tex but he seemed immune to her promptings, pretending he didn't understand.

A part of her had figured that working for a doctor she would get to meet a lot of great guys, that she would flirt a bit and maybe date some of the eligible ones but that hadn't materialized either. So far all she'd gotten were a bunch of old coots who thought they were God's gift to women and who ogled her boobs so brazenly she sometimes wished she could punch them in the snoot. But a receptionist didn't punch patients in the snoot. A receptionist just sat there and beamed and entered appointments into Dr. Tex's calendar.

No wonder Vesta looked like a shriveled old prune. Sitting in this dumb chair behind this dumb desk listening to dumb stories from dumb sick people would make anyone shrivel up and turn into an old hag. It was happening to her, too. She could feel it. Her face was drying out and new wrinkles were popping up each time she looked in the mirror.

It was bad for her karma, too. All this sickness and disease. Soon it would start to rub off on her and she would get sick herself. How Dr. Tex could stand it she didn't even know.

The door opened and a new patient walked in. This one looking even more hopeless than the others. She had a bandage wrapped around her head, walked with a distinct stoop, had a pair of sunglasses firmly placed on her nose, and a scarf wrapped around the lower portion of her face. As she approached the desk, she even seemed to stagger.

"Can you please help me?" the woman asked in a weak whisper.

"Do you have an appointment?" Scarlett asked, barely managing to keep the annoyance from her voice.

"I want you to help me," whispered the pathetic creature.

"Just take a seat and I'll call the doctor," she said.

Suddenly the woman opened the old coat she was wearing and revealed the dress she had on underneath. The dress was soaked with blood! "Take a look at this," croaked the woman. "Does this look normal to you?"

Scarlett was one of those people who hated the sight of blood. In fact she abhorred it. She suddenly felt faint now, and a little woozy. "Is that… blood?"

"I don't know. What do you think?" asked the woman. "I got up this morning with a pain in my chest. And when I looked there was all of this red stuff coming out of me."

Scarlett watched, bug-eyed, as the blood seemed to be pouring out of the woman's chest, pumping steadily, spurt after spurt.

"Just take a look, will you? I don't feel so good. And if this is blood, why is it coming out of me when it should be staying in? Is that normal behavior for blood you think?"

"Doctor!" Scarlett yelled. "Doctor—I've got an emergency!"

"Just give me your best diagnosis," said the woman. "Is this a bad thing?"

Just then, the woman uttered a gurgling sound, and collapsed on the floor.

"Doctor Tex!" Scarlett was yelling, then ran around the counter and knelt down next to the woman. She didn't want to put her hands on her—all that blood!—but still had a quick peek. Where did all this blood come from? "Doctor Tex! I need you in here right now!"

And as she peeled back the layers of clothing with her fingernails, more blood pumped out. The woman was bleeding out! On the office floor! What a frickin' mess!

Suddenly the woman drew down her scarf. Her lips moved. "Come... closer," she whispered.

Scarlett drew closer.

"You gotta give me mouth-to-mouth," the dying woman croaked.

Scarlett flapped her arms. "I don't know how to give mouth to mouth!"

"If you don't... I'll die right here... right now," the woman said weakly.

"Oh, no," said Scarlett. "Don't you die on me. Don't you dare die on me!"

The woman produced a terrible cough, and more blood was pouring out of her chest. "This is the end... Scarlett. You killed me... with your incompetence..."

She stared down at the patient. "What did you just say?"

"If I die now, it's all your fault, Scarlett. You're a murderer. You murdered me."

She narrowed her eyes, then peeled back a layer of clothes and saw a plastic little contraption pinned to the inner layer with a clothespin. She picked at it with her nails and saw that it was a tiny hose, 'blood' spurting from it. With a disgusted sound, she gave it a good yank.

"Hey! You're going to break the tube!" said Vesta Muffin, for that's who the patient was. She'd taken off her glasses and was now glowering at Scarlett, who was glowering back.

"You miserable old woman!" Scarlett said.

"Who are you calling old? We're the same age!"

Scarlett pulled at the plastic thingy and suddenly a baggie popped out from Vesta's clothes, still half filled with a syrupy red liquid.

"Corn syrup and red food coloring," said Vesta. "If it's good enough for Hollywood, it's good enough for me."

"How dare you give me a scare like that!"

"I got you good, didn't I?" said Vesta.

The door to the inner office opened and Tex walked out. "What's with all the screaming?" When he caught sight of his mother-in-law on the floor, covered in blood, he did a double take. "Vesta? Oh, my God, are you hurt?"

"It's fake!" Scarlett cried, holding up the bag and plastic tube. "She tricked me!"

"I didn't trick you—I caught you!" said Vesta, now taking out her phone. "I got the whole thing on tape, missy." She gestured with the phone. "This is going straight to the FBI. You're going down for impersonating a doctor and practicing medicine without a license!"

"I wasn't practicing medicine!" Scarlett screamed. "I was simply trying to help a dying woman!"

"Without a license! You're going down! This is the end of you!"

"Vesta," said Tex, pinching the bridge of his nose. "Can I see you in my office? Now!"

"Don't bother," said Scarlett, grabbing her purse and hiking it up her shoulder. "I'm out of here. Consider this my resignation, Dr. Tex. I've had it up to here with this nonsense." She turned to Vesta. "You won. I hate being a receptionist. I hate the smell of death and decay. I hate the doddering old fools who can't take their eyes off my chest. I hate the blood and the disease and this boring, GODAWFUL job! Goodbye, Dr. Tex. Have a great life, Vesta."

And with these words she stalked off towards the door, then out into the world beyond, and immediately felt the rush of relief. It told her she'd done the right thing.

CHAPTER 38

"Vesta," said Tex. "This is the final straw. This is…" He gestured to her blood-soaked dress, the blood-soaked floor, the blood-soaked everything. "This is madness."

Vesta could see how her son-in-law might take a dim view of her actions. But sometimes when a viper enters your world you need to take executive action to drive it out.

"I had to do it, Tex," she said now. "Scarlett Canyon is bad news. I had to get rid of her."

"You jeopardized my career! You put in crank calls, sent a bunch of homeless people into the office, promising them free medical care, and now this." He was clutching at his hair, a clear sign of distress.

"I'm sorry, Tex. But you replaced me with a younger model! How do you think that makes a girl feel?"

He was pinching the bridge of his nose again. "I did not replace you with a younger model. For one thing, you and Scarlett are the same age. And for another, you quit!"

"Because you refused to stand by me. Family always looks out for family, Tex."

"You quit our family!"

"I told you before. I didn't quit our family. I just saw an opportunity and I took it. If someone offered you a position on *General Hospital* wouldn't you take it, too?"

He was staring at her. "*General Hospital* is not a hospital. It's a TV show."

"Those doctors work hard to save the lives of their patients, Tex. Hard-working, devoted doctor like you would fit right in. And with that full head of hair you look the part, too. You could be the new Dr. Alan Quartermaine. I always like Dr. Quartermaine."

"Didn't he die?" asked Tex now. He would never admit it but Vesta knew that he enjoyed the occasional episode of *General Hospital*. He'd been taping the show for her for as long as she could remember and often sneaked in an episode when he couldn't sleep.

"Oh, yes, he did, but they got some great surgeons in General Hospital. They just might be able to bring him back. Or replace him with a fine doctor such as yourself, Tex."

"Why, thanks, Vesta," he said, standing a little straighter. "I always dreamt of working in a big hospital, you know. I mean, it's nice to be a small-town doctor, but it does get lonely sometimes. To be able to confer with a colleague. Tackle some of the more challenging cases. It would sure be a great opportunity."

She patted him on the shoulder. "General Hospital would be happy if they could add you to the roster. Sure, it would be a big loss for Hampton Cove, but they'd live."

He stared off for a moment, a slight smile on his lips, and she could see him envisioning a future as a hospital doctor—member of an elite staff of the country's top physicians. Then he blinked and was himself again. "Look, Vesta. Why don't you come and work for me again? This whole Scarlett business wasn't working out for me anyhow, and I need a competent receptionist. So what do you say?"

"You mean kiss and make up?"

He grimaced, the kissing part clearly a bridge too far.

"I'm just messing with you, Tex. I don't say this often but you're a good man."

In fact she never said it. You had to be careful with men. Their egos were such that you had to use compliments sparingly, or else you could end up with a blowhard for a son-in-law. Better keep them on a short leash so they didn't end up being the boss of you.

She pinched him on the cheek. "Sure I'll be your receptionist again, Tex."

Tex brightened. "You will?"

"But first I have to clean up the mess this Scarlett woman made," she said, staring down at the floor, hands on her hips. "What were you thinking when you hired her?"

Probably he wasn't. That was another thing about men: they took one look at a set of big knockers and they were gone. She looked up just in time to see Tex walk up to her, arms wide.

Uh-oh.

And then he hugged her.

"Let's leave the past behind us," he said warmly.

She grimaced. "Uh-huh. Sure, Tex. Let's."

As soon as the hug was over, she returned to her desk and Tex returned to his office. And since she was an old lady and didn't feel like cleaning up Scarlett's mess, she called the cleaner and told her they'd had a medical emergency and to come round right away.

And as she settled in her chair and started a new game of Solitaire, she thought with a satisfied grunt that life was finally back to normal again. And not a moment too soon, either.

CHAPTER 39

As we walked along Main Street, admiring its myriad shops and the felines associated with their owners, I had the distinct impression that all was not well in the cat community. A red cat was hissing at a black cat, which was hissing right back, its tail distended to its furthest limit, a Russian Blue was trying to hit a Siamese across the ear, a Scottish Fold was cowering before a British Shorthair, who stood thrusting out its chest with a sneer on its lips, and a Sphynx cat was running circles around a Turkish Angora.

Gazing out at this battlefield from his perch on his owner's checkout counter was Kingman, shaking his head at so much feline folly.

"What's going on, Kingman?" asked Dooley as we joined the store owner's piebald.

"Madness," said Hampton Cove's feline Nestor. "Pure madness." Then he directed an irritated look at me. "Is it true that you called me a pompous old windbag, Max?"

"Oh, for crying out loud," I said, rolling my eyes. "No, I did not!"

"Milo's been here, hasn't he?" said Dooley.

"He's the one who told me," said Kingman. "I practically couldn't believe my ears."

"So don't," I advised my friend. "Milo is a mythomaniac, Kingman."

"That's almost the same as a nymphomaniac," Dooley added knowingly.

"He makes stuff up so he can create trouble between cats."

"And humans, too," said Dooley. "Remember what he told Odelia about you?"

I did. The cat was a menace. I spread my paws. "All this is Milo," I told Kingman. "All this fighting and bickering is his doing. He's been hard at work tearing up the social fabric of our once peaceful and loving cat community."

"Well, maybe not all that loving," said Kingman dubiously. "I distinctly remember Shanille once calling me a braggart simply because I told her Wilbur gives me foie gras from time to time—only as a treat," he quickly added when I cocked a surprised whisker at him, "and only ethical foie gras, where the birds aren't forced to gorge, of course."

"Of course," I said. We might be cats but that doesn't mean we're animals.

One of the cat fights on the street had escalated into a minor war, with two cats coming to blows. Usually when cats fight one cat will hold up its paw and make to hit the other one, then doesn't. The other cat then returns the favor. Almost like a beautiful ballet.

There was nothing beautiful about the skirmish that had now broken out, though. These cats were whizzing around in a circle, a maelstrom of yowling and screeching and fur flying when nails hit their marks.

"Oh, enough already!" bellowed Kingman, and descended from his throne. He pranced up to the two cats, slapped one with his left paw and one with his right, then said, "Stop it, you two! You should be ashamed of yourselves, Shanille and Harriet!"

Only now that the whirring movement had stopped did I finally get a good look at the cats involved in the fight and to my astonishment Kingman was right: they were our very own Harriet and the conductor of cat choir, now both panting and missing a few patches of fur. Shanille even had a nasty scratch on her nose which was bleeding profusely.

"Explain yourselves," Kingman said, now fully assuming the role of a King Solomon.

"She's trying to seduce my boyfriend!" Harriet panted.

"And she's been saying that I'm a slut!" Shanille retorted.

"I did not!" Harriet cried. "You take that back!"

"I will do no such thing," said Shanille. "I will not be insulted by a common Persian!"

"No anti-Persian racism here, Shanille," said Kingman sternly. "And what do you have to say about the accusation? Are you trying to lay your paws on Brutus?"

"Of course not! I don't even like Brutus! He's been saying some very nasty things about me!"

"Like what?" asked Kingman, who couldn't resist a nice morsel of juicy gossip any more than the rest of us could.

"Brutus says I don't observe Lent, but I do! I always observe Lent."

"You abstain from eating meat during Lent?" asked Harriet, horrified.

Shanille raised her head proudly. "I do. So you better tell your boyfriend he's a liar."

"Brutus didn't say those things," said Harriet. "You're lying."

"Milo told me and Milo knows. Milo lives with Brutus," said Shanille. "So there."

I groaned, and locked eyes with Harriet. She knew, too. "Oh, dear," she said.

"Who told you about Shanille having an affair with Brutus?" I asked.

"Oscar." She nodded. "And he probably heard it from Milo."

"Milo," I said, extending and retracting my claws. "Always Milo."

"Did I hear my name?" suddenly a voice rang out.

We all looked up and there he was. The treacherous cat himself.

Harriet rounded on him. "You told Shanille Brutus says she doesn't observe Lent," she snarled, and something of the fight she'd just engaged in must have still come through in her voice, for Milo moved back a few paces.

"I'm sure Brutus is making that up, Harriet. I would never say such things."

"You didn't?" asked Shanille, surprised.

"Of course not, Shanille," said Milo. "I know what a God-fearing cat you are. You're an example to us all."

If he wasn't tearing cats down, he was building them up. Nice strategy.

"You told Oscar that Brutus was having an affair with Shanille," said Harriet now.

"Oscar said that? But that's terrible! I always knew there was something fishy about that cat. But then he does work for a fishmonger," he added with a sly smile.

The cat was slick, I had to give him that.

"Look, you have to stop spreading these lies," I told him. "Cats are getting hurt."

"Spreading lies? I don't spread lies, Max," he said with an expression of such innocence he could have fooled even me. "Am I a born socializer? Yes, I am. I love my fellow cats and I love shooting the breeze and even the occasional crude joke. But lying? Spreading rumors and gossip? I would never do that." He was holding up his paw. "Scout's honor."

"You were a Cat Scout?" asked Dooley, impressed in spite of himself.

"I was only the most decorated Cat Scout in the history of cat scouting," said Milo proudly. "They gave me so many medals that I finally told them to stop. It was becoming embarrassing. Also my human ran out of space on the mantel."

"There's no such thing as cat scouting," I said, then turned to Kingman. "Is there?"

But Kingman was holding up his paws and walking away. "I'm not getting involved, cats. You're old and wise enough to know a lie when you hear one."

And with these words, he hopped back onto the checkout counter and dozed off.

CHAPTER 40

Odelia walked into the police station just as Yasir Bellinowski walked out. The crime kingpin had the gall to give her a lascivious grin, which she bluntly ignored.

"Hey, Odelia!" Dolores yelled from her perch behind the glass.

"Hey, Dolores," she said, walking up to the desk. "Is Chase in?"

"Oh, he's in, all right. Listen, honey. What's this stuff I keep hearing about your granny moving in and Chase moving out? Correct me if I'm wrong but shouldn't it be the other way around?"

"Chase never moved in," said Odelia, wondering if these were the rumors traveling around town.

"Still," the wizened front desk officer grunted. "I'd rather have a man sleeping in my bed than my grandmother, if you see what I'm saying."

Oh, she saw what Dolores was saying, all right, and she heartily agreed. "I can't very well kick her out, can I?"

"Didn't she use to live with your mom?"

"She did. They had a falling-out."

She really wasn't ready to discuss family business with outsiders, though, so she was determined to leave it at that. Dolores was determined not to. "What happened? She and your dad don't get along? I heard she quit that receptionist job at the doctor's office."

"I think it will all work itself out," she heard herself say—quite lamely, too.

"Sure, honey," said Dolores dubiously, grimacing like one denied the kind of information she feels entitled to. "But if I were you, I wouldn't keep that man waiting. He's one hot hunk, and there's plenty of women working out of this here police station that wouldn't mind getting hot and heavy with him—if you see what I'm saying."

Once again, she saw exactly what Dolores was saying. "I think I get the picture."

"So you better stop slacking, baby girl," said Dolores. "And get fracking."

"Thanks for the advice," she said curtly, then stalked off.

Get fracking my ass, she thought. If anyone had to stop slacking it was her dad, who urgently needed to patch things up with his mother-in-law. Before she drove them all crazy.

She arrived at the police precinct proper, and one of Chase's colleagues, Sarah Flunk, gestured in the direction of the interview rooms. She walked on, passing her uncle's empty office, and suddenly wished the big guy was back from his hiking trip already. Without him at the station things kinda felt a little frazzled.

She found Chase in the interview room, reading from a file and looking dazed. She gave the doorjamb a quick knock and stepped inside.

"I just saw Yasir Bellinowski," she said.

He placed down the file and rubbed his face. "I talked to him."

"And?"

"Nothing. He's one slippery little weasel."

She took a seat across from the cop. "Did you show him the pictures?"

"He said to talk to his personnel manager."

"What about the rose?"

"He wasn't impressed."

They were both silent for a beat, then Odelia remembered something. "I just met Olaf Brettin."

"*Daily Inquirer* Olaf Brettin?"

"The one and only. He was paying a visit to Dan."

"And?"

"You mean did he confess? No, he did not."

She gave him the CliffsNotes version of their brief conversation and Chase blew out a sigh. "We're not getting anywhere with this, Poole."

"I hear you, Kingsley."

"So what are we doing wrong?"

"You're the cop, Chase. You tell me."

He drummed his fingers on the table. "We need to find Harlos and Knar and lean on them until they give up their boss."

The two men Max and Dooley had mentioned turned out to be two low-level criminals associated with Yasir Bellinowski. Jean Harlos and Markus Knar had a rap sheet an arm long and a reputation for doing whatever their client paid them to do, even murder.

"So it's pretty clear, isn't it? Bellinowski is our guy," said Odelia.

"Yes, he is, but like I said, the guy is as slippery as an eel."

"Once you catch Harlos and Knar, you'll have him dead to rights."

He nodded, but didn't look convinced.

A knock at the door had them both look up. It was Sarah again. The copper-haired officer with the fine-boned freckled face gave a quick smile. "Deirdre Dickerson is here to see you, Detective. I put her in the Chief's office."

"Deirdre Dickerson as in Dick Dickerson's daughter?" Chase asked.

Sarah nodded and rapped the door before retreating.

Chase and Odelia shared a look of surprise, then both got up.

"Better see what she wants," said Chase.

"You want me there?"

"Why not? You're here now, aren't you? And maybe she'll feel more inclined to talk when there's a woman present."

"Women usually feel pretty disposed to talk around you, though, if Dolores is to be believed," said Odelia.

Chase grinned. "What has Dolores gone and said now?"

"That there are a lot of women officers who wouldn't mind getting down and dirty with you—especially now that I kicked you out of my house so I could move my grandma in."

"Don't listen to Dolores, honey," said Chase. "She's a great cop and I love her to pieces but quite frankly she's full of crap. And I say this with the greatest respect."

"Uncle Alec always says Dolores is the station's barometer. If he wants to know what's going on all he has to do is take her out for a drink and he's completely up to date on the latest gossip, grievances, office politics, feuds and every family issue of every officer."

"Your uncle takes Dolores out for drinks?"

"At least once a month."

"Chief Alec works in mysterious ways his wonders to perform."

CHAPTER 41

Deirdre Dickinson was a tall young woman with a sandy-colored bob, a tilt-tipped nose and a pronounced chin. She got up when they entered.

"Detective Kingsley?" she said. She looked a little anxious, Odelia thought.

"That's me. And this is our civilian consultant, Odelia Poole."

Deirdre nodded nervously. "I just wanted to know when my father's body will be released. I would like to organize the funeral as soon as possible."

"I would have to check with the coroner's office," said Chase. "But I imagine it won't be long now. Please, take a seat."

Deirdre did, and so did Chase and Odelia, Chase on Uncle Alec's side of the desk, and Odelia right next to Deirdre.

"I'm so sorry for your loss, Miss Dickerson," said Odelia, leaning forward and placing a commiserating hand on the woman's arm.

Deirdre nodded and looked down. Her eyes were red-rimmed and it was obvious she'd been crying. "I loved my father, Miss Poole. In spite of the horrible things people say about him he was not a bad man. He just did what he thought he had to do to make it in his line of work."

"Did… you have a good relationship?"

"Yes, we did. In private, my father was a sweetheart. Not the bully they made him out to be."

"There's a rumor," Odelia began, and Deirdre looked up sharply.

"Don't believe the rumors, Miss Poole. I know people say Daddy cut me out of his will but there's absolutely no truth to that."

"I heard you were suing him?"

Deirdre shook her head decidedly. "Vicious gossip started by Daddy's enemies. We had a wonderful relationship."

"Now that you're here, I wanted to show you something," said Chase, and took out the picture of the rose. He placed it on the desk in front of Deirdre.

"What is this?" she asked, looking up.

"It was found in the safe. Where your father died," Chase explained.

Deirdre's eyes shot full of tears at these words, and she quickly took out a tissue and pressed it to her nose. "This is all so horrible. He didn't deserve to die—and he certainly didn't deserve to die in this way. Who would do such a terrible thing? And why?"

"Does the name Yasir Bellinowski mean anything to you?" asked Odelia.

Deirdre shook her head, trying to compose herself. "Is he the man that did this?"

"He's one of the leads we're pursuing," said Chase.

"He's a gangster, isn't he? A mobster? My father published stories about him."

"Did he ever mention Bellinowski to you?"

"Daddy never talked about his work. He liked to keep his family life and his professional life strictly separate. He even forbade us from reading the *National Star* when we grew up. Of course me and my sisters would sneak copies home from school and read them anyway." She smiled a weak smile. "We were very proud of him. All of us were. Even Mom."

Odelia remembered reading about Deirdre's mom. She was Dickerson's second wife, and originally hailed from France, where she'd returned after the divorce. Dickerson had gone on to marry two more times, but those marriages had ended in divorce as well.

"I know the rumors, Detective," Deirdre said. "I know how they say that I did it. Or at least one of us. To get our hands on Daddy's money. But I can assure you we would never hurt our father. He was a family man and doted on us. Even after he divorced our mother." She looked up imploringly. "Please find whoever did this, Detective. These *monsters* can't be allowed get away with this. They really can't."

And with these words, she finally broke down into sobs.

Odelia rubbed her back, but generally felt helpless. She couldn't imagine anything ever happening to her father or mother. She'd be devastated, too. And when she locked eyes with Chase, she could see he was thinking the same thing. There was a determined look in his eyes. He was going to bring Yasir Bellinowski to justice. Whatever it took.

CHAPTER 42

That evening, a homey scene at Odelia's masked a deeper, more horrible truth: a usurper was working away in the background, chipping away at the foundations that made ours such a warm nest. I would have warned Odelia, but she was so busy with her investigation, hunched over her laptop, a frown marring her lovely features, that I didn't have the heart to disturb her.

I was on the couch, Dooley next to me, watching *Jeopardy* with Gran, while Harriet and Brutus were nowhere to be found, and neither, for that matter, was Milo.

I knew he couldn't be far away, though, and the fact that he was close troubled me, making it impossible to relax.

Now cats are generally vigilant creatures by nature, but I was actually ill at ease, my tummy churning and making strange noises, and that had never happened to me before.

"Where is Brutus, Max?" asked Dooley.

"I don't know."

"Where is Harriet, Max?"

"I don't know."

"Where is Milo, Max?"

"I don't know!"

"No need to shout," grumbled Dooley. "If you don't know, just say so."

I didn't want to point out that I just had, so I bit my tongue.

"When is Gran going to fix the garden?" asked Dooley, who was in a questioning mood. It generally happened when *Jeopardy* was on. He probably thought he was Alex Trebek.

"I don't know, Dooley," I grumbled.

"There's nothing to fix," said Grandma. "The garden is fine just the way it is."

We both directed a look at the disaster area Gran had reduced the garden to, and both decided it was better not to comment. The mausoleum project had apparently been abandoned, just like the Versailles project that preceded it. I didn't mind. The piles of sand and the holes were wonderful to dig into and made a nice change from my litter box.

They also provided a great opportunity for Harriet and Brutus to hide when they went on one of their nookie sessions. Though judging from the distant and frankly disturbing way Brutus had behaved today, I had a feeling there wouldn't be a lot of that going on tonight.

"Did I tell you guys that Tex and I reconciled?" asked Gran now. She was unusually chatty. Possibly because she'd managed to watch all of her soaps and was now fully caught up. Quitting her job had given her oodles of time to do so, and she'd made good use of it.

"That's great," said Dooley.

"Does this mean you're moving back in with Marge and Tex?" I asked.

Dooley's excitement diminished. He had his doubts about Chase moving in with Odelia, and the prospect of the two of them making lots of babies, which would inevitably push out

Odelia's cats. Even though I told him many times this was not the case, he still wasn't too keen on the idea.

"Nah," said Gran. "I like it here. Tex and I have made our peace—he finally apologized for kicking me out of his office and confessed that he needed me—but that doesn't mean we have to live together. Frankly when two strong personalities like ours spend too much time together we inevitably clash. So it's better if I stay with Odelia. I never crash with Odelia. She has one of those soft, yielding personalities that suit me a lot better."

We both directed a curious look at Odelia, but she hadn't been listening. Phew. It's never nice to be called a 'yielding' personality, which is a fancy word for a pushover.

"So Tex actually apologized?" asked Dooley.

"Pretty much," said Gran, shoving a Cheez Doodle into her mouth.

"Well, I'll be damned," said Odelia suddenly, and we all looked up.

"Did you finally get those winning numbers?" asked Gran.

"Just something to do with the case," said Odelia, then abruptly got up. "I'm sorry, you guys. I need to pop out for a bit. I'll be back as soon as possible."

And with these words she hurried out the door and was gone.

Gran shrugged. "Hormones," she said knowingly. "They hit you when you least expect it."

CHAPTER 43

Odelia was in her car and hurtling along the road when she remembered she'd totally forgotten to take her phone. She slammed the wheel with the heel of her hand. Too late to turn back, though. She needed to see this through. Fifteen minutes later she took the turn onto Uncle Alec's street, practically losing a hubcap at the corner as her tires screeched dangerously, then parked in front of her uncle's house and got out.

Pressing her finger to the bell, she was relieved when the door was yanked open and Chase stood before her, a box of Chinese food in one hand, a fork in the other, and a spot of something yellow on his plaid shirt. "Odelia? Were we doing something tonight?"

"I know who killed Dickerson," she said, moving past him and into the house. She paced the living room as he sat down and finished his dinner. "Remember how I told you about Olaf Brettin visiting Dan at the office?"

"Uh-huh. So?"

"I couldn't stop thinking there was something I missed.

So when I got home I surfed the web. Did you know that Brettin had a daughter?"

"Yeah. I think I read something about that. Didn't she die?"

"Suicide. Three years ago. So I just happened to watch the video of the eulogy her father gave at her funeral."

"As one does," said Chase laconically.

"He called her 'his rose!'" she said excitedly.

"His rose."

"His rose! Give me your phone. I'll show you."

"Why don't you show me yours?" he asked with a grin.

"I forgot mine at home," she said, not in the mood for banter.

He handed her his phone and she quickly found the YouTube video, then scrolled to the moment Olaf Brettin had spoken the fateful words. The man was clearly undone as he stood at the church lectern. 'This tragedy would never have happened if I'd paid more attention,' the tabloid editor said, a crack in his voice, his speech interspersed with sobs. 'You should have come to me, my sweet Lavinia. But like an absent father, I was so busy, so immersed in my own world, that I never even noticed the cries for help you posted. Until it was too late. My sweet, darling Lavinia,' he said, turning to the lily-covered coffin, 'my rose.'

"See?!" Odelia exclaimed. "Rose! I'll bet that's what he used to call his daughter."

Chase wasn't impressed. "A lot of fathers call their daughters their rose, their flower, their whatever. This doesn't mean he killed Dickerson. Unless Dickerson killed this... Lavinia."

"He might as well have," said Odelia, taking a seat at her uncle's dinner table. She noticed the room looked a lot nicer than before. Her uncle's house used to be a pigsty. Ever since

Chase moved in it had improved significantly. "Lavinia Brettin killed herself, right?"

"Okay."

"Rumor has it that there was a sex tape involved."

"Christ."

"Yeah. So what if Dickerson got a hold of this tape and threatened to publish excerpts in the *National Star*?"

"What would be the purpose of that? It's not as if Lavinia Brettin was a celebrity."

"No, but what if he used it to blackmail her father?"

Chase narrowed his eyes. "Why would one tabloid editor blackmail another tabloid editor? What did Dickerson have to gain?"

"Only one way to find out," she said, getting up.

"You want to go there now?"

"Of course. Don't you?"

He shook his head. "Look, we've got our killers, and we've got the guy who paid them, and we know why he did it. So we've got motive, opportunity, means—the works."

"It doesn't hurt to follow up a secondary lead, does it?"

It seemed to hurt Chase, though, for he threw a quick glance at the television. She rolled her eyes. "Don't tell me. There's some silly game on tonight?"

He looked insulted. "The Red Sox are playing the Yankees. Biggest game of the season."

"Don't you usually watch these things with Uncle Alec?"

A smile spread across Chase's features. "He's coming home tonight. Just in time for the game."

"Look, if you're not interested in catching this killer, I'll just do it myself," she said, and made for the door.

"Wait up," he said, grabbing his coat. "I'll come with."

"You just might make it home in time for the game," she said.

"Promises, promises."

With Odelia gone, and Gran glued to the television, and Harriet and Brutus and Milo nowhere to be found, I had time to revise the plan I'd made to get rid of the lying intruder. My original plan had been to take a mental note of all of his lies and contradictions and to present them in a nice orderly fashion to Odelia, as proof of our guest's duplicity.

Problem was that Milo had told so many lies that it had proven impossible to keep up. Frankly I couldn't even remember all the lies he'd told and probably neither could he.

But then I caught sight of Odelia's phone, which she'd apparently decided to leave behind, and a new plan formed in my mind. A plan that wouldn't involve expending valuable mental energy keeping up with Milo's lies. I would simply record them on Odelia's phone!

And before you tell me that cats don't use phones, let me cure you of that misconception. Ever since Steve Jobs introduced the world to the power of the touchscreen, life has become so much easier for us cats. All we need to do is swipe left or right or whatever, and apply paw to screen and voila! Instant access to the magical world of the Internet.

Around nine o'clock Odelia still hadn't returned, and Gran was starting to yawn. Bedtime for the old lady, I knew. Or at least the start of bedtime prep.

"Why are you looking like the cat that swallowed the canary?" asked Dooley. Then his jaw dropped. "You swallowed a canary, didn't you?!"

"No, I did not swallow a canary, Dooley. Where would I get a canary?"

"I don't know. Maybe you found one out in the backyard."

"For your information canaries don't inhabit our backyard, so no, I didn't swallow one. The reason I look so pleased is because I think I finally landed on a great scheme to get rid of Milo once and for all."

Dooley nodded knowingly. "You're going to kill him, aren't you?"

"No, I'm not going to kill him, and I resent the implication. I'm not a killer, Dooley."

"Too bad. If there's one cat that needs a good killing it's Milo."

"I'm going to record him saying bad things about Odelia, and then I'm going to play them back to her and then she's finally going to know what kind of cat he really is!"

If Dooley was excited about my crackerjack idea he didn't show it. "I don't get it," he said. "How are you going to record him? Did you call James Bond and ask him to loan you one of those recording devices?"

"Who needs James Bond when you have that?" I said, pointing to Odelia's phone.

He eyed it curiously. "You're going to *call* James Bond on the phone?"

"No! Every modern phone has a recording device built in."

Now he was impressed. "Hey, that's cool. You mean we're going to spy on Milo?"

"Exactly! We are going James Bond on his ass."

Just then, the cat I'd been hoping to see came waltzing in, cool as a cucumber.

"Hey, you guys," he said. "How's it hanging?"

"How is what hanging?" asked Dooley.

"It."

"What's it?"

Milo grinned. "If you have to ask, I won't tell you."

Dooley blinked. He wasn't good at this kind of wordplay and it showed. I sidled up to Odelia's phone while Milo wasn't looking, and with a few swipes and taps of my paw pads fired up the recording function. "Oh, Milo," I said sweetly.

"Mh?" said the cat, who was languidly stretched out on the couch, watching *America's Got Talent*. Two kids were trying to induce three cats to play the Star-Spangled Banner on the xylophone. They weren't doing a good job.

"You never told us how you really feel about Odelia," I said, taking a seat next to him.

"I love her," said Milo without missing a beat. "You should be proud to have landed a human like Odelia, Max. You, too, Dooley. Best human ever. My human will always be number one, of course, but Odelia is a close second."

I was disappointed. "Isn't there anything you don't like about her?"

"Nothing," he said decidedly. "She's simply perfect. Best human any cat could wish for."

"Don't you think it's disappointing that she plays favorites?" I asked.

"She doesn't. She loves all of you guys equally. Just like a good parent should." He smiled. "Not that she's your mother, Max. I know she's your human. But she's as near to a mother as you can get. Don't you agree, Dooley?"

"Um…" said Dooley, looking from me to Milo and back. "She's not perfect," he said finally. "She does have her faults. For one thing…" He opened his mouth, then closed it again.

"You can't come up with a single flaw, can you?" said Milo, chuckling. "Of course you can't. I'm telling you, Odelia is perfect and I love her to bits. And so do you, right?"

"Oh, yeah," I said, desperately trying to salvage something from this wreck. "Though I don't like it when she snores. And sometimes when she thinks we're not looking she picks her nose."

"Oh, that's right!" Dooley cried. "She totally does!"

"Every human picks their nose, you guys," said Milo. "Now you're just nitpicking."

"Sometimes she smells funny," I said.

"That's okay. All humans smell funny."

"She sometimes uses the same shirt two days in a row."

"Who doesn't?"

"She eats with her mouth open."

"We all do, right? I mean, I know I do."

"She burps! She totally burps," said Dooley, now getting into the swing of things. "Especially when she drinks Coke."

"Oh, heck, I wish I could burp," said Milo. "That's one of those human habits I'd love to try sometime."

"She-she breaks wind!" I said, desperate now.

Milo yawned. "Look, I don't know about you guys, but it's been a long day. I think I'll take a nap before I head out again. I've got cat choir tonight and I told Shanille I wouldn't miss it for the world."

And without waiting for a reply, he made himself comfortable on the couch and promptly dozed off.

I stole over to the phone, switched off the recording app, and stole back to the couch, to stare at Milo as he slept. Oh, he was clever. Too clever. But sooner or later he'd slip up. And then I had him.

Dooley was staring at me staring at Milo, shook his head, and walked out.

I had a feeling I was very quickly losing my wingman's trust and admiration.

CHAPTER 44

Odelia parked her old Ford pickup in front of a nice little rancher.

"Far cry from Dickerson's mansion," said Chase.

"I guess the *National Star* really does sell a lot more copies than the *Daily Inquirer*."

"Or maybe Mr. Brettin likes to live in modesty."

They got out and walked up to the front door. Chase, in his capacity as police officer, took it upon himself to ring the bell. Moments later, shuffling sounds on the other side of the door announced that they were in luck, and then Olaf Brettin appeared. He was casually dressed in jeans and a denim shirt. "Oh, hey, Miss Poole. So we meet again."

"We do. This is Detective Kingsley, who is with the Hampton Cove Police Department. Can we step in for a moment?"

If the presence of a cop on his doorstep caused the tabloid editor concern he hid it well. "Oh, sure. Come on in. Is this about the Dickerson investigation?"

"It is," Odelia confirmed, as they followed Brettin through

a cozily appointed hallway—with a nice painting of a man on a horse—and into the living room, where more paintings of horses adorned the walls. There was also a white Stetson hanging from a peg, a clear sign Olaf Brettin was into the Old West.

"That yours?" asked Chase, admiring the hat.

"Yup. I like to wear it when I go riding," said Brettin. "I got the boots, the vest and the belt buckle, too, if you'd like to see. I even got the neckerchief."

"You got the gun, too?" asked Chase, cocking an eyebrow.

Brettin laughed. "Now that I don't got, Chief."

"We have a question for you, Mr. Brettin," said Odelia.

"Please call me Olaf," said Brettin.

"The thing is, remember I asked you about the picture of a rose that was found near Dickerson's body?"

"Uh-huh. And I told you that doesn't ring a bell."

"Your daughter… died a couple of years ago, didn't she?"

She was studying a painting on the wall that depicted a beautiful young woman.

"She did," said Brettin, his joviality slightly diminished now.

"I watched a video of the eulogy you gave at her funeral. You called her your rose."

Brettin's smile had completely dimmed. "Lavinia *was* my rose. The light of my life. When she died I thought I'd die, too. I didn't, even though a part of me did die that day."

"What happened?" asked Chase, a softness to his voice Odelia appreciated.

"She… took her own life, Detective. A, um, video was made—silly thing." He was staring off now. "She was young, and in love, I guess. And you know how young people are. They're into making these… selfies and things." He swallowed. "So she made one of those sex tapes. Nothing unusual about that. She and this boy she was seeing, they were really into each other. There was even talk of an engagement. She'd introduced him to us—me and Abbey. That's my wife Abbey over there," he said, indicating another portrait, this one depicting a strikingly handsome woman with clear blue eyes.

"So she made the tape," prompted Chase when Brettin stopped talking.

"Yes, she did. And somehow that tape got out. Someone hacked Lavinia's phone, found the tape, and a bunch of pictures, and threatened to post everything online."

"That's horrible," said Odelia.

"Yes, it was," said Brettin. "Lavinia, of course, was shattered."

"Was this a blackmail thing?" asked Chase.

"Yes. But not aimed at Lavinia. Aimed at me. You see, I was making inroads in markets that had previously mainly been Dickerson's province. The Midwest, for one. And he didn't like it. And Dickerson being who he was, he decided to play dirty. So he had someone hack my phone but probably didn't find the kind of dirt he was looking for so he extended the hacker's scope to my family, my wife and daughter. He must have been over the moon when he discovered that private video and pictures. Pay dirt," he scoffed bitterly.

"Are you sure this was Dickerson?" asked Odelia.

"Oh, yes. He called me. This was the day after Lavinia had gotten the message about the video being posted online. Dickerson said a little birdie had dropped that same video into his mailbox, and how he wanted to express his concern from one family man to another."

"He actually threatened you?"

"No, of course not. Dickerson was too smart for that. He just wanted me to know that he had the video, and that if I didn't back off, he was going to have it posted online."

"That's... criminal," said Chase, shaking his head.

"You should have reported him to the police," said Odelia.

Brettin looked sad. "What was there to report? That Dickerson had received an anonymous message from the creep who'd hacked my daughter's phone? I get anonymous tips every day. Pictures, videos—heck, it's part of the tabloid business model. 'We pay cash for videos.' Dickerson would have made damn sure nothing connected him to the hacker."

"But you knew he was behind the hack."

"Oh, yes. And he knew I knew. That was his whole spiel." His expression softened. "One week later Lavinia took her own life. She couldn't live with the knowledge that that video was out there. I told her I'd take care of it. That no one would ever see it. She must not have believed me. And seeing the line of work I'm in, maybe she was right not to trust me."

"I'm so sorry," said Odelia. She felt for the man. This was a horrible story. And showed what a ruthless crook Dickerson had been.

"I blame myself, you know," said Brettin. "I was Dickerson's target, and my beautiful flower got caught in the crossfire. And so did my wife. Abbey never recovered. She died six months later. Her heart simply gave up. They say you can't die from a broken heart but I can assure you that you can. The only reason my own heart is still beating is probably because I'm too stubborn to die. But a big part of me died the day I buried my daughter—my rose."

"So... did you have Dickerson killed, Mr. Brettin?" asked Odelia softly.

He glanced up, then shook his head. "I'm not a killer, Odelia. Even though I'm glad someone took the law into their own hands, it wasn't me."

"But... the rose."

"I'm not the first person Dickerson destroyed. There are

countless others. And I'll bet lots of people use the image of the rose to refer to a loved one. No, you're barking up the wrong tree, Odelia—Detective. I may have wished Dickerson harm, but I didn't act on it."

Just then, the editor's phone jangled and he picked it up from the table with a frown. "Yes, Mr. Paunch," he said, much to Odelia's surprise. She hadn't heard from President Wilcox's friend in quite a while, and had hoped he'd lost her number. "Is that a fact? No, I didn't know the President was the youngest billionaire in history. That is news to me." He rolled his eyes at Odelia. "So it's official? President Wilcox is Sexiest President Alive? That's quite an achievement. I didn't even know such a category existed. Yes, I will mention it in the next issue of the *Daily Inquirer*, Mr. Paunch. And give my regards to the President."

"Was that Otto Paunch?" asked Odelia.

"Oh, you know Mr. Paunch?"

"He's been calling me non-stop with little tidbits about the President."

"Did you know President Wilcox has been voted Sexiest President Alive three years in a row?"

"He also has the softest hair," said Odelia. "Soft like a baby's bottom, I've been told."

"It wouldn't surprise me," said Brettin with a smile.

"I thought the President only worked with the *National Star*?"

"Oh, I think he works with any publication that will sing his praises."

"But he was very chummy with Dick Dickerson, wasn't he?"

"He used to be," Brettin acknowledged.

Dua Lipa demanded Odelia's attention by belting out her signature tune and she was surprised to see it was her uncle.

"Uncle Alec?"

"Hey, honey. Look, there's some kind of fracas going on downtown."

"Downtown? You're back?"

"Just arrived. It's your cats, Odelia. They're trying to tell me something but you know I don't speak feline. You better get down here ASAP. It looks serious."

CHAPTER 45

Milo had just dozed off when Harriet came in, all atwitter. She motioned for me and Dooley to meet her in the backyard. The moment we set foot outside, convening amongst the mounds of dirt Grandma had dug up, she cried, "It's Brutus! He's gone!"

"Gone? Gone where?" I asked.

She gave us a pained look. "The pound!"

"Why would Brutus go to the pound?" asked Dooley. "Does he know cats there?"

"No, he doesn't know cats there, Dooley! He just kept telling me the pound is paradise and how I should come with him—to escape Max's reign of terror!"

"My reign of terror?" I asked. "I don't have a reign—and definitely not one of terror."

"He seems to think you're some kind of dictator. And that we're your slaves. He said the only way to escape this prison camp is to head down to the pound—where cats are cats and are free to live their lives untethered by the chains you bind us with."

This was all news to me. I didn't even know how to lay

my paws on a pair of chains. "This all sounds very suspicious to me," I told Harriet. "Where would I even get chains?"

"He's gone completely bananas," Harriet agreed, giving us an imploring look. She would probably have wrung her hands if she had hands. Instead, she merely screwed up her face into a pitiable expression. It was obvious she was in the throes of extreme emotion. "We have to save him, Max. If he sets paw inside that pound they'll lock him up and throw away the key."

"Why would they throw away the key?" asked Dooley, intrigued. "Wouldn't they need it to open his cage so they can feed him?"

"Cage!" Harriet cried. "Can you imagine Brutus locked up in a small cage?!"

I could, and the thought frankly made my stomach turn. I'm not claustrophobic, per se, but I definitely don't like small spaces. Or cages, which are a form of small space, I guess.

"What if they want to clean out his cage?" asked Dooley, still pursuing his own line of thought. "Wouldn't they need a key to open it? Or do they install new locks each time? That just seems wasteful."

"Please, Max," Harriet said. "Let's save Brutus. I know you two haven't always seen eye to eye but you're friends now, aren't you? You don't want him to languish in some cage?"

No, I certainly didn't. What was more, I had a fairly good idea who was responsible for Brutus's sudden wish to escape my so-called reign of terror. Only Milo could have planted such a ridiculous notion into his head. "Let's go," I said therefore. "Maybe we can catch him before it's too late."

And so our mission to save Brutus commenced. Dooley was still brooding on locks and keys, Harriet looked as if she was ready to call in SEAL Team Six to save her mate, and I wondered how we were ever going to get this Milo menace out of our lives before he did more harm. Yes, I know he was leaving in two weeks, but considering how much damage he'd done in just a few days, I could only imagine how much worse things could get.

It was quite a long walk to the pound, and Brutus had a nice head start, so we broke into a trot and put some haste into our mission. Once Brutus entered the pound it was game over for the black cat.

It was a testament to Harriet's despair that it only took us twenty minutes to reach destination's end, and the horrible building soon loomed up in our field of vision.

It wasn't one of those places I enjoyed visiting. In fact the further away from the pound I stayed the better I felt. But our friend was in need, and so there we were.

"I don't see him," said Harriet nervously as we surveilled the squat gray-brick building from across the street. It looked like an army barracks, or a prison, or even a police precinct.

Dark, ominous, and absolutely evil, it didn't look like no paradise to me.

"Let's check the back," I said. "Maybe we can look in through the windows."

"If this place has windows," said Dooley, and he had a point. The only windows I could see had either been bricked up or were covered with the kind of thick safety glass that is impossible to see through.

Still, we'd come this far, so we needed to see our mission through. So we crossed the street—after checking left then right then left again, like our mama taught us—then stealthily moved around the building. There was nothing but a strip of wasteland behind the pound, which neighbors had happily used to dump their rubbish: broken bicycles, old couches, mattresses, even a car wreck provided a backdrop to Hampton Cove's scariest building.

"There!" Harriet cried suddenly. "It's Brutus!"

I half expected her to be pointing at the mangled body of the former butch cat, but Brutus looked fit as a fiddle, staring into the only window that seemed to offer a glimpse of the pound's innards. We quickly joined him but he barely looked up when we did.

"Brutus!" Harriet said. "What has gotten into you!"

He shrugged, still staring intently through the grimy window. "Milo told me that the pound was paradise," he said in a low, dispirited voice. "Look at that. Does that look like paradise to you?"

We all looked where he was looking. And I knew I was looking at hell when the scene unfolded before my eyes: rows and rows of cages, with dogs of every variety locked up inside. Most of them looked absolutely listless, huddled up near the back of the cage, lying on the concrete floor. Some of the dogs were barking up a storm.

"Newcomers, I'll bet," said Brutus softly. "Listen to them."

We listened. "Let me out!" a Labrador was yelling. "This is a mistake! I don't belong here! I have a family! Let me out!"

"All I did was root around in the trashcan," a Poodle was lamenting. "I like trashcans. What's wrong with that? There's always something new to be found in a trashcan. So when will this punishment be over? And what are all these other dogs doing in here? Are they all punished, too? What is this place? A prison for dogs?"

"More like a concentration camp for dogs, buddy," said a Beagle sadly.

"Where are the cats?" asked Dooley. "Maybe they're treated better?"

"You wish," scoffed Brutus. He tracked a path to the right side of the building, and sank down in front of another grimy window, affording a glimpse inside.

This was obviously the feline part of the pound, with

dozens of cats locked up in cages, looking equally demoralized and unhappy.

"Oh, this is just terrible," said Harriet. "Poor cats!"

"Milo tried to convince me this was paradise," said Brutus. "Now I see he was just lying, as usual." He directed an apologetic look in my direction. "I'm sorry, Max."

"Sorry for what?"

"He said you were a dictator. That I was your minion, having to kowtow to you. I should have known he was full of crap. When did I ever kowtow to you? We butted heads so many times we both have the bruises to prove it." He placed a paw on my shoulder. "I'm sorry for believing those lies about you, buddy. I feel like such an idiot."

"Well, if the shoe fits…"

He laughed. "I deserved that."

Dooley was still looking through the glass. "You guys. Do you think this is where Milo lived for the first part of his life?"

"Yeah, I think he wasn't lying about that part," said Brutus. "His human probably picked him up here."

"Don't you think… this is why he turned into the cat he is now?" asked Dooley. He looked up. "This could all be some kind of… survival mechanism."

We were all so surprised that Dooley would even be aware of such a big word that we simply stared at him.

He went on, "I mean, this place is like prison for cats and dogs, right? So maybe this is why he lies so much—to protect himself from the harsh realities of life? And why he sets cats up against each other. So they wouldn't pick on him?"

"Direct their attention away from himself. Divide and conquer," I said, nodding.

"Dooley, you're a lot smarter than you look," said Brutus.

"Hey, thanks, Brutus," said Dooley, suddenly chipper.

"It's no excuse for Milo's behavior, though," said Harriet sternly.

"No, it's not, but it definitely explains a lot," I said. I thought I understood our new housemate a little better now. And even though I didn't approve of what he did, I was beginning to see things from his point of view. Entering a potentially hostile environment, with four other cats to contend with and one human to dole out punishment and reward, he must have automatically reverted to his old ways of sowing discord and making fantastical statements.

Poor cat. Suddenly I felt Milo was to be pitied more than to be censored.

And I would have had a lot more to say on the subject if a stray cat hadn't suddenly been streaking past us, looking extremely excited about something.

"What's going on?" I asked.

"Big to-do in town!" he yelled. "Kit Katt's been spotted! Kit Katt and Koh!"

CHAPTER 46

We didn't linger at the pound. Instead, we hauled ass in the direction the other cat was going and soon we were going well and going steadily, as more and more cats joined the stampede.

"Looks like every cat in Hampton Cove will be there!" cried Dooley excitedly.

"Who doesn't want to meet Kit Katt and Koh?" I said, equally excited about the prospect of meeting our heroes in the flesh.

"What are they doing in Hampton Cove?" asked Harriet.

"Probably filming new episodes for their show," said Brutus.

"Maybe they'll let us guest star!" Dooley said.

"To guest star on a show you have to be exactly that, Dooley," I said. "A star."

"We could be extras," said Harriet, the prospect clearly enticing.

By now it looked like a minor migration was taking place, and I saw and nodded a greeting at many a familiar face. The closer to the town center we got, the bigger the crowd.

Almost like going to a rock concert, if rock concerts weren't so terribly loud and rock music so perfectly horrible to listen to. Nope. Cats do not like rock music. Let me be clear on that.

The action seemed to be taking place near the old industrial zone, on the other side of town. A few deserted factories awaited demolition, to be replaced with a commercial park. The factory where all activity was centered was the old Beluga Watchcase Factory.

The brown-brick five-story structure was derelict, with windows shattered and ivy covering a big part of the building. Cats seemed to have converged on a window on the ground floor, and sat staring inside, much the same way we'd been trying to get a peek at the pound innards just before.

"Why would Kit Katt and Koh be filming their show in such a horrible place?" asked Harriet, regarding the decaying factory building disdainfully. "It will show our lovely little town in a very unfavorable light."

Like any town, Hampton Cove has its eyesores, and these remnants of the past are never featured on the brochures doled out by the local tourist board. Harriet was right. Why would the production team of our favorite show pick this horrible spot to film the new season's episodes?

"Maybe Kit Katt is trapped here by a gang of crooks," Dooley suggested. "And it's Koh to the rescue as usual."

That was a great explanation, and I perked up. But when we approached the heart of the hubbub, we encountered nothing but irate cats, all screaming at the top of their lungs about something.

"It's an outrage!" one Exotic Shorthair was yelling. "An absolute outrage!"

"I knew she was too good to be true!" a Maine Coon screamed. "I said so from the start!"

What it was they were so upset about was difficult to

determine, as they were all screaming and venting their anger but hard to pin down to the particulars of their outrage.

We moved to the front of the milling masses and finally made it all the way to the source of the uproar. A window offered a look at what had once been the factory floor where diligent workers had manufactured watchcases by the thousands, to be used in the famous and elegant Beluga watches. Now all that remained was a cement floor and a bunch of furniture.

"Looks like someone lives here," said Harriet over the din of the other cats.

She was right. There was a bed, visibly slept in, a table with pizza boxes and Chinese food cartons scattered on top of them, a couple of chairs, and a couch where two men were watching television, unconcerned about being watched by Hampton Cove's cat population.

On TV, a CNN breaking news story was unfolding, with footage of Virginia Salt being shown. The actress who was now better known as her alter ego Kit Katt, was being hounded by a camera crew as she made valiant attempts to walk from her car to her house.

"What's going on?" I asked anyone who would listen.

Next to me, suddenly Shanille materialized. "Oh, hey, Max. Haven't you heard? Kit Katt hates cats! Can you believe it? She's been secretly filmed kicking a cat!"

"What?!" cried Harriet. "That's not possible. She's Kit Katt! She loves cats!"

"That's only for the show," said Shanille, eyeing Harriet with some trepidation. She clearly hadn't forgotten the cat fight she and the feisty Persian had gotten into before. "In real life the actress who plays Kit Katt likes to kick cats for fun!"

And as we watched, a rerun of the footage was shown. It was clearly shot with a smartphone, as the footage was shaky and the lighting was lousy. Filmed at night, it showed Victoria Salt stumbling out of her house, a garbage bag in hand. She was unsteady on her feet, and had probably been hitting the bottle a little too enthusiastically. Three cats were enjoying a leisurely evening atop the trash container when Victoria came upon them.

First she seemed to hurl a few well-chosen insults at the cats, then she was throwing the garbage bag at them, and when one cat didn't move fast enough, she kicked it so hard it flew through the air and landed ten feet away before skittering away as fast as it could.

She then teetered back into the house, and that's where the short reel ended.

"Oh. My. God," said Harriet. "Kit Katt hates cats!"

"What if that had been Koh?" asked Shanille. "Can you imagine?"

"I can," said Harriet, and it was obvious the two lady cats were fast friends once more.

"I don't like this, Max," said Dooley. "Kit Katt was my hero. And now she's not."

"How the mighty have fallen," Brutus grumbled, shaking his head. "What a mess."

All around us, cats were expressing their anger and disappointment, and it was obvious now that there probably wouldn't be a new season of *Kit Katt & Koh*, filmed in Hampton Cove or elsewhere.

And that's when I saw it. One of the men had gotten up from the couch and now stood staring out the window, mouth agape, eyes wide, at the sea of cats gathered in front of the old factory building. He stirred his colleague, and now they both stood goggling at us.

I was goggling, too. For one of the men was short with a strawberry nose and a purple spot on his upper lip. The other one was tall with a wispy little mustache.

I'd found them. I'd found Dick Dickerson's duck poop killers.

CHAPTER 47

Odelia drove at breakneck speed through Hampton Cove's suburb, making Chase grip the dashboard and admonish her not to kill any pedestrians or other vulnerable road users. She made it to the other side of town in what probably was some kind of world record, and parked her car right next to Uncle Alec's in front of the old watch-case factory, now deserted.

Or at least that's what she thought. In front of the factory hundreds of cats had gathered, and on top of the hood of Uncle Alec's car, Max, Dooley, Harriet and Brutus sat.

Her uncle greeted her jovially. He looked healthy and rosy.

"Hey, Uncle Alec," she said, getting out of the car. "Where's Tracy?"

"Flew out to Paris two hours ago. Shooting another beer commercial."

"Hey, you guys," she said to her four cats. "What's going on here?"

Chase, who'd joined her, gave her a strange look.

"Dammit, Poole. You scare me sometimes. Do you know you sounded like you were talking cat just now?"

She'd totally forgotten about Chase. So she laughed lightly. "And what if I was?"

Now he laughed, then Uncle Alec also laughed, and then they were all laughing.

Very funny.

Max was talking, though, and she listened intently. Then she shot a quick look in the direction of the factory building. "I have a hunch we better check this out, Chief," she said.

"A hunch, huh?" her uncle said with a twinkle in his eye.

"Check what out?" asked Chase. "I don't get it."

"You know our Odelia," said Uncle Alec. "Her and her hunches. We better take a look, son." And he started in the direction of the small feline assembly. By now they were dispersing, moving in groups of twos and threes and fours, and they all looked outraged.

She didn't wonder. If what Max had just told her was true, a lot of *Kit Katt & Koh* fans would be extremely disappointed. It was the other thing he said, though, that was more important.

"You better be careful, uncle," she said as they approached the building.

"Careful about what?" asked Chase, continuing being mystified.

"Odelia thinks Dickerson's killers may be holed up in there," said Uncle Alec.

"Well, I'll be damned," Chase muttered, and reached for his gun. Unfortunately he wasn't wearing his gun belt. Or any of the other police paraphernalia, and neither was Uncle Alec. Both men were in civvies.

"I'll call for backup," grunted Alec, and took out his phone.

Soon the scene would be crawling with cops as well as cats.

She just hoped Max was right—not that she doubted his astuteness.

They approached the front of the building, and Odelia gestured to the window where the cat presence was still most pronounced. "They're in there," she said, drawing a curious look from Chase. She shrugged. "Just a wild guess."

"Don't tell me. Another one of your mysterious sources, huh?" said Chase.

He and Alec moved over to the ground-floor window and positioned themselves on either side of it, then took a quick peek inside. Odelia waited from a safe distance. She wasn't a cop, and these were two professional killers, presumably working for a well-known mobster. She wasn't about to get in their line of fire. And she'd just ambled up to the factory entrance, the door hanging off its hinges, when suddenly two men came bursting through.

As a reflex action, she stuck out her leg, and the shortest one crashed to the ground. The tall one dawdled for a moment, then moved off at a respectable rate of speed. Chase had spotted him, though, and broke into a run to intercept the guy. Like a freight train gaining momentum, he barreled into the guy and tackled him to the ground. Ouch.

Uncle Alec came walking up to the short guy, who was rubbing his head and directing a nasty look at Odelia, and yanked him up to his feet, then proceeded to place him under arrest. From a distance, Odelia could see that Chase was extending the same courtesy to his tall friend. Cop cars were driving up, sirens wailing and lights flashing, and within minutes both men were safely tucked away inside two squad cars, and outfitted with nice shiny handcuffs.

"Now let's take a look inside, shall we?" Uncle Alec suggested.

A small team of cops entered the building, Alec, Chase and Odelia in the lead, and made their way to the room where Harlos and Knar had been holed up all this time.

A small table covered with the remnants of several fast-food meals attested to their presence here, and so did the bed, the couch and the chairs. And as they carefully searched around, suddenly Odelia's attention was drawn to a calendar attached to a clammy concrete support post.

On the 16th an entry was written in a childish scrawl: 'Shake down Craske—Yasir.' And for the 17th the same person had written 'Shake down Fido—Yasir.' What interested her the most, though, was the entry for the 20th: 'Take out Dickerson—Brettin.' In small print a series of digits had been added. The combination to Dick Dickerson's safe.

Next to her, Chase had materialized, and was studying the calendar with similar interest. Then he let out a deep sigh. "And here I thought the schmuck was innocent."

CHAPTER 48

Alec and Odelia were seated in Uncle Alec's office. They were both silent. It's not every day that a police chief returning home from his vacation manages to take down a mobster and unravel a plot to murder one of his town's most prominent citizens in one fell swoop.

Chase had picked up Olaf Brettin, and this time it wasn't a social call. In fact it was probably safe to say Brettin wouldn't be wearing his white Stetson for a long while. Jean Harlos and Markus Knar had confessed to the murder of Dick Dickerson and the occasional work they did for Yasir Bellinowski, who'd lawyered up but would also go away for a long time, no matter how good his lawyer was.

"Sad story," said Alec finally. "I like Olaf. Liked his wife, too."

"You knew Abbey Brettin?"

"Sure. She was a sweet lady. Great kid, too."

"Lavinia."

He nodded. "Real shame. Dickerson did a terrible thing there. Monstrous."

"Do you think the jury will feel the same way?"

"I'm sure they will. Extenuating circumstances and all that. Still, people just can't go around killing other people. That way lies anarchy."

"But you can understand why he did it."

"Of course I can. Any human with a heart can. I just have to imagine this was you and maybe—just maybe—I'd have done the exact same thing."

"I still don't understand how Harlos and Knar could be so dumb to write down their assignments."

Alec smiled. "You know what they told me? That they'd seen a documentary on Edward Snowden so they knew smartphones could be hacked and decided to play it smart and write everything down the old-fashioned way so nobody could catch them."

"They probably shouldn't have written anything down."

"Those two boys are not the brightest bulbs."

"That's the understatement of the year."

"What did Chase say?"

"About what?"

"About your sudden 'hunch?'"

She grimaced. "I probably didn't handle that as well as I should have."

"No, you did not. You want to be more careful, honey. Unless you want to let him in on your little secret?"

"I think it's too soon for that. He might not understand."

"Sooner or later you're going to have to tell him."

Yes, she did. Though later sounded a lot better than sooner.

"I hear your grandmother and Tex made peace?"

"They have. She still refuses to move out, though."

Alec suddenly looked grim. "We'll see about that."

"You lied to us, Mr. Brettin," Chase said.

"Of course I lied. What did you expect?"

The tabloid editor looked a lot less rosy than the last time they met, Odelia thought. She was looking through the one-way mirror into the interview room, her uncle next to her.

"You can see why I did what I did, can't you?" asked Brettin. "He killed my daughter!"

"There are other avenues you could have pursued," said Chase.

"What? The man was smart. There was no way to prove he did what he did."

"Look, whatever he did, that still doesn't excuse murder."

"Do you have children, Detective?"

"No, I don't."

"I hope one day you're blessed with a family the way I was blessed. Lavinia was my heart. My life. The moment she was gone it was as if the light went out of my world. The only thing I could think of was how to punish the man who'd taken her from me. Dick Dickerson was not human, Detective. He was a monster. And monsters don't deserve to live."

Odelia turned away and left the small room. She'd heard enough. Now it was time to go home and be with her family again. She felt for Olaf Brettin, she really did, but Uncle Alec was right. If everyone started to take the law into their own hands, the world would not be a fun place for very long.

"Mom. You can't do this," Marge was saying.

"And you can't force me to change my mind," Vesta insisted stubbornly.

Marge and Alec had called this emergency family meeting

to try and talk some sense into their mother. Tex was still at the office, Odelia was home, and now it was just the Lips, gathered in Marge's kitchen, having this thing out once and for all.

Vesta wasn't budging, though. She'd folded her arms across her bony chest, and had jutted out her chin, a clear sign she'd made up her mind and that was all there was to it.

"Can't you see Odelia has a real shot at happiness here?"

"She has a better shot with me there to guide her along."

"Chase won't even come near the house since you moved in!"

"Which just goes to show: sometimes you think you know a man until you discover that you don't. I mean, what kind of man is afraid of a little old lady?"

"I don't think he's afraid of you, Mom," said Alec now. "He just doesn't want to inconvenience Odelia. He's a real gentleman that way."

"I think he's scared of me—which should tell you something about the guy."

Alec laughed. "Oh, for crying out loud, Mom. Don't you want Odelia to be happy?"

"She's very happy with me. We're like peas in a pod. BFFs for life. A girl needs her grandmother, there's no two ways about it. She knows I'll be there for her always."

"A woman also needs her man, and you're standing in the way of that," Marge insisted.

But Vesta simply rearranged her features into her most mulish expression and gave her the kind of stare Marge remembered from when she was a little girl. Frankly she wouldn't blame Chase if he were afraid of Vesta. Most men were. Heck, most humans were. She was a little scary. She also could be very sweet, but right now there was no sign of that.

"Is this about Tex?" she asked. "Are you still upset he cancelled your credit cards?"

Vesta shrugged. "Water under the bridge as far as I'm concerned. He begged me to come back so I did. We're good, Tex and I. In fact we've never been better."

Marge directed a quick look at her brother, who nodded, then dug into her purse and brought out an envelope and slid it across the kitchen table at her mother.

"What's that?" Vesta inquired frostily.

"Just open it and you'll see."

Vesta narrowed her eyes suspiciously, but couldn't contain her curiosity. She picked up the envelope and tore it open. A credit card dropped out and fell onto the table. Vesta stared at it, then slowly picked it up. It was a red-and-gray AARP Chase Bank credit card.

"I'm not with the AARP," said Vesta, taking a firmer grip on the card.

"Doesn't matter. There's plenty of advantages for everyone," said Alec.

"I read that the Sapphire Preferred Card offers travel rewards."

"When do you ever travel, Mom?" said Alec.

"There's a hundred dollar cash back," said Marge.

Vesta's grip around the card was tightening, her cheeks now flushed and her eyes glittering like Gollum when he took possession of the one ring. "What's the catch?" she finally asked.

"Move back here," said Marge. "Give your granddaughter some space."

Tex wouldn't be happy, but that couldn't be helped. At least Odelia had a shot at landing herself an actual date with Chase again if the cop wouldn't find his date's grandmother breathing down his neck when they got home from the movies.

"Fine," said Vesta finally. "I'll take your blood money."

The credit card had disappeared into the folds of the flowery dress she was wearing.

"That's great," said Marge, much relieved. "You won't regret this, Mom. We're also getting you that new mattress you asked about—the one with the memory foam, we're installing a faster modem and a new computer so you can surf to all of your favorite websites a lot faster. And Tex has promised to look into that cruise you wanted to go on."

A smile had appeared on Vesta's lips, and for the first time in a long time she looked satisfied. Then the smile disappeared, as if wiped away with a squeegee. "You could have saved yourselves a lot of trouble if you'd just listened to me in the first place." She got up and grumbled, "The lengths an old woman has to go to to get anything done in this place."

"So when are you moving back?" asked Alec.

"Let me sleep on it a couple nights. I'll let you know."

And with these words she was off at a surprisingly quick pace.

Marge leaned back. "I swear to God, Alec, if she doesn't move back here this week you have my permission to bodily drag her over and handcuff her to the bed."

Alec grinned. "I'll bet by now she watched plenty of YouTube videos on how to get out of those handcuffs. That mother of ours is one tough old goat, hon."

"And don't I know it," Marge sighed.

CHAPTER 49

It had been an eventful day, so I was glad to be home again. Gran was out, and so were Odelia and the rest of the family, but when we arrived at the house Milo was ensconced on the couch as if he owned the place—which by now he probably thought he did—so I decided it was time for a heart-to-heart with our annoying visitor.

"Where have you been?" he asked when I trotted in through the pet door.

"Your former home," I said, and watched his response.

A slight smile slid up his face. "Slumming, have you?"

"Why did you send Brutus to the pound?" I asked.

"It seemed like a good idea at the time."

"You wanted to show him what it was really like, didn't you?"

He didn't respond.

"How did you end up there?"

He shrugged. "I merely was part of the entertainment. The all-star band to entertain the inmates. Like Elvis Presley with his *Jailhouse Rock*."

"Oh, don't give me that crap, Milo," I said. "You may fool others but you don't fool me."

He gave me a quick sideways look. "No, I guess I can't." He paused, seeming to think things through, then finally relented. "Fine. I was part of a litter of five. All of us were relegated to the pound, along with our mother. Punishment for her human's stupidity, I guess. What human doesn't understand that cats have a tendency to get pregnant? At any rate, I spent a good chunk of time down there, watching my brothers and sisters be doled out to deserving new owners, as well as my own mother. Finally my time came and I ended up with Aloisia and I was glad for it."

"She treats you well?"

"I can't complain. Only problem is that she doesn't allow me to go outside."

"That's not very nice."

"It's her way of protecting me. In fact this vacation at Odelia's is the first time I've been allowed out for years. And it's been a lot of fun."

"Why do you keep spreading lies and setting cats up against each other?"

His mouth closed with a click of his incisors. "I'm not sure I like your tone, Max."

"I know you don't, but I still want you to answer me."

He glared at me for a moment. "You're way too smart for your own good."

"Is it because you developed lying as a coping mechanism at the pound?"

"And now you lost me, Mr. Amateur Shrink."

"I think it is. I think you learned to survive by creating trouble amongst the others—anything so they wouldn't notice what you were up to. Did you steal their food when they weren't looking? Drink their milk when they were fighting amongst themselves?"

Milo laughed. "You think they serve milk in there? You are so naive, Max."

I studied him for a moment. "What if I convinced Odelia to talk to Aloisia? Tell her to give you more freedom? Install a pet door, just like the one we have? That way you wouldn't be confined to the house. You could even come and visit. Go to cat choir. Be free."

He was regarding me suspiciously, as if trying to detect either a flaw in my reasoning or duplicity in my offer. He must have realized I wasn't kidding, for he finally said, "Why would you do this for me, Max? I haven't exactly been very nice to you or the others."

"I don't think you're a bad cat, Milo. In fact I think deep down you're a decent one."

"You don't know me very well, do you?"

I shrugged. "I guess I don't. But I'm willing to take a chance on you. Are you willing to take a chance on me?"

For the first time since I'd made Milo's acquaintance he was speechless. Finally, he said, with a lump in his throat. "I know I'll probably regret this but… I am, Max."

"Great. That's settled then." I held up my paw. "Put it there, 'bro.'"

After a moment's hesitation, he did put it there, and we shook paws on it.

Just then, the others walked in. "Hey, did you hear about *Kit Katt & Koh*, Milo?" asked Dooley.

"No, what happened?" asked Milo.

"Only that Kit Katt likes to kick cats for a living."

"She doesn't kick cats for a living, Dooley," Brutus said. "She was clearly drunk."

"Drink brings out the inner you, Brutus," said Harriet. "So she's a cat hater."

"That's not necessarily true," said Brutus. "And I don't think she *hates* cats."

And as the others chattered on, I saw that Milo was quietly smiling to himself. We locked eyes for a moment, and he gave me a nod of understanding. 'Thanks, Max,' he mouthed silently, and I mouthed back, 'You're welcome.'

EPILOGUE

Tex was watching on as Chase expertly turned the burger patties on the grill. I think everybody was happy Tex wasn't in charge of the proceedings. Dr. Tex may know his way around a human gallbladder, but he can't grill a burger if his life depended on it. Somehow they always end up looking like charred coal, which apparently humans don't enjoy.

I know I don't like to eat my food charred into oblivion, but then I'm a cat, and I like my food raw and bloody. Others, like our good friend Clarice, a feral cat, like to eat their food while it's still breathing, but then Clarice has always been something of an extremist.

After the great upheaval, life in Hampton Cove had gradually returned to normal. Dickerson's killers were in jail, Netflix had put *Kit Katt & Koh* on hiatus while its star went into rehab, and an anonymous benefactor had launched a campaign to offer all of the pets at the local pound new homes. Rumor had it that benefactor was Brenda Berish.

I told you. Once people fall in love with cats they become fans for life.

A row of cats was now lined up on Marge and Tex's patio: me, Dooley, Harriet, Brutus and... Milo. Over the last couple of days the erstwhile terror had settled down and was starting to become almost like a regular feline. He still had a ways to go, though, considering that just that morning he'd convinced Dooley that if you pull a cat's tail really hard a nugget of gold drops out of its mouth. Ever since then Dooley has been telling Odelia to pull his tail so she can become a millionairess.

"So what's happening with Tracy?" asked Marge as the entire family convened around the table. "When is she going to join us?"

"Soon," Uncle Alec promised with a smile. And when Marge tried to heap a pile of fries onto his plate he quickly declined. "I'm trying to lose weight," he announced, patting his ominously large stomach fondly.

Odelia cocked an eyebrow. "Is this Tracy's doing? If so, I like her even more."

"That woman is such an avid hiker that if I hope to stand a chance keeping up I need to lose at least thirty pounds. At one point she said she thought there was something wrong with her ears as she kept hearing this strange thumping sound. I didn't have the nerve to tell her that was my heart beating so fast I thought it would pop out through my throat."

"I think it's great that you've decided to take better care of yourself," said Marge.

"And I think this Tracy is one overbearing female," said Grandma. "I mean, look at you, Alec. You're perfect just the way you are."

"Thanks, Mom," Alec muttered, munching down on a piece of lettuce.

"A real man got heft," Gran continued. "Nobody likes a skeleton."

Chase joined the others, placing a plate of perfectly grilled patties on the table. Tex, holding onto a bottle of beer, held it up in a salute. "I want to congratulate the law enforcement members of this family on a job well done. You, too, Odelia."

"Thanks," said Odelia. "I think it's all very sad, though."

"It is," her mother agreed.

Tex had brought out the small television he'd recently purchased and they watched for a moment as President Wilcox laid a wreath on a grave, then held his hand to his chest while the National Anthem sounded.

"Why did you write that the President is the Sexiest President Alive, Odelia?" asked Marge. "I don't think he's that sexy."

"I have a great new source," said Odelia. "He keeps calling me with all kinds of exclusive scoops." Just then, her phone sang out a song and she picked it out. "Oh, look, it's him. My source." She picked up. "Yes, hi, Mr. Paunch. Thank you. Yes, I thought it was a lovely article, too. Especially that bit about the President being voted Best Dressed Politician by the White House Correspondents' Association. Yes, I think he's a very natty dresser, too."

She'd switched her phone to speaker, so we could all listen in to her exclusive source. His voice sounded awfully familiar, though. As if I'd heard this Mr. Paunch before somewhere.

"And Odelia," Mr. Paunch was saying, "this is a real scoop for you right here. President Wilcox has just been informed that he's a shoo-in for an actual Nobel Prize!"

"Wow, that's amazing," said Odelia, her eyes gleaming. "A real Nobel Peace Prize."

"Not just the Peace Prize. He's getting the Nobel Prize for Literature, too."

"Literature? I didn't know the President was a writer?"

"Oh, sure. He's only one of the best writers in the world. Bestselling writer."

"What... books did he write?" asked Odelia, clearly confused.

"Oh, you name it, he wrote it. Amazing, huh? I thought you'd be impressed."

Odelia looked up when her mother was pointing at the screen, where the President of the United States was talking on the phone now. And as he talked, it quickly became clear that his lips were forming the exact words that were coming out of Odelia's phone.

Otto Paunch... *was* President Wilcox!

"Oh, and another little scoop. My good friend Van Wilcox is also in line to join the ranks of EGOT winners. That's an Emmy, Grammy, Oscar *and* a Tony! He's the first President in history to pull off such a hat trick. Amazing, huh? Yeah, he is a great man. In fact he's the greatest man in a long line of great men. The greatest great, you might say. So how abou—"

Odelia switched off her phone, gazing dazedly at the screen, where President Wilcox could be seen shouting into his phone, then looking annoyedly at the little gadget, before tucking it away again and shaking his head at so much insolence.

"I think... I've just been played," said Odelia uncertainly.

"Don't worry, honey," said Grandma, patting her on the arm. "We've all been there."

"And here I thought *you* were the nymphomaniac," Dooley told Milo.

"Mythomaniac, Dooley," Harriet was quick to correct him.

Even Milo could see the humor in that, for he laughed loudly.

"How about another burger?" said Tex, breaking the

embarrassed silence that had descended upon the company. "I'll do the honors, shall I?"

"No!" Marge shouted before Tex reached the grill.

Chase, who'd turned off the TV, took over from the doctor, and soon the party was in full swing again.

Milo drifted off in the direction of Grandma, who was now feeding him pieces of burger and even bits of coleslaw. Harriet and Brutus had snuck off into the garden next door, where they planned to make good use of those hills and valleys Gran had created, and then it was just me and Dooley.

"Milo seems fine, doesn't he?" said Dooley. "He hasn't told a lie all day."

"Except for the part about pulling your tail," I reminded my friend.

"The jury is still out on that one," said Dooley. "No one has pulled my tail so he could be right."

I pulled Dooley's tail, hard, and he yelped in surprise. "See?" I said. "No gold."

He eyed me sheepishly and rubbed his tail. "I really hoped he was right."

"Maybe I didn't pull hard enough," I said, and made to pull again.

"No! I believe you," he said quickly.

"At least spitting out nuggets of gold beats scooting your poop across the carpet."

"I think we all learned a valuable lesson, Max."

"Which is?"

"If something sounds too good to be true, it probably is."

I looked at Dooley, surprised. "Those are regular words of wisdom, buddy."

"I read that on Odelia's calendar."

Of course he did.

"You know? If Milo went into politics, he could be one of the greats," said Dooley.

And so he could. But fortunately for humans Milo is a cat, and cats aren't eligible to go into politics and lead countries. Then again, maybe if they were, the world would be a better place. No politician licking his own butt in the middle of a speech would ever be able to be taken seriously when declaring war on another nation or making budget cuts and lowering pensions. And no stump speech would go over well if the one giving the speech suddenly yawned in the middle of a sentence, stretched and promptly fell asleep.

But wouldn't it be fun to watch the video on YouTube?

EXCERPT FROM PURRFECT ALIBI
(THE MYSTERIES OF MAX BOOK 9)

Prologue

Marge Poole surveyed the scene. She wondered if they'd set out enough chairs. The event she was staging was without a doubt the biggest and most ambitious one she'd ever taken on. Even though the Hampton Cove library had been remodeled five years ago with exactly this kind of literary event in mind, and a small conference room had been added for writers to hold readings, Marge had never expected ever to land the bestselling thriller writer in the world for one of her Author of the Month evenings.

But there he was. Chris Ackerman. Author of such bestsellers as *The Connor Conundrum* and *The Dixon Dilemma*. America's favorite writer and the most-borrowed author of all time. The scribe was seated on the small stage, peering through his reading glasses and going over his notes, an expensive-looking golden fountain pen poised in his hand. When he noticed Marge nervously bustling about, he fixed his pale blue eyes on her.

"Wasn't Burke supposed to be here by now?" he asked.

There was an edge to his voice, and Marge didn't wonder. A long-standing feud between Chris Ackerman and Rockwell Burke, the well-known horror novelist, had existed ever since Burke had announced that he felt Ackerman's books were the work of a hack and a dilettante and had discounted his prose as bad writing. In fact it had surprised Marge a great deal when Burke had accepted to host the evening, and interview Ackerman on stage.

Perhaps the horrormeister had had a change of heart. More likely, though, it was because his own once flourishing career had hit a snag, his last three books not selling as well as he'd hoped, at which point his publisher must have insisted he try to turn things around by associating himself with the reigning king of the *New York Times* bestseller list.

"He'll be here," Marge assured Ackerman, who was glancing at his watch.

"He'd better," grumbled the famous writer. In his early seventies now, Chris Ackerman was a ruddy-faced heavyset man with a quiet air of self-confidence. "If he doesn't show up I'll have to tell the audience what I really think of him." He chuckled. "That his best years are behind him, and that I hated every book he's put out for the past decade."

"You don't really mean that," said Marge, shocked at the harsh words.

"Oh, but I do," said Ackerman, adjusting his glasses to owlishly stare at Marge. "My publisher told me not to engage, but if Burke stands me up all bets are off." He wagged a finger. "I'll bet he's doing it on purpose. Promising to make nice then making a fool of me."

"I'm sure he's simply delayed," said Marge, checking the door to the left of the stage. "His publicist would have told me if Mr. Burke had decided to cancel at the last minute."

"Not unless he wants to make a fool of me," Ackerman repeated.

Marge checked her own watch. One hour until showtime. There was still plenty of time for Rockwell Burke to show up. Then again, the man's publicist had promised Marge he'd be there on time, so he could go over some of the questions with Ackerman.

Marge, a fine-boned fifty-something woman with long blond hair, chewed her lip and walked the short distance between the conference room and the library proper. She wondered if she'd unlocked the front doors. It worried her that no one had shown up yet. Usually when she organized her Author of the Month evenings at least a few people arrived early, wanting to secure a good seat—or an autograph from the featured author. And with Chris Ackerman as the featured speaker she'd expected the town to turn out en masse.

The Hampton Cove library wasn't a big operation. In fact it was downright modest. But it had a nice selection of books, DVDs and CDs, a computer room where users could surf the Internet, a cozy kids' corner with a pirate ship where the kids could sit and read, a colorful fish tank, a collection of stuffed animals, and cheerful artwork by a local artist.

Breezing past the checkout desk and the newspaper stand, she quickly moved to the door, where her husband and her mother stood peering out at the courtyard in front of the library. The size of a postage stamp, the courtyard nevertheless featured a fountain and a few stone benches. At this very moment, though, it was as deserted as the library itself.

"Where is everyone?" asked Marge.

Vesta Muffin, a septuagenarian the spitting image of Estelle Getty, lifted her bony shoulders. "Probably at home watching *The Bachelor*. Which is what I would be doing right now if you hadn't roped me into this meet and greet with your childhood crush."

"He was never my crush," said Marge, checking the doors to see if they weren't locked. They weren't. "I just like his books, that's all. He's an amazing writer."

"I like him," Tex said. A buff man with a shock of white hair, Tex always kept a Chris Ackerman on his bedside table so he could read a couple of chapters before going to sleep.

"Too bloodthirsty for my taste," said Gran, adjusting her large, horn-rimmed glasses. "All those serial killers and crazy maniacs. How many serial killers do people really think are out there? Give me EL James any day over your creepy Chuck Peckerwood."

"Chris Ackerman."

"Huh?"

"Chris Ackerman, not Chuck Peckerwood."

"Whatever. I'm just saying. If there really were as many serial killers as Ackerwood wants us to believe, the streets would be crawling with them and we'd all be dead right now, murdered in the most gruesome way possible."

"It's fiction, Mom. It's not supposed to be real."

"EL James is real. Christian Grey is out there. In fact the world is full of Christian Greys. Only problem is the world is also full of Anastasia Steeles who hog all the Christian Greys and leave nothing for the rest of us shlubs."

Tex chuckled. "I doubt billionaires are anything like Christian Grey," he said. "Real billionaires don't look like runway models. They look like Bill Gates or Warren Buffett."

"How would you know?" said Vesta. "You're not a billionaire."

Tex agreed that he wasn't. Still, he said, he believed Christian Grey to be just as fictitious as Chris Ackerman's trademark serial killers.

Marge didn't think Christian Grey, real or not, would fancy a crusty old lady with tiny white curls and a big attitude problem. But since she didn't want to get drawn into the argument, she decided to keep her comments to herself. "I don't get it. Last month we had Jacqueline Rose Garner and people showed up an hour before the start of the event."

"Which just goes to show you people are fed up with murder and mayhem. They want love and passion. Speaking of which, did you know Chase asked Odelia out on a date?"

"Yes, she told me. Chase took her to Villa Frank. Too bad it's tonight. She really wanted to be here so she could meet Chris and Rockwell Burke."

"You can't beat love," said Vesta in uncharacteristically sentimental fashion.

"He took her to Villa Frank, huh?" said Tex, rocking back on his heels. "I took Marge there for our wedding anniversary. Remember, honey? You loved their steak pizzaiola."

"Oh, I did. And how about that almond joy sundae? That was to die for."

For the next forty-five minutes, conversation flowed back and forth, mainly focusing on Tex and Marge's daughter Odelia and Odelia's boyfriend Chase Kingsley. People finally started showing up, though they were in no great hurry to take their seats, instead opting to chat with friends and acquaintances. For most people these Author of the Month evenings were more an excuse to socialize than to come and listen to an author read from their work.

Just then, there was a soft yelp coming from the conference room. Marge immediately whipped her head around. She listened for a moment, but when no other sounds came, she relaxed again. "I better go and see if Burke has arrived yet," she said.

"I'll come with you," said Tex.

"No, you better stay here and welcome the guests," said Marge.

She retraced her steps to the conference room. Chris Ackerman was still where she'd left him, seated in his chair on stage. Only he seemed to have fallen asleep, his notes having dropped from his hands and scattered all around him on the floor. Oh, my.

"Mr. Ackerman?" she said, threading a path through the chairs. "Are you all right?"

Even from ten feet away she could see the star of the evening wasn't all right at all. The first sign that something was amiss were the drops of a dark crimson substance splattered on the sheets of paper on the floor. Even before it dawned on her what those drops represented, her eyes fixed on a strange object protruding from the writer's neck.

It was the golden fountain pen, its nib now deeply embedded into the man's neck.

The world's bestselling writer... was dead.

Chapter One

Odelia Poole, star reporter for the Hampton Cove Gazette, wasn't used to being wined and dined in quite this fashion. Chase Kingsley, her boyfriend and local cop with the Hampton Cove Police Department, hadn't just taken her to any old place. Ever since he'd asked her out, he'd been highly secretive about the itinerary for their date, and only when he'd picked her up in his squad car and entered the Villa Frank parking lot had she caught on that this wasn't going to be a quick burger at the local diner but an actual fancy date.

Good thing she'd dressed up for the occasion, her off-the-shoulder red pencil dress pretty much the fanciest thing she had hanging in her closet. She'd bought it on the instigation of her mother, who insisted she have at least one nice thing to wear for galas, movie premieres, chamber of commerce banquets or the occasional fancy reception. Her usual costume consisting of jeans, T-shirt and a sweater the dress made her feel slightly self-conscious, especially since there was some bust involved. Watching Chase's jaw drop when he'd come to pick her up had been more than enough to dispel those qualms, though.

"You look lovely," he said, not for the first time.

"You don't look so bad yourself," she purred.

That was an understatement. Chase, usually a jeans-and-check shirt man himself, had gone all out as well, dressing up in an actual tux for the occasion. His long dark brown hair was combed back from his brow, his square jaw was entirely free of stubble, and his muscular frame filled out that tux to the extent that Odelia had no trouble picturing what he looked like underneath. Then again, the man was no stranger to her bed. Or at least he hadn't been until her grandmother had decided to move in and cramp his style.

But now that Gran had moved out again, the coast was clear, and it was obvious that Chase intended to move in on a more permanent basis—possibly the whole reason for splashing on a night at Villa Frank, one of the more posh places in Hampton Cove.

She took a sip from her wine and felt her head spin. It was more the way Chase was looking at her right now than the alcohol, though, his green-specked blue eyes holding a promise that she hoped he intended to keep.

"So what movie have you picked?" she asked.

"I thought I'd go with a golden oldie. *Bringing Up Baby*."

"Ooh! I love Katherine Hepburn."

"What about Cary Grant?"

"He's fine, I guess," she said with a coquettish flutter of her lashes. In fact he was more than fine. Cary Grant had always been one of her favorite actors. More than today's movie heroes, he had charm, style and charisma and that elusive *je-ne-sais-quoi*.

"Phew. I hoped you'd like my selection."

"I love it." She didn't mention that she'd already seen the

movie about a dozen times on TCM. On the big screen it would look even better, of course. Their local movie theater was holding a screwball comedy retrospective and she was happy Chase was a fan, too.

"So what do you think is Cary Grant's best movie?" she asked now.

He pressed his napkin to his lips. Their menu had consisted of shrimp scampi and lobster stuffed flounder with a side of pasta and marinara sauce and brickle for dessert: toasted almonds, ice cream and whipped cream. A real feast. And the evening wasn't over yet. Not by a long shot.

"I like the Hitchcocks best," Chase said. *"North by Northwest, To Catch a Thief, Charade..."*

"*Charade* isn't a Hitchcock," she told him. "It's Stanley Donen's Hitchcock homage."

Chase grinned. "Of course you would know that, Miss Movie Buff."

"I like *Arsenic and Old Lace*. Oh, and *Mr. Blandings Builds His Dream House*, of course."

"Huh. I thought you'd have gone for the more romantic ones."

"I guess I'm a funny girl at heart," she quipped.

"Yes, you are," he said, and gave her one of those looks that made her melt like the toffee-flavored ice cream on her tongue. "Not only funny but smart, beautiful, compassionate..."

Her cheeks flushed, and not just from the fireplace they were sitting close to. "Keep this up and I just might let you get frisky through the second act of *Bringing Up Baby*."

"Oh, I'm counting on it."

She dug her spoon into the caramel-colored ice cream. "Is it just me or is it hot in here?"

Chase cleared his throat. "I heard your grandmother moved back in with your parents?"

And there it was: the reason he'd asked her out on a date in the first place. Or at least that's what she hoped. They'd been going out for months now, and it was time to put their budding relationship on a more permanent footing. Since Chase bunked with Odelia's uncle, having not had much luck renting a place of his own in town, moving in with her was the logical thing to do. And oh boy was she ready. And she'd just opened her mouth to confirm that her grandmother had, indeed, moved back in with her folks when both of their phones started to sing in unison.

"Huh," said Chase with a frown. "It's your uncle."

"My mom," said Odelia with a smile, and tapped the green Accept icon. "Hey, Mom. What's up?" When the garbled words of her mother flowed into her ear, though, her smile quickly vanished. "Wow, slow down. What are you talking about?"

"He's dead!" Mom practically shouted into the phone. "Chris Ackerman is dead and now they think he may have been murdered and that I had something to do with it!"

As her mother explained what happened, Odelia fixed her gaze on Chase, whose jaw was clenching while he listened to what Uncle Alec, the town's chief of police, had to say.

Looked like Cary Grant and Katherine Hepburn would have to take a rain check.

Chapter Two

I won't conceal I was having a tough time at it. To be honest I don't think I'm cut out to be a teacher, and teaching a bunch of unruly cats was definitely not my idea of an evening well spent.

"We'll watch it again until you discover when Aurora picked up the all-important and vital clue," I said, and tapped the rewind button on the TV's remote. When my audience groaned loudly, I added, "And no buts. If we're going to do this, we need to do it right."

"But, Max!" Brutus cried. "We've seen this movie three times already!"

"And we'll see it three times more if that's what it takes," I said stubbornly.

"*The Bachelor* is on," said Harriet. "I love *The Bachelor*. Can't we watch that instead?"

I gave her a stern-faced look. "No, we can't. *The Bachelor* won't teach us the things we need to know as cat sleuths. Aurora Teagarden will."

Unfortunately Odelia had only taped one Aurora Teagarden movie, even though I'd asked her to tape all of them if she had the chance. Instead, she'd taped a movie called *I'll Be Home for Christmas*. Which featured a dog, and as everyone knows, no cat wants to be seen dead watching dogs on TV—or in real life, for that matter—so that was a definite no-no. Besides, there was no mystery, only a silly romance plot and a lot of tinsel.

I watched the screen intently, then paused the movie just when Aurora opened her mouth to say something, her face a mask of concentration. "See? This is the moment she realizes who the killer is. See the way her forehead crinkles? How her eyebrows draw up?"

"She looks constipated," said Harriet, tapping her paw against Odelia's leather couch.

"Do I look like that when I get an idea, Max?" asked Dooley.

"You would if you ever got an idea," said Brutus with a grin.

"I get ideas," said Dooley. "I get ideas all the time. Just now I got the idea that Odelia's been gone a long time, and that I hope she'll be home soon."

"That's great, Dooley," I said. "But that's not the kind of

idea we're talking about."

"So tell us exactly what we are talking about, Max," said Brutus as he suppressed a yawn. Even though he, unlike Harriet, wasn't a big fan of *The Bachelor*, it was obvious he wasn't remotely interested in my lecture on modern sleuthing techniques either.

"We're talking about being perceptive," I said. "About not missing even the teensiest, tiniest clue. For all we know a cigarette butt can lead us to the killer. Or, as in this case…" I pointed to the screen. "Pizza boxes tucked underneath the kitchen sink."

"Are the pizza boxes a very important clue, Max?" asked Dooley eagerly.

"They are," said Brutus before I could respond. "They're a clue to this couple's eating habits. It tells us that they like pizza." He was grinning again, clearly enjoying himself.

"The pizza boxes tell us that these people took the missing students hostage," I said, directing a censorious look at Brutus. "It tells Aurora—and the viewer—that the missing students are, in fact, somewhere in the house. So yes, Dooley, the pizza boxes are a very important clue. They're that all-important, telling a-ha type of clue you want to find."

"Pizza boxes," Dooley repeated reverently, as if memorizing the words.

"They're an important clue in *this* particular case," I hastened to add. "In any other case they're probably completely irrelevant."

Dooley looked confused. "So… pizza boxes aren't *always* a clue?"

"No, they're not. It all depends on the circumstances. In this case the pizza boxes—"

"Oh, enough about the pizza boxes already!" Harriet cried, lifting her paws in a gesture of despair. "Can we watch *The Bachelor* now? I'll bet Jock's dinner with LaRue is still in full swing. We just might catch dessert if you turn off this Aurora nonsense right now."

"I think I need to see it one more time," said Dooley. "I think I missed something."

Harriet looked as if she was ready to pounce on Dooley, but restrained herself with a supreme effort. "What don't you get, Dooley?" she asked instead in clipped tones.

Dooley was shaking his head confusedly. "Well, it's those pizza boxes. I don't see how Aurora goes from seeing the empty pizza boxes to finding those missing students."

"God give me strength," Harriet muttered, very expressively rolling her eyes.

"Why don't you let us do the thinking from now on, Dooley?" Brutus suggested.

"You think so?" said Dooley.

"Yes, unlike you I do think. In fact I think so much I don't mind doing a little thinking for you, too, so that you can…" He gave Dooley a dubious look. "Do whatever it is you do."

"I could… help you search for those pizza boxes," said Dooley hopefully.

"You do that," said Brutus, patting the other cat on the shoulder. "You do that."

I now realize I may have committed the ultimate faux-pas. I've neglected to introduce you to my merry band of felines. Let me rectify that right now, by introducing myself first. My name is Max, and I'm Odelia Poole's feisty feline sidekick. I'm strapping, I'm blorange, and I'm proud to be of assistance to my human, who's probably one of the finest humans a cat could ever hope to be associated with. She also stems from a long line of females who can converse with felines, which makes her an honorary feline in my book.

The three cats lounging on the couch are (reading from left to right) Dooley, who's a gray Ragamuffin and my sidekick (yes, he's a sidekick's sidekick), Brutus, a black musclehead who likes to think he's the bee's knees (or more appropriately the cat's whiskers) and finally we have Harriet, who's by way of being Brutus's mate. She's also a pretty, prissy Persian but don't tell her I said that because she can be quite catty. And she has some very sharp claws.

"I think I saw a pizza box yesterday, Max," Dooley said now, showing the kind of zeal and initiative a feline sleuth worth their salt should strive for. "If you want I can show you."

"That's all right, Dooley," I said. "We can go into that when we start the practical part of this introductory training."

"Practical part?" asked Harriet. "There's a practical part?"

"Of course there is," I said. "First we learn the basics, then we apply them to a real-world situation."

"I still don't get why you get to teach this course, Max," said Brutus. "What makes you think you're qualified?"

"I'll have you know I've solved quite a number of high-profile cases," I told him.

"You couldn't have pulled those off without me and you know it. In fact before I arrived in town you hadn't solved a single case. Not a one. Admit it, Max."

I was puffing out my chest to give him a proper rebuke when all of a sudden there was a commotion at the door. It flew open and Odelia burst in.

"I need you guys to come with me," she said, panting as if she'd just run a marathon. "There's been a murder." She fixed us with a meaningful look. "My mom is implicated."

ALSO BY NIC SAINT

The Mysteries of Max
Purrfect Murder
Purrfectly Deadly
Purrfect Revenge
Box Set 1 (Books 1-3)
Purrfect Heat
Purrfect Crime
Purrfect Rivalry
Box Set 2 (Books 4-6)
Purrfect Peril
Purrfect Secret
Purrfect Alibi
Box Set 3 (Books 7-9)
Purrfect Obsession
Purrfect Betrayal
Purrfectly Clueless
Box Set 4 (Books 10-12)
Purrfectly Royal
Purrfect Cut
Purrfect Trap
Purrfectly Hidden
Purrfect Kill

Purrfect Santa
Purrfectly Flealess

Nora Steel

Murder Retreat

The Kellys

Murder Motel

Death in Suburbia

Emily Stone

Murder at the Art Class

Washington & Jefferson

First Shot

Alice Whitehouse

Spooky Times

Spooky Trills

Spooky End

Spooky Spells

Ghosts of London

Between a Ghost and a Spooky Place

Public Ghost Number One

Ghost Save the Queen

Box Set 1 (Books 1-3)

A Tale of Two Harrys

Ghost of Girlband Past

Ghostlier Things

Charleneland

Deadly Ride

Final Ride

Neighborhood Witch Committee

Witchy Start

Witchy Worries

Witchy Wishes

Saffron Diffley

Crime and Retribution

Vice and Verdict

Felonies and Penalties (Saffron Diffley Short 1)

The B-Team

Once Upon a Spy

Tate-à-Tate

Enemy of the Tates

Ghosts vs. Spies

The Ghost Who Came in from the Cold

Witchy Fingers

Witchy Trouble

Witchy Hexations

Witchy Possessions

Witchy Riches

Box Set 1 (Books 1-4)

The Mysteries of Bell & Whitehouse

One Spoonful of Trouble

Two Scoops of Murder

Three Shots of Disaster

Box Set 1 (Books 1-3)

A Twist of Wraith
A Touch of Ghost
A Clash of Spooks
Box Set 2 (Books 4-6)
The Stuffing of Nightmares
A Breath of Dead Air
An Act of Hodd
Box Set 3 (Books 7-9)
A Game of Dons

Standalone Novels
When in Bruges
The Whiskered Spy

ThrillFix
Homejacking
The Eighth Billionaire
The Wrong Woman

ABOUT NIC

Nic Saint is the pen name for writing couple Nick and Nicole Saint. They've penned 80+ novels in the romance, cat sleuth, middle grade, suspense, comedy and cozy mystery genres. Nicole has a background in accounting and Nick in political science and before being struck by the writing bug the Saints worked odd jobs around the world (including massage therapist in Mexico, gardener in Italy, restaurant manager in India, and Berlitz teacher in Belgium).

When they're not writing they enjoy Christmas-themed Hallmark movies (whether it's Christmas or not), all manner of pastry, comic books, a daily dose of yoga (to limber up those limbs), and spoiling their big red tomcat Tommy.

Sign up for the no-spam newsletter and be the first to know when a new book comes out: nicsaint.com/newsletter.

www.nicsaint.com

facebook.com/nicsaintauthor
twitter.com/nicsaintauthor
bookbub.com/authors/nic-saint
amazon.com/author/nicsaint

Printed in Great Britain
by Amazon